The King's Siege
(A Tudor at War)

by

Anne Stevens

Tudor Crimes: Book XIX

Foreword

Henry, King of England, is intent on war with France. To this end he is gathering a huge army which he hopes to get across the Channel without notice. Twenty thousand foot soldiers, six thousand horse, and fifty cannon, with all their gunners and ammunition, must simply appear around Calais one day, ready for war.

That the king is looking for a last great battle is obvious to all, but few realise that his grandiloquent celebration of English military might is based entirely on an easy victory over a dysfunctional Scottish army, and liberal helpings of Miriam Draper's powerful poppy distillation.

King François has done the unthinkable; he has entered into a treaty of military support with the Ottoman Empire. The most powerful Roman Catholic country in Europe is now a bedfellow of the dreaded Mussulmen, whose aim it is to impose the teachings of Allah on the civilised world at the point of a sword.

Because of this, the Holy Roman Emperor, Charles V, is allied to Henry and will support him in any action he takes against François. With such an assurance, the king feels confident enough to raise a great host. Almost forty thousand soldiers and camp followers sit on the quaysides of

England, waiting for the order to embark for Calais.

Henry's mental state, coupled with his badly infected and ulcerated leg, drives him into making some strange decisions which, on reflection, he must reverse. Just the year before he has Archbishop Cranmer arrested, and charged with heresy. The public outcry is so great that Henry's advisors urge him to release the primate at once. The king does so, and reinstates him as the Archbishop of Canterbury, with increased powers. Then he turns his rage on an unsuspecting Stephen Gardiner, Bishop of Winchester. It seems that the bishop had purchased land that the king coveted, and so angered him. He too is soon released, with what can only be seen as a grovelling apology.

The changes effected by Thomas Cromwell have made Henry into a 'democratic' king, who must listen to both the people, and his parliament. The days of arbitrary arrest and execution are coming to an end, and the new social order ordained by Cromwell is coming into being.

Miriam Draper is happy. She is the agent for transporting and supplying the kings huge army, and she stands to make yet another fortune from it. Will, her husband, counsels for peace, but knows it is a futile gesture. His overwhelming defeat of the Scots at Solway Firth has enlivened the nobility, and they want war. War means more land to hand out, and the chance of plunder.

Queen Kathryn spends her time soothing Henry, and keeping him from some of his more insane acts. She treats him like a small child, and brings him little treats and gifts to distract him from the daily business of running the country. That is best left to men like Sir Richard Rich, Sir Rafe Sadler, Sir John Russell, now a Lord Warden, the Duke of Norfolk, and Sir Richard Cromwell.

Unfortunately, Richard Cromwell, perhaps the steadiest of them all, is no longer at court. In a move that has shocked his friends, he has decided to withdraw from public life forever... having lost his great love to the wild caprices of an increasingly dangerous, and dissolute, monarch.

1 *March to the Drum*

The great, enclosed courtyards of both Whitehall and Westminster Palaces are seething with a mass of armed men, the like of which has not been seen since the heady days of the magnificent victory at Agincourt. Men with muskets are busy learning how to drive home their forked rests in readiness for the weight of their heavy gun barrels, whilst others are being drilled in the close order use of the long pike, and the broad sword.

Out in Gravesend, teams of men are busy learning how to load their cannon with the new sort of chain shot, and others are being given the secret of 'forming square', a sure way of breaking enemy cavalry. The whole of England, it seems, is drilling, and preparing itself for the coming war. Only the French are unaware of the coming conflict, and the onslaught that is being prepared against them.

"How goes it, General Draper?" The king is standing in a high gallery, overlooking the Whitehall drill field. "Are they ready yet?"

"Is any man ever ready for war, sire," Will replies. The king is wearing a metal breastplate, and a heavy steel helmet on his head, and he looks quite ridiculous. In his own mind he is girded for war, and thinks himself to be like mighty Achilles, about to slay Hector before the walls of

Troy. He is ready, and thinks that every man in England should be ready.

"You sound as if you would rather not fight this coming war," Henry says to his Examiner General. "Do you not think our cause is a worthy one, Will?"

"The French king is weak, sire," Will replies. "But give him the chance, and he will back out of any military confrontation. To this end, he will probably surrender land to you. If we can extend the Calaisis, it will become an area as large as Kent and Suffolk. Then we need not make war."

"That is so, Will, but I would hold it under the French king's sway. I cannot allow that, for the sake of my honour. We must *take* what we want from François, and force him into a fight against us."

"And if we lose?"

"I have ten thousand men under arms here, and another five thousand at Gravesend," Henry explains. "With the garrison at Calais numbering another six thousand, I can put twenty one thousand men, and over fifty cannon, into the field at a day's notice. Within a month I can have the northern troops too; another thirty thousand men. We cannot lose."

"Norfolk is an old man," Will tells the king. It is an obvious enough thing to understand, but the king seems not to see the inherent danger. "What if he is not up to commanding your army?"

"It is his prerogative," Henry replies, with a shocked expression on his ruddy face. "Norfolk is always the first noble in the land. It has been so since the Plantagenets. He must lead my army into battle, and drive the French back onto Paris."

"Sire, he is far too old," Will persists. "He is in his sixty ninth year, and his health is failing him. I doubt he has the enthusiasm for war that he once had."

"Enough, General Draper," the king snaps. "Norfolk shall command, with his son Surrey as second in command. You shall retain command of your Examiner Company, and of the Genoese crossbowmen that the Draper Company have hired. That is enough to keep you busy."

"I seek no advancement for myself, sire," Will tells the king. "Rather that you choose a better man for the task. Charles Brandon is a good general, and he knows the French. Let him lead your army to glory."

"My Lord Suffolk may attend, of course, but he is not to interfere with Norfolk." The king has made his mind up, and nothing will sway him. He is aware of how well Norfolk has done in the past against the Scots and the French, and he believes him to be right for the task. That the duke's victories are all twenty or thirty years in the past quite escapes his notice.

"As you wish, sire," Will Draper says. "The tides are favourable from tomorrow, and the Draper Company cogs are ready to sail. If we pick our spot carefully, we might land most of the army before the French even know they are at war."

"That's the way," Henry says. "Get our fellows ashore and into them, before the bastards are awake."

"Are we to send a declaration of war?" Will ask the obvious question, for all the secrecy in the world counts for nothing if you must first let the enemy know you are going to war with them, but to act without warning is deeply dishonourable, and an unthinkable move.

"I have asked the Holy Roman ambassador to deliver the message for me," Henry replies. "He is going to Paris anyway, and can give François my declaration when he arrives. I expect that to be the day after tomorrow."

"The day after we land?" Will sees the cunning of this action. Face is saved because the message is entrusted to a diplomat who fails to hurry, and the army is landed without opposition. Once there are twenty odd thousand men in the field, the French king will have no choice other than to beg for terms, or to take up arms, and fight.

"A clever move, Your Majesty," says Will. He is sure that the idea is not Henry's but suggested by a sharper mind, such as Rafe Sadler's, or even Richard Cromwell's.

"Yes, it was suggested to me in a letter from Antwerp," Henry says, slyly. He is, quite *unofficially*, aware that Mijnheer Cornelis of that city is none other than Thomas Cromwell, but chooses to remain *officially* blind to the fact. Cromwell might well have hoodwinked the king, but he will make clandestine use of the man now. "Master Cornelis is a shrewd fellow, and still loyal to the crown."

"Really, sire… a gentleman from Antwerp, you say?" Will Draper plays along with the king's little pantomime, content that it will not cause him any immediate trouble. If Henry wishes to use Tom Cromwell's cleverness, then he must accept that the Draper Company protects him, and thus holds the reins. "Then may his good will stay with you, and his advice continue to flow."

"It shall," Henry says. "His good advice will earn my good will, and we shall all benefit from our little secret."

"Then he is for war?" Will asks.

"He says very much as you do… that the French king will run away and then try to buy me off with land." Henry wants his war, and so he twists the advice of Tom

Cromwell to fit in with his dream. "François is a stingy bastard, and will not offer me enough, so I must take it. I rather think that half of his kingdom will suffice."

"Why lose ten thousand men taking half, when you can have a third without us firing a single musket?" Will asks, but he knows it is in vain. The king will ignore his good advice and force a war on the French that will be no good for anyone.

"I want Norfolk to advance at once," Henry says, as if the Examiner in Chief has not even spoken. "None of this waiting for supplies nonsense, or for the rain to stop falling. It is your task to push the duke onwards, Will. You must goad him into the fight, and never let him slow down."

"Old men are always cautious," Will tells the king. "The duke fears losing more than he welcomes winning. Let Suffolk take command."

"No!" Henry turns away, and the interview is ended.

*

If Will expects any sympathy or support from his wife, he is sadly mistaken. She is busy over her accounts with Pru Beckshaw, and scarce looks up when he enters her counting house in Hackney.

"The king is mad," he tells Miriam. "No matter what I say, he is intent on going to war."

"Then stop trying to dissuade him, husband," Miriam tells him. "Men must have their wars, now and then. This one will be a fairly bloodless affair, with two ageing monarchs making rude noises at one another, and then circling about like two toothless fighting dogs."

"Henry will want his battles." Will helps himself to a flagon of decent Italian white wine that stands on the desk by his wife's right hand. He pours a cup out, and then breaks off a piece of hard cheese to chew upon.

"Can you see Norfolk risking an open fight?" Miriam says with a clear insight into how nobles like to make war. "If he loses, Henry will want his head, and if he wins, the king will claim the honours. No... they will march about, then return home after a few skirmishes."

"Then it is a complete waste of effort," Will tells her. "What is the point of it all?"

"The point, my dear is this." Miriam gestures to her account ledgers. "Henry has hired out twenty five of my cogs for transportation of troops and supplies. That is eleven shillings a day for each cog, for the duration of the war. Then I am contracted to supply fresh meat, vegetables and drink for twenty thousand men. Add to this the fees for hiring out our

Genoese crossbowmen, and we stand to make a pretty enough penny."

"Even if we do not fight?" Will is, as always, mystified by the intricacies of finance. "What if we just flounder about for a month?"

"The longer the better, Will," Pru Beckshaw explains. "I think the company will make a fine profit. The cog hire will bring us in over three hundred pounds a month, the victuals another seven thousand, and the hire of our mercenaries yet another three thousand pounds."

"Then I hope we do not fight," Will says, "for even one Englishman to die for so ignoble a war would be a shame."

"War happens, my love," Miriam says with great pragmatism. "Why can we not make a profit from it? Over ten thousand pounds for a month is a tidy sum."

"Henry need only land his army on French soil, and demand some concessions from François," Will explains. "The French are so badly prepared that he will surrender land and castles to keep the peace. Henry might end up with an entire county, without a single fight."

"You miss the point, husband," Miriam tells her irate man. "Henry does not wish peace. He thinks to lead the charge against the French again. It will make him feel young once more."

"He has a younger wife to make

him feel young," Will replies. "Cannot Queen Katheryn dissuade him from his folly?"

"Katheryn is to rule in his name whilst he is abroad," says Miriam. "She shall hold the king's seal, and her word shall be law. Henry must trust her very much."

"Rather he does not trust the Seymour brothers," her husband muses, quite correctly. Both Ned and Tom are pushing themselves forward too hard, and the king fears they have designs against him. "Ned already commands the navy, and Tom Seymour gathers favours in from every place. Half of the nobles in England borrow money from him, and the rest seek his friendship. I doubt either will last much longer with such thrusting ways about them. Besides, they cannot get along with one another for more than an hour."

"Tom is for France, alongside the king," Miriam tells Will. "Whilst Ned must stay in London and keep the navy up to the mark."

Tom Seymour will find some excuse to remain in London," Will tells his wife. "He will not leave Prince Edward to his brother's care alone."

"Perhaps you are right," Miriam concedes. "Ned is a man with too many plans for his own good, these days."

"Does he still dote on his

nephew?" Will asks, somewhat sarcastically. "Or has the shine worn off?"

"Now Prince Edward is under the protection of Queen Katheryn, along with the princesses, he seems content to let things be. I suppose he cares only that the child is cared for, and readied for his future role."

"True enough. With Henry dead, Ned Seymour will be in a position to make himself into the Regent to the King's Body."

"The king's body?" Miriam shudders. "What a horrid way of putting it."

"An archaic form only," Will tells her. "It means only that he be a regent above everything that is the king's, without hinderance. His power will be great, unless the Privy Council can hem him in in some way."

"The wolf shall rise high, and fall low," Pru Beckshaw mutters, as her eyelids flutter. Miriam touches her elbow, and offers her a sip of wine.

"Are you well, dear Pru?" she asks. "What ever do you mean by saying such a thing?"

"I spoke?" Pru is confused. It has been almost two years since she was afflicted with a prophetic vision, and this sudden effort tires her out.

"Never mind," Miriam Draper tells her. "I doubt it meant anything."

Will Draper drinks his wine, chews on his hard cheese, and keeps his peace. To him, the meaning of Pru Beckshaw's words is more than clear. The Seymour family have, for most of the last hundred years, occupied a lush part of Wiltshire, where the great grandfather built himself an almost fortress-like house. He named it Wulfhall, and Ned Seymour is the latest in a line of ravenous wolves to occupy it. Pru is never wrong, he thinks, and Ned Seymour will rise above all men, until he suffers a great fall from grace. It is a reassuring thought, and something for the Examiner in Chief to look forward to.

"We sail on the morrow," Will tells his wife. "I thought it only right to see you before I go."

"You are in with those that are to be the first to land then?" Miriam asks. It is a pointless question, for she knows her husband can do nothing else. His idea of honour demands that he be first ashore with his men, and not safely in the following boats.

"I must," Will tells her. "I shall land with half of the Examiners and prepare the way for Henry to arrive. He will expect everything to be in good order. John shall bring on the rest of our people with the next tide." John Beckshaw is Pru's husband, and the second in command of the King's Examiners.

"Then go with my best wishes, husband," Miriam tells him. "This war is not for any noble cause, so do not think to act nobly. Do your duty, and nothing more. The children and I want you back, safe and sound."

"They are well?" Will asks. "I see them so little, what with the king's demands on me."

"They thrive, husband," Miriam replies. "Though Gwyllam is growing to be a handful. He insists on being called William, and has his playmates call him 'Will'. I scold him, but it does no good."

"He is his father's son," Will tells her, with a small smile. "Let him be, and see where it takes him. I think he is of my own nature, and shows it by taking my name. It is no great leap from the Welsh to the English, is it?"

"I want him to be a lawyer," Miriam says. "Not an adventurer, ready to fight other peoples wars for them."

"You mean like me?"

"One hero in the family is enough," Miriam says, firmly. Whatever her eldest son wants to call himself, he will finish his ordinary schooling in another year, then be placed at one of the best universities in Cambridge. He will study both the law, and commerce under the best tutors, until his eighteenth year, then join her within the company. It is her intention to keep him from harm, and turn him into a man of business. "Gwyllam shall take the company on to ever greater things."

"Things change," Will tells her. "Look at how the king's fancy for war affects us all. Your precious mission to find another way to the far off East is abandoned, and the ships are now employed for other purposes."

"It is merely postponed, not abandoned," Miriam tells him. "Once this war is done with, Ibrahim and his men will sail west."

"Poor Ibrahim. He is convinced that he will fall off the edge of the world."

"The world is not flat," Miriam says. "The Portuguese assure us of that. Ibrahim will sail around it for me, and find another … quicker… way to Cathay."

"For commerce's sake?" Will shrugs. "We are already rich, my dear. Why bother with so fraught an adventure?"

"I cannot help it, my love" Miriam replies, truthfully. Her urge to provide for her family is almost overwhelming. "I am compelled to it, as you are compelled to do as you must."

"Then let us both follow our compulsions," Will says, "and God help us both." They kiss then, and Miriam neglects to mention that she has her swiftest cog waiting for her. On the next tide she will sail for Antwerp, along with her closest companions and, once there, take up residence in the grand Palais de Juis.

*

The streets are crowded with people more than usual, for it is the 15th day of June, and the feast of St Vitus. Despite the new church frowning on such 'saintly' beliefs, the common man must have his day of fun. St Vitus lends himself to frivolity, as he is the saint who looks over those with the shaking sickness named after him, and both dancers and actors are under his watchful eye.

The populace take to capering about the streets, dancing wildly, and generally drinking to excess, all of which contributes to a congestion of the city's roads. Will Draper sees that he must abandon his horse to the care of one of his men, and proceed on foot. The summons, from Mush, is urgent, and he must get on.

After a walk through muddy streets, awash with slops and excrement, he finally comes to a more elegant part of the city. The well built villa stands out from its neighbours, as a model of modern building, and two men stand guard at its gate.

"General Draper, to see Sir Richard Cromwell," he says, and one of the men salutes him.

"Corporal Wilmott, sir," he says. "I was by you when we beat the Swiss in Flanders."

"A great day," Will replies, and takes a couple of coins from his purse. The man waves them away and gestures for him to go straight inside. Mush is standing in the hall, by an unlit fire. He looks worried, and his smile at Will's arrival is forced.

"Welcome, brother in law," he says. "I hope you can be of some help to us. It is Richard."

"Is the great ox unwell?" Will asks. Richard Cromwell is a giant of a man in so many ways. He is worth any five men in a fight, and can argue his cause with anyone brave enough to contradict him. Despite his almost ogre-like presence, he is generally liked, even loved, by all those who really know him.

"He claims to be dying," Mush explains. "I came here to take him out carousing, and found him abed, with his servants almost in mourning."

"You jest," Will says, but he can see how upset his friend is. "He is in his bed now?"

"Go up, and see for yourself," Mush tells him. "I can get no sense from the fellow."

Will Draper climbs the steep staircase, and is shown to Richard Cromwell's bedroom by a tear streaked young serving girl. He removes his hat, and goes in. Richard is propped up in his bed, bolstered all about with pillows. He is grey faced, and looks but half the man he once was.

"Richard… you are unwell… what is it?"

"Time to die, Will," the big Welshman replies. "I felt death's wings flutter by me this last night. I am not long for this world."

"Nonsense," Will says, as heartily as he can muster. "I think you have been imbibing too much wine these last few days, and you are hung over. A few raw eggs in brandy will soon settle your stomach."

"No, old friend," Richard replies. "I am done with this life now. In truth, I was done with it on the day my dearest Lady Jane met her wicked end. I   shall curse Henry Tudor for that vile deed with my very last breath."

"Come now, old comrade, you cannot allow that to cause you so much upset now," Will says. The two men have had their differences in the past, but their love and comradeship remains constant.

"I am not upset," Richard says, glumly, "I am simply dying."

"Of what?" It is a good question, for Will knows that one must die of something. "It is St Vitus' day today, so are you going to dance yourself to death, old fellow?"

"Do not bait me, friend," Richard

tells him. "I can feel the canker within me. It is by my heart, and will have me before long. All that remains is for me to make dispositions of my property and other wealth. Can you act for me in this matter, Will, or must I find myself some expensive lawyer to take down my last words?"

"I can write down your wishes for you," Will says, "but it is a futile action, for you will be up and calling for one of Miriam's pies before nightfall." It is a shrewd enough guess, but one that is not to come about. Despite all of Will and Mush's cajoling, the big Welshman refuses to get up from his bed. He is, he tells them, warm, comfortable, content and ready to meet with his maker.

"Soon, I shall be in the arms of Almighty God," he explains, "and whom amongst us can want for more?"

"Perhaps Almighty God is not quite ready for your arrival," Mush says. "In my faith we are told not to be so damned righteous as to think that we know what God's purpose is. We must do our best, and let His will be done. I am sure that the immediate fate of one portly Welsh border bandit's son is of little interest to Him just at this moment."

The jibe about Richard's antecedents will usually raise the big man's hackles, and get him into a heated argument about his honest 'Williams' side of the family, but this time, it does not. Richard simply shrugs his shoulders, as if none of it matters anymore and looks out of the window. The view over the crowded rooftops is not inspiring, so he turns his gaze back onto Will Draper, and it is full of a sadness he cannot put into words.

"Let me die here, Will," he says. "Find paper, and fetch ink, old friends, for I must have my words taken down, before it is too late. My last words to a world that is as tired of me, as I am of it."

"That is just boredom," says Will. "All you need is something to lift your spirits and you'll be as right as rain. Come home with me now, and let Miriam make us a fine dinner. We can invite anyone you wish."

"Pray, do not volunteer your wife's services so readily," Richard replies. "She is busy making ready for her trip to Bristol. Is not the fabled Prince Ibrahim, Son of Kush, almost ready to sail for the New Found Land again?"

"Go with him," Mush says. "So great an adventure would turn you from this morbid path."

"And see me fall off the very edge of the world?" the Welshman asks, with a glint of humour in his eyes. "I think not. Let Ibrahim ben Rachid and I both meet our maker in our own ways. Is he still using the Hebrew '*ben*'?"

"Yes, he says it confuses his enemies if he is neither a good Christian, a failed Mussulman, nor a black Jew. The man is quite the fool, of course, but the adventure is postponed for now," Will tells them. "The men and ships are for the French war instead, by order of the king."

"The man is raving mad," Mush Draper groans. "Can this stupid war be so important?"

"The king thinks so," Will replies with a sigh. "He thinks it will firmly fix his royal name in posterity."

"Murdering so many innocents will do that," Richard Cromwell says. "Now, shall you help me, or must I send for some smooth lawyer to attend to my private business?"

"God forbid such a thing," the King's Examiner says. "Why pay a lawyer when you can use a friend for the same purpose freely?"

"Then we *are* friends?" Richard Cromwell asks. "You forgive me?"

"For what?" Will replies.

"That terrible business in Norfolk," Richard says. "All those men… hanged without trial."

"I was younger then, and did not understand the political necessity of those men's deaths." Will is still sure the deaths could have been avoided, but the years have passed, and it does not do to linger over past hurts and slights. If so, they fester, until you can think of nothing else.

"And I was younger too, and did not understand the immorality of my actions," Richard tells his friend. "Either way, they would have died. Uncle Thomas decreed it thus, you see. To let them live would have threatened the monarchy. I cared back then. Now, I would just let them go, and be damned to the politics of it all."

"And I would probably hang them all," Will says. "How the world does change, old friend. Your soul is at peace, whilst mine grows ever more in need of succour. Are you absolutely sure you are ready to die, and this is not just the product of indigestion, and a morbid imagination?"

"My time is near," Richard tells him. "I feel it in my heart. Help me, Will."

There is nothing else for it. Will Draper fetches paper, quill and ink, then settles down at Richard's writing desk. He looks up, and his friend smiles, gratefully at him.

"Ready."

"Then let us begin," Richard murmurs. "To my pompous young ass of an eldest son, Henry Cromwell, I leave the three Huntingdonshire estates, and their livestock, valued at thirty thousand pounds; with an annual income of two thousand eight hundred and fifty pounds, per annum, together with the sum of five hundred pounds... the interest on which is to be paid annually. Said amount is to be given to the poor of this parish as he sees fit. To my second son, the more dissolute, and beloved, Francis, I bequeath *stewardship* of my London house, and the income from such properties as I own within the city walls. This bequest is to remain intact, and may not be sold, or gifted to any other person, save by royal decree. The annual rental of these twelve houses is to be paid to him on the first day of January, each year. Upon his death, probably at the hands of an angry husband, ownership is to pass to his children in equal portion. My holdings in Ramsey, some three thousand a year in rentals, I leave to my third son, to do with as he sees fit."

"Slower, Richard," Will says. "You are powerful rich, and I am powerful slow. Let my quill catch you up." Mush, who is sitting by the window, nursing a mug of rum, sweetened with sugar and the juice of a lemon, takes this moment to speak.

"Forgive me, Richard, but my *mathamaticking* is not what it should be. I am aware that Henry... a fine, boring lad, and Francis, who enjoys his life to the full, make up the number two, but where does this third child come from? Lady Frances, may God bless your late wife's sainted memory, never mentioned him to me. Does the child happen to have a name?"

"He does. It is Morgan Williams… for his grandfather, and he was born in the spring of 1518. A full month before I was contracted to wed Lady Frances Murfyn, the daughter of the Lord Mayor of London. Uncle Thomas thought it an advantageous match for Austin Friars at the time. Morgan's mother was a very pretty dairymaid on my father's farm, and he was raised there."

"Bastards cannot usually inherit," Will says with the cold precision of reality. "I think your legitimate sons will contest the bequest, and tie things up in Chancery for many years."

"I cannot leave him penniless," Richard replies. "He is a fine boy, and runs the local village school. We are known to one another, as father and son, yet he has never sought out any financial help from me. How should I proceed if he is to benefit in equal portion to the others?"

"You must avoid naming him as your bastard," Will tells him. "Rafe Sadler had a similar case only last year. The father left a portion of his estate to '*the son of an old friend*'. As he was not named as an illegitimate child, but a friend's offspring, there could be no objection. The bequest went through unopposed."

"Then word it so, my dear friend," says Richard Cromwell. "I cannot see the boy going without because I did not marry his mother. Poor Meg died in childbirth, and I am all he has left."

"Then I shall put down that you leave the bequest to Master Morgan Williams, so that he might continue with his excellent work as headmaster of a school for the children of the poor. Such magnanimity is expected in rich men's wills, and is seldom opposed. It is how they think to get into Heaven. Is that all, or do you have anything else we do not know about?"

"Morgan is, to my knowledge, the end of it," Richard replies, "save for a child born to one of Queen Katherine of Aragon's ladies in waiting when I first came to court. Kate is almost sixteen now, and thinks herself to be the daughter, and only child, of a gentleman farmer in Oakley, which lies in Northamptonshire."

"Then you should provide," Will says. "Why not place a thousand in trust, naming the gentleman as beneficiary, and then his daughter upon his death?"

"As you wish," Richard says. "Though you might make it five thousand. The gentleman concerned is aware of the situation, and will not think it odd. I find myself to have an embarrassment of riches just now, so five thousand will do the girl nicely."

"Damnation, Richard," Mush Draper says, with a conspiratorial chuckle, "just how much money are you worth? I have made my own fortune under Henry, and with Miriam's help, but nothing like the amounts you talk of."

"That is all, under my Cromwell name," the ailing Welshman explains. "Though I have done nicely as Dick Williams. I am a partner in the company of Bulstrode, Slye and Williams, and it acts as a safe conduit to the king. I let it be known that any royal requests notified to my company will go to one of the king's leading advisors… Sir Richard Cromwell… and corrupt men of business queue up to employ our services. It is customary for the fellow to pay over a purse of twenty-five pounds to become a client, and another twenty-five pounds for each request we champion. Messieurs Bulstrode and Slye tell me that we seldom have less than ten clients on our books at any one time."

"Then it makes you about five thousand a year?" Will guesses. "Who do you wish to leave so excellent a business to?"

"I want Miriam to take over my share holding," Richard tells his friend. "Though your sums are somewhat out. Last year I cleared over forty-five thousand pounds. If one of my clients wants a certain tax repealed, and another wishes it to stay, I allow Henry or the Privy Council to decide. Either way, I have at least one satisfied customer. I apologise to the one who has lost out, and refund him his twenty-five pounds, then boast to the winner of our success, as Master Slye presents him with our account, usually for a thousand pounds. He explains that we have risked much in obtaining so favourable a result, and the client, who stands to make at least ten times as much, gladly pays up."

"Miriam does not need it, my friend." Will knows his wife controls much of the mercantile business between England and Flanders, and that she is, at only thirty-three years of age, worth ten times as much as Richard Cromwell.

"Then let her endow a hospital, or a university with it," Richard says. "Why, for all I care she can use it to buy back the Holy Land from the infidels who now possess it. I trust her, Will. She can see that the money is spent most wisely."

"Very well. If that is the last of it, all that remains is a decent bequest to the king. He considers his patronage to be worth a great deal, so expects a show of gratitude in return. It is the custom, and will make things go easier when the will is read."

"Yes, that is so. To Henry Tudor, King of England, Ireland, and France, Supreme Head of the protestant Church of England, I leave the pick of my best stallions, in the hope that he is thrown whilst out hunting, and breaks his bastard neck. He should choose *Satan*, if he knows his horse flesh... but the name will put him off, for he has ever feared the occult arts. Instead, he will pick '*The Prince*'. You might also bequeath him enough money to pay for the beast's upkeep for life. Shall we say a hundred pounds?"

"Henry might think you to be stingy," Mush advises. "You will want him on your side, if you ever do actually die."

"Then leave him the Abbey of Buckton Parva, along with its entire income," Richard Cromwell says, with a wry grin upon his face. "The damned place is a money pit, and costs me more than it is worth. Let Henry buy a new roof for the main hall, and deal with a hundred Roman Catholic yeomen who still want to say the popish mass every Sunday. The place is a poisoned chalice, and it will bring him nothing but ill luck."

"Very well. I shall have Rafe draw it up in legal form later today, and it shall be ready to sign on the morrow. Can you wait until then, or is the Angel of Death pressing you for an answer?"

"I shall manage." Richard frowns then. "You see that I leave nothing to my many friends, no doubt? It is only that they have all prospered well under the guidance of Uncle Thomas, and do not need it."

"You cannot say that of Tom

Wyatt," Mush puts in. "He is poorer now than when we first met, thanks to his profligate nature."

"Ah, yes, I forget our impoverished poet." Richard thinks for a moment, then gives a feeble grin. "Let him receive the sum of ten thousand pounds, Will … upon the publication of his first set of legitimate poetic works. That should certainly concentrate his mind well enough. Enough about me now though. How do you fare, old friend? Do you prosper still?"

"Well enough," Will replies. "Though Miriam's overseas business is set for a few problems."

"Oh, why?" Richard asks.

"Because the king, bless his heart, is set on invading France," Mush says from the door. "It is a great folly."

"I was over there last year, for but a little while," Richard Cromwell says, softly. "It was but a raid, and we did kill many of the French for little gain. The king shook my hand and told me I was his greatest soldier."

"Then he needs you now," Will says.

"Let him rot for all I care," Richard replies from his sickbed. "He will send ten thousand men against some impoverished French town, sack it, and claim he is the new King of France. Then, six months later, he will get bored and return to England, leaving poor Suffolk in charge. Charles Brandon will raid through Picardy and lay siege to Beauvais."

"That is certainly the approved way of things," Will says, hoping to get his friend involved enough to forget about his ridiculous premonitions of death. "You would do otherwise then?"

"Yes, I would, were I not on my deathbed," Richard Cromwell replies, stubbornly holding on to his belief that he is about to meet his maker. "I would leave a garrison to hold what we have, and invade Normandy. François will think we mean to snatch the fertile Loire valleys, and raise the *Oriflamme* banner against us."

"That is so," Will agrees. "He can call on fifty-thousand foot, and ten thousand knights. With such a force he can block us in the Loire and force us to retreat to the coast."

"Just what King François expects, my dear old friend." Richard Cromwell, who is surprisingly pert for a dying man taps a finger against his nose, knowingly. "Only I would not be there. I would leave a few hundred men to hold one of the towns, along with a troop of cavalry to provide a screen. François will advance on us, and expect us to either retreat, or stand our ground with less than fifteen thousand foot and a couple of thousand horse. Instead, I would lead the main army eastwards, around the French, and race for Paris."

"That would be a huge risk to take," Mush says, "but the idea appeals to me."

"Of course it does, because you are a thief at heart," Richard tells him. "We cannot match the French numbers in open battle, but we can man the walls of Paris quite easily with a few thousand good men."

"François will have to turn about," Will reasons. "He cannot let us keep Paris."

"He will march his tired army back the eighty odd miles he has just marched over, whilst the troops in Flanders, and the men behind him in the Loire valley, will harass his rearguard all the way." Richard Cromwell makes a gesture that says '*there, you must see it all*'. "Each time he stops and turns to fend us off, the Paris garrison will sally forth and raid his front ranks. After a few days, he will start to understand that his food supply, which is controlled by Paris, has dried up. That is when he will wish to negotiate. You must tell Henry not to give an inch."

"Cannot you tell him?" Mush Draper asks, ingenuously.

"How can I do that, you damned fool?" says Richard, his voice shot through with petulance. "I will be dead!"

*

The streets of Antwerp are always

clean and inviting, thanks to a city council who are well funded, and organised by the shadowy presence of the Draper Company. The English mercantile house invest money in the harbour, and create hundreds of jobs in the docks, and throughout the town.

Mijnheer Tomas Cornelis is a citizen of the city, and he often likes to stroll about the streets and harbour after dark, thinking deep thoughts. This night, he is with the young man who visits him so regularly that his neighbours whisper that he is a bastard son or some such.

"It is a fine evening," Cornelis, alias Cromwell, says as they walk along the quayside. "We should savour it."

"Yes, master," Kel Kelton replies. "For it is the last peaceful one we will see for a while. The first troops will land in Calais on the morning tide."

"Yes, I know. Henry was not for dissuading, but I hope to guide him onto a more sensible path. If he but lets Francois buy him off, all will end well, without the slaughter of an Agincourt or a Crecy."

"Henry wants a last battle," Kel replies.

"Then he truly is a damnable old fool," Tom Cromwell says. "Modern warfare is no longer about gallant charges. It is about who has the most cannon, and how many muskets you can bring to bear. If he tries to emulate his 'battle of the spurs' his charge will be shredded by chain shot."

"Will Draper thinks as you do, sir," says Kel, "but Henry will not listen. He insists on Norfolk leading the army, with Suffolk in support. A fine pairing, I think."

"Just so. They absolutely loath one another," Cromwell says with a chuckle. "I think they will fight one another more than either will fight the French."

"The voyage to the New Found Land is abandoned," says Kel. "Henry wants the ships, and the men too. Ibrahim is joining Will Draper instead."

"Ah, my Prince of Kush." Thomas Cromwell recalls the audacity of how the Moor once turned up at the royal court, claiming to be an Abyssinian prince, and how he had almost fooled the king into an act of great folly. "Let us hope he acquits himself better than he did in his last escapade. A flying engine indeed!"

"To be fair, master, it was meant to be a floating machine," Kel says. "Its purpose was to allow a man to float down from a great height."

"And did it?"

"Well, no. I suspect that the traitor Gibbison was somewhat surprised to find himself plummeting to the earth. He must have thought himself saved, until the moment Ibrahim's contraption failed, and sent him into that tree."

"Ibrahim is that sort of a fellow."

Tom Cromwell smiles at the sheer bravado of the fellow. "He causes chaos wherever he goes. I hope Will keeps him in check, or he might invade France, all alone, and make himself the Caliph of Paris."

"He will be watched," Kel says. "I was thinking of joining up with…"

"No." Cromwell is emphatic. "You shall not go off on such a wild goose chase, my boy. Maisie would never forgive me if I let you run off to war."

"But it will all be over within a month, sir," Kel protests. "I could…"

"No, I say." Thomas Cromwell has lost enough friends, and he does not wish to lose any more. "Let Will Draper and Norfolk attend to this pointless war, and you carry on with your duties for me."

Kel Kelton sighs, but agrees to Cromwell's demands. There is little point in trying to argue with him. Instead, he will slip away on the morrow and join up with Draper's Examiners in Calais. His master will be furious, of course, but he will soon forgive him. Wars come along so infrequently, and Kel Kelton thinks that he cannot miss out on this chance for glory.

The two men stand and watch one of Miriam Draper's cogs being loaded with its cargo. There is nothing for them to say now, except the trivia of day to day life.

"Your nephew Richard is sickening, and dying again."

"Really?" Tom Cromwell shakes his head in sorrow. "He is not the same since Jane died. How I wish we could have saved her from so wicked a fate. Is he abed again?"

"Yes, and he has drawn up his will."

"That is different, at least," Cromwell muses. His nephew has predicted his own demise on several previous occasions, but he has never gone quite so far as to make out a will. "The boy can be so morbid. Still, he will soon relent and return to court."

"I hope so, for he is sore missed," says Kel. "With the king abroad, it will be for Queen Katheryn to act as temporary Regent of England, and she will need his support against the Seymours and that festering turd, Sir Richard Rich."

"Ah, yes. Rich. I found him, you know. He has worked for me at Austin Friars, then for Sir Thomas More, Stephen Gardiner, and old Norfolk. He is consistent only in that he betrays each of us in our turn. You asked for permission to kill him once, and Alonso Gomez and Mush have each offered the same service. I should have listened back then."

"I can still…"

"No. It is too late. His party is strong, with his men in every law court in the land, and almost as many agents as I once employed at Austin Friars. Do him to death now, and they would simply carry on, but with a new head."

"Then he will eclipse us all," Kel warns, and his master just shrugs at the prospect.

"Pru Beckshaw once predicted he would die alone in his bed, a very old, very rich man," Cromwell replies. "She is never wrong. Now, you must return with me to my office, where I can drink wine with you, and while away the hours until it is too late for you to disobey me and go off to war."

"Master... I would never..." Kel starts, but Thomas Cromwell holds up a staying hand, and smiles at the young man. Kel will resent him for his actions, of course, but he will be alive to resent him. "We shall travel south, in due course. Be content to be a spectator, my boy. Think of the children."

"Their mothers can look after them, and I have left enough gold to see them all through their lives."

"Then think of the mothers," Cromwell snaps. "Both Maisie and Lucy adore you. Though one can survive without you, one cannot. Lucy is a half caste, Kel. She is half Portuguese and half Moorish, and would have no legal rights. Then her children are bastards, and unable to inherit."

"You leash me like a greyhound, Master Tom," Kel grumbles. "Cannot a man wish for glory?"

"Wish, yes, but that is as far as it must go," Cromwell says. "You are my *Sejanus*, and I dare not lose you."

"Sir, my blood cries out to fight," Kel says, and Cromwell clenches his fists in frustration, and anger.

"Oh, that makes it perfectly alright then," he snarls. "You may be torn apart by a cannon's shot, or skewered on a pikestaff. Then again, you might be run through by some Frenchman who is a better swordsman than you. No, I say. You are the man for a brawl, or a sudden killing of an enemy, but not one for a battle. You have never faced a massed charge by heavy cavalry, boy."

"And you have, I suppose?" Kel replies. The words are out before he can stop them, and he wishes he could have bitten off his own tongue.

"I have," Cromwell tells the young man, "and I turned tail, and ran for my life. Indeed, I would still be running now, had I not fallen over a wounded man. I pulled him onto my horse, and saved us both. that man was Andrea Gritti, a son of a rich family, who would become Doge of Venice in his turn. It made me, lad, but only because I was running away. Had I stood my ground, i would have died that day, and that would have been that."

"I meant no…"

"I know. Now, let us play cards 'til

the light fingers of dawn creep over the roof tops."

"You are poetic, master," Kel says, but there is a sullenness in his voice that he cannot disguise, and it makes Cromwell sigh at the stubbornness of youth.

"Think how happy Maisie and Lucy shall be," he tells the young man. "We must not widow two women with the death of one husband, must we?"

2   Calais

The English fleet crosses the Channel without mishap, and sets the army ashore without any opposition. A great mass of men and equipment is unloaded, and invested within the bounds of the *Calaisis,* with skill and precision. Then the king arrives, with his ministers in tow, and things begin to go awry.

Sir Richard Rich wishes to extend his role as Attorney General over any conquered lands, whilst the Archbishop of Canterbury is keen to install the new Church of England credo. Charles Brandon, as Duke of Suffolk wishes to be given sole charge of any military action, and Norfolk seeks to deny him.

Suffolk uses his position as 'best friend' to the king to gain a private interview with him, where he will press home his request to command the army in France.

"Come now, Charles," Henry says. "Cannot you see that Norfolk, as my senior noble, must have precedent?" The king is in his chambers within the main tower of the fortress, and eager to settle any disputes that might thwart his ambitions.

"Only if he be fit for that service, Hal," Charles Brandon replies. "If Norfolk is too old, or infirm, you may then select the next in line without any difficulty." Suffolk is sure of his ground, as he has been carefully prepared by Rafe Sadler and Barnaby Fowler as to the legal aspects of the matter. "Put the old man aside, dear friend, and let me lead your army for you."

"Nothing would please me more, Charles," the king says. "We are like brothers, and I would dearly love to have you fight by my side."

"Then you will make it so?" Suffolk asks, a little surprised by so speedy a surrender.

"No, I cannot. Norfolk is quite fit enough for the task. I can only relieve him of his duties if he asks me to, or if he is found to be guilty of some offence against me."

"But, Hal... old Norfolk is always involved in some wild plot or other, and he..."

"Enough!" Henry lurches forward in his chair and snatches up his wine. "The duke has never yet been proven guilty of any single offence. Each accusation against him has been found unproven, or even malicious. I will not listen to anything more on the subject. Norfolk will lead, and you will follow."

"I shall return to England," Brandon tells the king. "I am sure to be better appreciated there."

"No, you will not, sir." Henry drains his goblet and bangs it down, hard. "You will do as you are damned well told.

You will command my artillery, and act as second in command to the army. Is that quite clear, My Lord Suffolk?"

"As you wish, of course," Suffolk replies, taken aback by the king's fierce rebuke. "I meant only that…"

"I know what you meant, Charles," Henry says with a sigh. "Do not try to thwart me in this matter. Thank me instead for my actions."

"Yes, of course, sire." Suffolk knows, from long years of experience, that he can push no harder. His friendship, cultured in boyhood, and nurtured into manhood, still has its bounds. Ultimately the duke must always defer to the king, rather than expect anything different. "I meant only to advise… not tell… and if you know better, then I must accept your greater wisdom."

"Yes, that's the spirit, my dear old fellow," Henry says, and his face lights up with a smile. "I know that Norfolk can be a terrible old boor, and his last battle was against a few rebels, but this is his last chance for glory, before I put him out to grass."

"You mean to have him retire?" Suffolk is astonished at the naïvety of this, as the Duke of Norfolk will grasp onto power to his last breath. If Henry suggests such a thing as his stepping down, the old duke will drop gentle hints about his army of twelve thousand men, camped on London's threshold.

"I do, for he is a veritable *Methuselah*," Henry replies. "Now, I really must get on. I have a war to prosecute, and a country to conquer!"

*

The Duke of Norfolk is famous for his great victories over the invading Scots and the French, but he has not fought a major battle for the best part of a quarter of a century, and things, especially militarily, do tend to move on apace.

"I need more pikemen," he complains to his son, who is in France with him, much against his will. Having once experienced the gut churning horror of a cavalry charge, he has no wish to see further military action, but he fears his father to much to stay at home and be thought of as a coward.

"You have five thousand as it is, sir," the younger man complains. "Why do you want more."

"It is the way to win this damned war, my boy,' Norfolk says, and he taps a gnarled finger against the side of his bulbous nose.

"How so?" Surrey asks, but in a conciliatory way, for he does not want his head to be slapped from his shoulders.

"A solid wall of pikes, two thousand men wide, and four deep,"

Norfolk explains. "They advance on the Frogs and force them to withdraw. Then the cavalry charge home on the broken enemy, but only if I have enough pikes, and the men to wield the bloody things."

"Forgive me, My Lord Norfolk, but your plan is badly flawed," Charles Brandon puts in from his place at the table. "Such a tactic can only end in…"

"I do not recall asking your opinion My Lord Suffolk," Norfolk snaps at his much younger second in command. "I have never yet seen a Frog, or a Scotcher, stand and fight against massed pikes."

"Thirty years ago," Suffolk replies, rather sarcastically. "Ragged arsed Highlanders with claymores, and chinless Frogs on horseback were easier meat back then." He has little faith in the duke's judgement, and writes daily to the king, begging for him to be removed from his command.

"They have grown no braver in all those years, I warrant," Norfolk tells him, with a smug smile. "Cowards, to a man."

"Cowards with muskets and new Venetian cannon, sir," the Duke of Suffolk reminds him. "At two hundred paces, I would have my musketry give fire. Even at that range, your pikes would take many casualties. Then I would have them retreat, as if running away. An English pikeman seeing that will not be able to resist. They will break ranks and charge home, confident of victory. They would be a hundred paces into their charge when the cannon begin to fire."

"What of it?" Norfolk asks. "Men have faced cannon before, and overrun them."

"Yes, the old style guns, but not these new cast metal cannon. They stay cooler and can be reloaded faster. The French will have the new grape and chain shot loaded. Have you ever seen either at work, My Lord?"

"I know of it," Norfolk says, with a dismissive wave of the hand. "The men must charge home, and take the guns."

"At one hundred paces, the chain shot will scythe through the air at waist height and cut down everyone in its way. Your 'solid' wall of pikemen will be slaughtered by the hundreds. Then the grape shot will come into play. Bags of musket balls packed into the cannon muzzles, and fired at fifty paces. Each bag contains two hundred musket balls. If any man is standing after that, the Frenchmen's own foot soldiers will charge home, and finish the job."

"I grant, we might take some casualties, of course," Norfolk replies, coldly, "but you exaggerate, sir. I doubt we will take but a quarter of our men in dead. Besides, my cavalry will be in support.

They can sweep around the French flanks, and be amongst the enemy in no time."

"Forgive me, Lord Norfolk," says Will Draper, who has put Suffolk up to doubting the old duke's plan, "but I must agree with My Lord Suffolk in this matter. I have witnessed chain shot at first hand, and it is a devastating weapon. To charge it head on is nothing short of lunacy."

"Did I ask your opinion, Draper?" the Duke of Norfolk snaps.

" *'My Lord'*, sir," Will says, pointedly. As a recent addition to the aristocracy, his title cannot be allowed to be ignored. "Or, if you wish, just Templar, as I would say 'Norfolk' to an equal."

"Equal be damned, you gabbling upstart," Norfolk roars, but subsides as soon as he begins. Will Draper is obviously looking to pick a quarrel with him, so that he might use it with Henry. "My pardon, My Lord Templar. It has been a long day. I forget that His Majesty, in his infinite wisdom, has elevated you to become one of my peers. However, a duke outranks a baron, and I must insist that you do not concern yourself in this matter any further, unless I so wish it."

"As you command, sir," Will says. "Just as long as none of my men are used in the initial assault on the French cannon."

"That smacks of cowardice," Surrey mutters, but Will catches the sly aside, and smiles at Norfolk's pimple faced son and heir.

"I bow to your superior knowledge of cowardice, Surrey," he says, "but my Examiners are not pikemen. They are general infantry, and light horse. With your father's permission, I will use them in a flanking manoeuvre and so come upon the French from the rear."

"Do what ever you wish," Norfolk says. "The main army will advance, line abreast, and throw the French back by sheer weight of numbers. My spies tell me that the French number less than twenty-five thousand."

"My agents put the figure at thirty thousand foot, eight thousand horse, a thousand muskets, and about thirty cannon. The cannon are all of the modern Italian type, wheel mounted, and easy to move about. They can fire at the rate of eight or ten shots to the hour. We are twenty five thousand foot, and six thousand horse. Our cannon are old ones taken from the walls at Calais. I doubt we can load and fire them above thrice in the hour. A full frontal attack will fail. Then who will tell the king?"

"This meeting is over," Norfolk replies, and he lurches to his feet. "I shall tell Henry that we are going to win, and that is that. Even if I lose half the army, or more, I shall break the French tomorrow."

Norfolk and Surrey leave the

chamber, and Suffolk can do nothing but shrug his shoulders in utter disgust. He has tried, but old Norfolk is far too pigheaded to listen to good advice.

"I did my best, Will," Suffolk says. "Half of those pikemen are my own fellows, and I have no wish to see them cut down like corn. The king supports the old fool, and will not relent, until he suffers a defeat."

"It will be too late then," says Will. "By noon tomorrow, what few men survive will be falling back to Calais. The war will be lost, and Calais shall come under siege. Henry will be forced to take ship back to England, with his tail between his legs."

"Then Norfolk's head will finally roll," Suffolk offers. "That is a result, is it not?"

"Not at the cost of fifteen thousand dead, Charles," Will says. "We must seek to find a way of lessening the effect of the duke's stupidity."

"How?" Suffolk is a Draper man, and will help out in any way he can. It does not benefit him if the French win, for he will have to put up with the king's moaning for years to come. Besides, he is the more humane sort of lord, and he does not wish to sacrifice thousands of his own people for a poor plan of action. "If you have a plan, share it with me, and I shall do what I can to forward it."

"I have a plan," Will says, "but it must be kept between the two of us."

"Then tell me." Suffolk replies, earnestly, "for I dearly wish to save my own troops from Norfolk's rank behaviour."

"Very well. Can your fellows sing, Charles?"

"With a cup of ale inside them, they can be almost poetic," Suffolk says, with a broad grin. "What have you in mind?"

"We must seek out Tom Wyatt, and enlist his help," Will says. "His skill with words might well keep us in with a chance of victory."

"You mean to defy Norfolk's direct order?" the duke asks. "He will then blame any defeat on you, and demand Henry exacts retribution."

"I shall not defy him," Will replies, with a knowing wink. "Let our troops be drawn up in full formation, with pikes to the fore, and musketry and foot behind. The enemy will bless their luck, and point every cannon in Christendom at us. I doubt they will even bother to offer us quarter."

"The French king says he will sweep us into the Channel, and take back Calais," Suffolk tells his friend. It is a gloomy prospect, but one that seems ever more likely. "I am a poor swimmer, Will, so must hope the little frog is wrong in his assumption."

"François does not have enough strength to dislodge us, Charles," Will explains. "He hopes to halt us here, tomorrow, and force us back into Calais, rather than let us advance on Boulogne and join the Emperor's coming siege. If we can manage that, he must fall back on Paris, and see if the city can withstand our joint assault."

"And if it falls?" Suffolk asks, as he wonders if there will be booty going begging after the French citadel surrenders. "What then?"

"If it falls to Emperor Charles, Henry will want to race on to Paris, and try to steal the city from his allies. If we take Boulogne, I very much think he will settle down to being the new king of a much truncated France. His holdings will increase by a third in land, and a quarter in revenue. Though he must leave a couple of strong garrisons to hold his new domains."

"A task for Norfolk and his son, I think?" Suffolk says, and they both laugh at the prospect of the duke and his loathsome boy being stranded in France for years to come.

"Yes, that would be a fine jest," Will muses.

"I doubt Norfolk would remain over long in his new command," Suffolk says. "He is as like to leave the idiot son in charge, and slip back across the Channel to

London. He cannot leave well enough alone, even when the king looks on him with utter disdain."

"Disdain today can turn into utter dependance tomorrow," says Will, with clear foresight. "Henry can change his mind in a trice, and see treason in a friend, where none exists. We must not underestimate old Norfolk, my friend!"

3   Plots and Plans

'It seems strange that our dear husbands are but so few miles away from us, yet we cannot see them." Prudence Beckshaw voices her thoughts, but knows full well that there is nothing to be done about the matter. "I pray they are keeping well."

"We should go to them," Miriam says. "We could deliver supplies, and provide them with much needed encouragement."

"My dear," Marion Giles puts in. "It is a hundred and twenty miles from Antwerp to Calais, across hostile French lands. We cannot contemplate such a journey, even though my foolish new betrothed is with the army."

"What, Egbert is with the Examiners?" Miriam asks, somewhat surprised. Egbert Towler is a notable forger of documents, but he is hardly the stuff of which fighting men are made.

"He spoke of courage, and valour," Marion says. "Like all men, he needs to prove his worth to us both. I suspect he thinks it will make him more manly in my eyes."

"But you are going to marry him," says Pru. "What more proof does he need of your devotion?"

"I cannot say," Marion is, at thirty four, fast reaching an age where men will cease to think of her as marriage material, and she craves the comfort of a warm relationship with a man she can love. Egbert is such a man. He is like her first husband, a parson who died too young, in so far as that he is kind, and listens to her. He admires her looks, but also her obvious intellect. "He begged Will to enlist him, and your husband obliged. Though he has placed him in charge of the baggage animals, and thus to the rear in any battle. I must pray for him."

"You must see him," Marion decides. "I shall have Captain Stubbs take us down the coast in my fastest cog. A night, and then half a day's sailing will see us safely into Calais harbour. Then we take horse, and gallop on towards Boulogne. The French straddle the road, and would offer a fight soon. We can be there before it starts."

"A fine plan," Pru tells her friend. "But the men will be angered at us roaming the *Calaisis* without an armed escort."

"Sergeant Tam Jones is in Antwerp," Miriam tells her. "He is almost recovered from his last wounds, and will be glad to escort us. There are at least another dozen Examiner troopers who are recovering from their last engagement. Most will be happy to join us. They will be our bodyguards."

"I would rather have Richard Cromwell with us," Marion says. "He is the strongest man I have ever seen, and quite fearsome to the enemy."

"You will have to make do with his uncle," Thomas Cromwell is at the door, and listens to every word with avid pleasure. "My nephew is still in his bed, and swearing to die. Kel will be pleased at the chance to get nearer to the fray. When do we leave?"

"Master Tom, you cannot leave Antwerp," Miriam replies. "It is far too dangerous. The army will recognise you at once."

"I shall wear a cunning disguise," Cromwell tells her. "Besides, with this long beard and my ever balding pate, I am not the man I was, even two years ago."

"But, master…"

"I will go with you," Cromwell insists. "No more time wasting. Have Captain Stubbs land us at *Dunkerque*. It is a shorter sail, and will bring us to the army a half day sooner."

"What if we lose?" Pru asks. "How will we escape from the carnage?"

"Who knows?" Tom Cromwell shrugs. It is many years since he fought in a scuffle, and a lifetime ago since he fought the French outside Venice. "I am a great believer in the old adage that '*something will turn up*'. You see, it *usually* does."

*

The Duke of Norfolk is content.

He has just explained his master plan to his stunned junior officers, and sent them off to get an early night for the battle on the morrow. That few of them now expect to survive another night is of little consequence to him, as he is convinced that, providing they do not step back, he will win a famous victory.

"What if Draper is right?" the Earl of Surrey asks of his father. He hates the entire Draper edifice, but he respects the man's ability to always come out on top. "What if the French slaughter us with their cannon fire?"

"What if they do?" Norfolk says, like a true general. "My man, McTavish, knows about these things, and he calculates that they cannot reload fast enough to cut down every wave of men. He tells me that though the first line of pikes will be virtually annihilated, the second and third rows will fare a little better. By the time the fourth line of pikes reaches the French guns, they will still be reloading them. My lads will then murder the French gunners, and so win the day. Simple *mathamatickery*, boy."

"But each line holds three thousand men," Surrey calculates. "You will lose about ten thousand men, just to overcome their cannon. What of their reserves… their heavy cavalry?"

"Oh, they will probably run away," Norfolk replies with a blasé shrug. "They usually do, you know. Agincourt saw horse against bows, as did Crecy… and our lads won the day on each occasion. That's the problem with these French, you see. Cowards, to a man… the lot of 'em."

"It will be a grand slaughter to watch," Surrey tells his father.

"To watch?" Norfolk grins at his son's naïvety. "You shall have a place of honour, my lad. No man alive can say a Norfolk shirks his duty. Your place shall be at the front of the second line."

May you die in your sleep, you bastard, Surrey thinks to himself, but he dare not utter a word. Having once experienced the gut churning horror of a cavalry charge into massed infantry, he understands that he is, above all else, an absolute coward. One way or another, he will avoid his duty on the morrow, and only advance once the enemy are broken, As for Norfolk, the younger man is more convinced than ever that he is past his best, and should be put out to grass. If only he could possess the courage to knock the old fool on the head… but he does not, and so must suffer the unending agonies of the coward.

*

The king leaves Calais at dawn, and begins the short journey out to where the English army await the French advance. He is in good company, for apart from the two hundred hand picked soldiers guarding him, he has Tom Cranmer, the Archbishop of Canterbury, Stephen Gardiner, Bishop of Winchester and Ambassador Chapuys in his entourage.

The first two are to lend heavenly support, whilst Eustace Chapuys is there as an observer for his lord, the Emperor Charles. Henry understands this well enough, and encourages the little Savoyard to stay close to him.

"Enemy country, my dearest Chapuys," the king tells the ambassador. "You must tell the emperor how I did brave it in person, rather than send on some poor stand-in to take my place."

"Your Majesty's courage is not in doubt, sire," Chapuys replies, from the comfort of his fresh horse. "My emperor often writes of his love and affection for you '*his most martial of brothers*'."

"He says so, does he?" Henry grins like a child with sweets to eat. "Then today I shall prove my abilities yet again. The French seek to fight, and I shall not disappoint them. I will smite them hip and… dear God, who is that terrible looking fellow?"

"Oh, it is only my personal servant, sire. Alonso Gomez is like a family heirloom. I once tried to discharge him, but he explained why he could never leave my service in so forceful a way that I have never since repeated the mistake."

"He looks like a born killer," Henry says.

"He is, Your Majesty," Chapuys replies. "Before he came to me, he was chased across Spain and Portugal by the Inquisition. By the time he left Lisbon on a fast ship, seventeen of their number lay dead in his wake."

"Dear Christ," Henry mutters, with sudden respect. "Yet he is not a gentleman?"

"No, sire. He is not a gentleman. Even by French or Venetian standards, he is nothing more than a wicked cutthroat. Here, let me demonstrate." Chapuys beckons, and Gomez spurs his mount until it comes level with him. "Alonso, do you recall when a certain lord sent four men to murder me in London?"

"I do sir," Alonso Gomez says, and his eyebrows knit together in remembered anger. "I regret that one of them escaped alive, but I simply ran out of knives."

"Should I ask you to guard His Majesty from harm, and a dozen ruffians burst in upon him, what would you do?"

"Why, kill them, master," the Spaniard says with mild surprise. What else would one do?"

"A dozen?" Henry scoffs.

"They cannot all get through the door at once," Gomez replies, casually.

"Two by two, and I will kill at least six before they can gain entry. Then I would abandon my throwing knives, and resort to sword and axe. I doubt they would press too hard."

"Dear Christ, fellow, come and work for me, and I will pay you most handsomely," Henry says.

"No, sire, I cannot. I swore an oath to stay with Señor Chapuys until his dying breath is gasped."

"A noble sentiment," Henry says. "You and your Spaniard must stay by my side today. See how a king fights, what?"

"An honour, sire," Eustace Chapuys replies, diplomatically.

'Bullshit', Alonso Gomez thinks to himself. If the French get close, this one will be on a boat back to Gravesend, and may the devil take the hindmost. It is a fact that the more one has, the more one does not wish to lose it.

They ride down to the place on the river where Henry's royal barge awaits, and board her. The sailors lay three gangplanks down, side by side, and four of their number carry Henry aboard on a specially built Sedan chair.

It is one thing to set out on horseback, but the king's leg will not stand the rough ride, and they dare not risk the wound opening again.

Sir Thomas Heneage has the barge

loaded with food, thirty heavily armed Royal Examiners, and enough wine to last the entire company a month. The crew of twenty oarsmen, a rudder man, and the captain have their instructions.

Heneage will see that the captain of the vessel makes only slow progress up the placid river, ensuring that the king's arrival is none too soon. The battle must be done with, before Henry sets foot on dry land once more. England needs a living king, more than a foolish and possibly dead hero.

*

"What about '*Her Song doth Kill me Softly*'?" Tom Wyatt suggests, as dawn's rosy hued fingers begin to spindle over the near horizon.

"How does it go?" Mush Draper asks. He is familiar with the bawdy stuff, but never bothers with the longer, more sentimental ballads. The overt sentimentality makes him feel quite nauseous.

"It is one I have been working on for some months," the poet replies. It has a certain gravitas, I believe. Listen to this:

> *I heard she doth sing a goodly song,*
> *sung with a certain rhyme,*
> *And so, I called to see her,*
> *and listeneth for a time.*
> *Then there she was, this young lass,*
> *a tonic to mine eyes,*
> *Easing my pain with a sweet voice,*
> *and thus shewing mine life*

with her words… Killing me sof…"

"Enough!" Mush Draper roars. We want to rouse the troops, not send them to sleep, Tom. What about something that bounces along?"

"Bounces along?"

"Y e s .   W h a t   a b o u t   t h a t *'Greensleeves'* the men are all humming?"

"You would need a few sopranos to get that one right," the poet replies. "Might Abe Wake bring his pincers along? Besides, it drags a little. The tune is strong, but the lyrics are a little wooden."

"Then what?"

"How about *'Forty hairy virgins'*?" Wyatt suggests. "Or *'The Milkmaid Doth Fal De Rah With Me'*?"

"How does that one go?" Mush asks.

"You know. And as she stooped o'er her pail I did *fal de rah* and *diddle de doh* with her."

"More like it," Mush admits to the deep voiced poet. "One of yours, Wyatt?"

"It is," Tom Wyatt confesses, with a smile. "The king did laugh for a week at the suggestive lyrics. He even paid off my wine bill for me."

"I should start with that," Mush advises. "Then go right on to another dirty one, without a pause. Anything smutty about the frogs?"

"Oh, I see. You want some cutting political comment," Thomas Wyatt says.

"You should have said sooner. What say you to a round of '*The Frog Who Sat on my Thumb*'?"

"That sounds promising." Mush needs only enough ribald songs to keep the army singing, rather than charging. "I take it that it concerns frogs and thumbs in a filthy way?"

"Of course. Listen to this.
A froggy did the Channel hop,
his holdings to expand,
but Norfolk Tommy cried out
'*stop*',
and kissed his pretty hand.
The Frog was taken with this plot,
and never saw the farce,
François took in Norfolk's rot,
and took it up the…"

"Yes, I get the gist of it," Mush says, almost crying with laughter. "I think that will do us well enough, my friend."

"So, we sing these songs, and send up great hurrahs," Tom Wyatt asks. "What then? The cannon still await our charge. We cannot sing the French to death, you know."

"Hold back, until you judge the time is right," Mush says, rather enigmatically. "Then press home for all you are worth."

"Very well," the poet replies, then looks about the spacious tented pavilion. "Where is Will?"

"He is away, on family business,"

Mush tells his friend. "It seems my sister and John Beckshaw's wife are in Calais, against his wishes, and he is seeing them on the next boat out of here."

"I wish him good luck with that," Tom Wyatt mutters, as he returns to his own tent. Miriam Draper has, in the years he has known her, never been diverted from her course, and she is not the sort to be 'put' on a boat without demur, or even a little bloodshed.

*

"Captain, me and the lads have no stomach for this," Corporal Jesse Hawks says to his troop commander. They are leading their horses away to the east of the english camp, as if heading for the broad road that runs around the coast, and safely back into Calais. "We seem to be sneaking away from a fight, and it ain't right."

"Not so, Jesse Hawks, for you are heading to a goodly fight with me," Jeremiah Cord growls back at the young trooper. "If you want to speak to me on the march, go through your sergeant… so that he might speak to his lieutenant, who may then ask to speak to me."

"But…" Jesse Hawks' voice trails away to silence as he sees the look of menace in his captain's eyes. "Yes, Captain Cord."

"Good. Now, bugger off back to your place, and warn the rest of the men to keep quiet, and obey orders." Hawks does as he is told, and the minor rebellion is quashed. The troop of five hundred Examiners, each armed with arquebuses, lances and swords, moves steadily eastwards, and by the time the camp is beginning to stir, and ready for battle, Will Draper and his Royal Examiners are many miles away from the proposed battle field.

*

"Desertion?" the duke cannot believe what his agent tells him. "Draper's men are gone, you say?"

"They rode out with muffled hooves, Your Lordship," Hob Newton replies. "It seems the man does not wish to fight for you this day."

"For the king," Norfolk says. "It is one thing to skulk off with his soldiers if we fall out, but to desert the king on the eve of a battle is nothing short of treason."

"Shall I have the papers drawn up, sir?" Hob Newton asks.

"No. We will let Henry find out for himself," the duke decides. "It will make the treachery of this priest's bastard seem all the worse in his eyes. Draper's head shall adorn a high spike before the week is done!"

*

"What is this?" The Duc de Ponet waves his hand over the tray that a servant is setting down before him in his sumptuous pavilion. There is a small, roasted fowl, some soft boiled eggs, cheese, and thin slices of bread, toasted in the French way.

"Breakfast, Milord?" the young man offers, and receives a swift kick for his temerity.

"That is not breakfast, Raoul," the duc sneers. It is something to feed my horse with. Where are the fancies? Or the fried lamb's kidneys? Has France run out of fresh strawberry compote?"

"No, sir, but Chef says the lambs are not yet hung enough to be succulent. He begs your forgiveness, and hopes the soft boiled eggs… duck and goose… are a tasty substitute."

"I see. I suppose one should not fight on a full stomach. What is there to drink… not English beer, I hope?"

"There will be plenty of that in a few hours, Milord," the servant says. "Once you have crushed the English."

"Well said, my boy," the duc replies, benevolently. "Forgive the kick up the arse. To make up for it, you shall ride beside me in the first attack.'

"Sir, I lack a horse." The servant holds his breath, for the Duc de Ponet's generosity is well known. "Else I would follow you into Hell."

"By the sainted Denis, and Our sweet Virgin Lady," the duc cries. "I hope all Frenchmen are like you this day…

young…"

"Raoul Dumond, sir," the lad says. "My father served your father at the infamous Battle of the Spurs. When the English charged without first discussing the terms of engagement."

"Yes, by God. That was a black day for the English," Ponet swears. "Such infamy won them the day, but left their king with no honour. His name has ever been mud since then. I hope he prays for forgiveness, each night. Boualtier, find a decent horse for young Dumond here. Then give him one of my lesser swords, and a leather jerkin. From now on, he is to ride in my personal demesne. Now, let us have at these eggs."

"Your Lordship," a herald comes into the pavilion, and bows low. "News from our scouts. The enemy are deserting in numbers. Some five hundred men left their camp an hour ago, and are heading for the coast road, whilst a hundred or so more are marching back to Calais in a more direct route. Are we to try and catch them?"

"Goodness, no," the duc tells the man. "The Duke of *Norfook* has sent word of how we are to dispose ourselves on the battle lines today, and I find his thoughts to be most gentlemanly. We are not to start until the eleventh hour, and if we are still fighting at three, we are to break off for the taking of refreshments. Quarter is to be given, and offered by both sides, and all gentlemen are to be given immediate parole, upon them giving licence not to fight any more this day. It is a sound and honourable way to fight a war."

"Sir, what if they win?" the young Frenchman asks.

"Win?" The duc shakes his head, and forks a soft egg into his mouth. "The Duke of Norfolk tells me his plan. He will charge us, as the English always do. Perhaps he might let his crossbows and muskets try to weaken us first, but that will not do. We are behind strong barriers, and can hold out against a few bolts, bullets, and arrows. Then he will send his men at us in waves. Tell the gunners to hold fire until seventy five paces, then flay them."

"It will be a complete slaughter, sir." The Royal Herald smiles at the thought of the plunder to come, and the ransoms that might be extracted. "Though once they break we cannot give chase from fixed positions."

"This is why I an the general of the army," the duc replies. He is in his late thirties now, and has spent his life putting down small protestant insurrections all over France. His physique is that of a strong man, just going to seed, but he is still a formidable fighter. Until now, he has never fought against a foe who is armed as well as he, and eager to spill his guts. Still, he will remain behind the wall of cannon, until the end is close, then rush out with his best gentlemen, and ride down those who seek to flee the field. "I shall have four hundred horse waiting, and we will bring ruin on the rest. I only hope that the Duke of *Norfook* is not a fast runner!"

*

Miriam is furious. She arrives in Calais, only to find a message from her husband. It tells her, in the starkest terms that he will have nothing to do with the coming battle, and that he is saving all the men in his troop that he can. He is going to make for the coast, and hopes she can send cogs to take him off the beach. To this end, she should tend to her duty, and then return to Antwerp… 'where our old uncle is in need of you'.

It makes her blood boil, until Tom Cromwell eases it from her grasp, and reads it through. He cannot stop himself from laughing, and he calls for young Joe to fetch him a jug of watered wine.

"Your mistress will need brandy," he jests. "I fear her husband's machinations have quite fluxed her this morning."

"What can it mean?" Miriam asks of him. "Will could never desert his post. How can I get together enough cogs at such short notice?"

"Who brought you this message?" Cromwell asks. "One of his troopers?"

"No, one of the loyal French, from Calais, who are with Norfolk." Miriam begins to see the light. "Ah, I see. This 'loyal' Frenchman will show the note to Norfolk, no doubt. It is some sort of a ruse."

"Your treacherous Froggy will also report to the nearest French officer too," says Tom Cromwell. "He will take the French gold and show them what Will writes, then come on here. You see that your husband did not bother to seal the letter?"

"Then he wishes his enemies to believe the contents," Miriam replies. "Yes, I see it all now. It is for me to read what is not written within, and act accordingly."

"Precisely. Will is not a fool. He knows I am with you, so why beg you to 'return to where our old uncle has need of you'?" Cromwell glows at his own cleverness, for he has arranged certain messages in advance with the Lord Templar. "Will means for me to collect together every available man, and bring them to the fore. He fears Norfolk will play the over cautious fool, and attempt to withdraw before coming to battle."

"Dare he?"

"Oh, there will be a very good excuse, no doubt. 'Draper ran away', he might say, or 'there was illness in the camp, and half my men were sick'. Yes, the Norfolk half, and poor Suffolk will be left with fifteen thousand men against three times that number. He will stand, like the honourable fool he is, and he will lose. No, we must advance with every pot boy, sick soldier, and garrison dregs we can find."

"Captain Stubbs has been landing my cogs up and down the coast for the past three days," Miriam tells Cromwell. "The crews, and hired Genoese crossbowmen number over nine hundred useful men, Uncle Thomas. They are already marching, and will meet us on the road. Stubbs is a general now, I think."

"Such foresight." Tom Cromwell curses himself that he has not thought of such a simple ploy, but admires his beloved Miriam for her sharp wits. "You might almost be my blood daughter."

"Yes, I am a sharp one, and no mistake," the woman replies. "Why, I even wonder at why you might think it perfectly safe to come here to Calais, surrounded by the king's men, with but a beard and a hat pulled low, and think yourself perfectly safe from discovery."

"Kel Kelton has my back." It is true, but also a lie, for that is not why he is safe from detection, or at least, arrest. "I am safe, dear girl."

"I can see Kel fighting the whole town for you, master, and dying for it, but that is not the full truth of the matter, is it?"

"Best not ask, my dear," Cromwell tells her, "for it is of no concern to you just now."

"Henry knows, does he not?" Miriam has suspected, ever since the messages between London and Antwerp increased two fold, and another two messengers were now allowed to take them along with Kel Kelton. "You write to him direct."

"Only at his request. I received a letter from His Majesty, three months since, addressed to Mijnheer Cornelis, and asking for my advice on certain agricultural matters. It made no mention of how he came to know of me, but stressed that any reply would be seen by his eyes alone."

"So, you wrote back?"

"I had Kel write it down at first, to disguise my hand. For the king's attention might have been a pure coincidence. I advised him on how to set the next tariff for the ports of Dover and Lowestoft, so as to best benefit the crown."

"And what then?"

"He wrote back… in his own hand, and mentioned that I need not use a scribe, as his knowledge of my own hand was long standing. He was telling me he knew, and did not wish it to become known, you see. Since then, we have conversed two or three times a week, and England begins to prosper once more. I warned him not to remove Norfolk from the leadership of his army, lest it foments trouble back in

England. Instead, I begged that he appoint Suffolk and your Will to oversee the fool."

"You still sign yourself as Cornelis?"

"Of course, and he writes as 'Hal', though his hand is easy to recognise." Cromwell decides he must divulge it all. "We are in cahoots, Miriam. Every step is planned, and we hope by this to settle many old disputes with the least amount of disruption. We have no intention of capturing Paris, and removing Cousin François from his dismal little throne. Instead, we are against Charles."

"What? The Emperor of the Holy Roman Empire is our ally," Miriam is surprised, which is rare for her. How can one declare war on the French, yet be against the Empire? "I do not understand. You are talking nonsense. No… forgive me, master… you never talk nonsense, so please explain."

"Of course. The Holy Roman Empire is twice the size it was fifteen years ago. Charles is a master of manipulation, and his armies are powerful. Too powerful for us to withstand. So, we must have an ally. That ally is, logically, France, but François is so shortsighted, and he would never dream of making a valid treaty with us. He would shirk his duty, and let the Spaniards do their worst, both in Italy, and against us. After all, we are now a nation of heretics and dangerous schismatics… so, who cares?"

"So we side with our natural enemy?" Miriam begins to understand just how complicated the layers of diplomacy really are. "You must explain in more detail, whilst my people assemble our forces."

"As you wish, my dearest girl. The king and… Mijnheer Cornelis… are of a like mind. The northern empire is quite willing to live in harmony with us, for half their population are protestants, and see us as a natural friend, but the stronger, southern parts… Spain and her Catholic allies… want us ruined. They see Venice as a thorn in their sides, so wish to conquer the whole of Italy, and they count us as a threat to their very souls. We are protestants, and so, we must be brought to heel one day.

"Therefore, we must do all we can to weaken them. To this end, we follow an old Roman maxim… 'keep your friends close, and your enemies even closer'. Henry signs a pact with the empire, thanks to poor Chapuys, who thinks it a wonderful coup on his part, as indeed does the emperor. The treaty calls for each party to come to the aid of the other if attacked, and support them 'in time of war'. I draw your attention to the wording. The aid is due, even if we are the aggressor. This absolves Charles the Self Righteous of a bad conscience, and allows him to gain some of the spoils without much effort.

"When we defeat the French this day, he will launch his armies into both the north and the south, and try to gobble up half of France for himself. We will be left with all we have by conquest, yet Charles will find that he is doing all of the fighting. What a sweet deal."

"Are you so sure? I dare say he will take the lands on the Spanish border without a fight, and the northern parts with ease. For the main French army will be falling back on Paris, with us chasing them."

"Yes, but we will not be," Cromwell says, with a joyful cackle. "Henry knows that taking France is a pipe dream. Once in Paris, François is safe. His fortress cannot be taken by storm, unless we have two hundred thousand men at arms, hundreds of the biggest cannon, and five years to do the job. We would die of old age, and be bankrupt, before we even breached one wall."

"Then what?"

"We defeat François today, then turn about and retreat to Calais. All bar Suffolk and your warlike husband. They shall break off with a third of our army, and our cannon, and invest Boulogne. With luck, the town will see they are abandoned to their fate, and surrender. Then we will have a much expanded holding in France…

three times the size of the Calaisis, and an increased revenue to pay for the war. By now, Charles is committed to the attack, but will find French armies, almost intact, save for today's mauling, coming to face them. They are strong enough to cause the empire some disquiet, for their forces are split betwixt north and south, and cannot join up. King François will say a silent prayer of thanks that we have withdrawn, and set about his new enemy. The resultant war will last at least two years, maybe even more, and end with both sides exhausted from a series of almost constant battles and sieges."

"Then we must remain neutral... I mean the Draper Company of course." Miriam sees the way to great profit, even through all this proposed carnage. "I shall continue to trade with both camps, as they require, but at 'war' prices. My ships run a greater risk, and the price of food always goes up in bad times. If I import grain from Egypt and Italy, they will force up the price, and I must pass that on."

"That is your business, my dear," Cromwell concludes. "I am but a poor, dead, advisor to the king. Now, shall we gird our loins, and set forth? Let every soul be included, even the women and the boys. Have them armed with anything that even looks like a weapon... at a distance. We are not going to fight, but to put backbone into

Norfolk."

"How so, master?"

"He will be told of a huge army of reinforcement coming to him, by his scouts, and that will force him to stand his ground. He will use us as an excuse to delay things, or so I hope. Will must have all the time we can give him. Once clear of the field, he must describe a huge arc, if he is to be successful."

*

The Duc de Ponet is just having the leather straps of his shoulder *Pauldrons* tightened onto the breastplate, when his herald comes in to report. He has already been fitted with a *Plackhart* to cover his abdomen, *greaves* on the lower legs, and the heavy *sabatons;* steel boots with spurs. The heavy steel leggings, and outdated skirt-like *faulds,* he dispenses with, like most modern knights. Only the gauntlets are to come, and they will be placed on his hands at the moment of engagement, along with a twelve foot lance, or sword, as required. It is just striking the eleventh hour.

"They are coming at us?" he asks the herald.

"No, sir. Not yet." The man seems nervous and is hopping from one foot to another. He does not wish to explain further.

"Then what are they doing?" the Duc de Ponet demands, running away from us?"

"No, sir... they are singing."

"What?" Ponet considers this, and finds it reasonable. They are protestants, and such men like to listen to sermons, and sing uplifting psalms. On the eave of there coming deaths it is wise to sing to God, and thus pave the way to Heaven's gate. "Are they offering up a salutary psalm?"

"No, My Lord, they are singing a filthy song about King François. It seems he bathes in asses milk, and that accounts for his stupidity. Then they do make great play about his genitals, and a certain farmyard animal."

"Ha! Let them sing away. Our men cannot understand a word of their filthy language anyway." Ponet sees that soon the song will end, and he can get on with his business of slaughter.

"They sing it in French, sir. A little crude, as if just memorised, but nevertheless, it is quite understandable. Our own men are either roaring with laughter, or demanding to rush into the attack. I fear to hold them in check."

"Dear Christ, but that would mean disaster for us. Without the chain shot we might lose. Have our fellows sing back at them, at once. Show them we can sing even dirtier songs about *their* king. What about that one which claims his wife used to fornicate with her own brother? That might shut the loathsome bastards up."

"As you wish, sir… but the battle is to commence at eleven… and *Norfook* might cry foul."

"How so, for is it not his own men who wish to sing, rather than fight like they should?" Ponet is indignant at this blatant change to the running order, and he resolves to chastise the English duke over it, once he is taken prisoner.

*

"Damn me, Suffolk, what are the scurrilous bastards doing?" Norfolk is agog with horror. He has sent word for the advance, but before it reaches the first line, lead by Mush Draper, they begin to sing. Soon all the army is joining in.

"Singing, Tom," Suffolk says.

"Why?"

"It is what men do before battle. They work up a fine rage, and then storm forward into the attack. If you are worried about it, send young Surrey to see what is amiss."

"My son is abed with a belly ache," Norfolk confesses. His son is a coward of the first order, and would rather die of shame than die violently on the point of a pike, or with a sword in the guts. "He might be well enough for the latter stages."

"Ah, the division of spoils?" Suffolk is unrelenting in his deprecation of the Norfolk family these days, and wants nothing more than their demise. If not for

Norfolk, he would command today, and there would be no need for all these ploys to win the day. "Then we must stand and listen to their ribald tunes a while, I fear."

"The enemy might cry foul."

"And do what? If they charge us, we will mow them down with crossbows, then trample them beneath our massed rows of pikemen. Our musketry will advance and chase off their cannoneers… poor hired fellows who will run at the first chance. If they refuse to fight, we just sit here, and wait for them to retire. then we take the open road to Boulogne."

"To Paris," Norfolk corrects. "We are for Paris, are we not?"

"Oh yes, Paris, of course. Paris, Boulogne… they are all one to me. Then Paris it is. Hopping François must make a stand soon, or Henry will be sitting on the French throne."

"And he will need a Regent to rule France for him." Norfolk is, as usual well ahead of his ability to think sensibly, and sees himself as the only contender for the post.

"You, I would suggest," Suffolk says. "I am needed by Henry's side, and you are the only man of a high enough rank to run the country."

"Why, thank you, Charles. I shall not forget your supportive words, but what about Ned Seymour. He is a wily, upstart bastard, and might contest it." Only Norfolk can think of the Seymour clan as upstarts, for they can boast a lineage going back three hundred years… to a time when Norfolk's distant ancestor was a common thatcher of roofs.

"Not if I whisper into Henry's ear, of how he does seem to be coming on so fast these days… and that his father was nought but an adulterous old swine who made his money from breeding pigs in Wiltshire."

"You really would do that for me?" Norfolk suspects he is being tricked. Suffolk does not love him, he knows, so why this sudden offer of help?

"I deeply dislike you, old man. That cannot be denied. But the Regent of France hands out gifts like sweets. I would expect the rights to wool importing, a contract for wine export at favourable rates, and a monopoly for all spice imports."

"Oh, commerce. I don't bother with such rubbish. It sorts itself out without me interfering. You may have exactly what you wish. Write it all down, and I shall sign it, as soon as I am Regent of France."

"Your word is enough, Tom Howard," Suffolk says. "I wish we could be better friends. So let me give you a final word in advice. Do not take your eyes off the Seymours, for that is where the poisoned dagger lies."

"I shall keep my best agents on them," Norfolk replies. Then he laughs aloud. "Oh, listen to that. Those bastards even know the one about me swiving twelve milkmaids, all in the live long day. Ho, but I do love to listen to it. Of course, it is not true. I managed them all, but it was nigh on two days, and I was fair broken afterwards. Let them sing of my ancient exploits for a while. It will hearten them to face the French cannon."

'And delay the battle for a few more minutes,' Suffolk thinks, as he scans the horizon. It is a clear day, and there is no sign of any help coming. Sooner or later, he must let Norfolk have his way, and send the English army into disaster. He will hold back the last couple of ranks, and try to withdraw them in squares. It will take time, but they might make it back to Calais alive. Perhaps four thousand out of twenty five is a poor return, but still a return. Then God answers his prayers in one way. Norfolk is damned if he attacks, and damned if he withdraws, but he might just decide to run away, and that would be even worse. The French would sweep around them, and invest Calais town at once. With the town under siege, the army would be stranded, and slowly starved into submission. Hungry men cannot last long.

"My Lord, reinforcements are coming!" The messenger is one of the rear lookouts, and he is covered in dust from the mad ride to the camp. A great cloud of dust, and men at arms coming on at the march. Thousands… but far too many to count."

"Good man, here." Norfolk tosses over a single silver coin, He is renowned for his rather parsimonious nature, and silver is better than the usual copper he gives out. "Hear that Suffolk. It must be the king with the men he swore to bring on to me. Five thousand of the best troops in England. Now we must prevail."

"At least, not run," Suffolk mutters to himself. "Soon, like it or not, there must be a battle. May God allow everyone to play their parts well, and give victory to the most deserving side."

In the field the men begin the tale of how Suffolk did marry the king's sister without consent, and nearly lost his head. It makes much of him losing others parts of his anatomy within his new bride, and is as dirty as anything that he has ever heard. Then, as if to equal things up, the pikemen begin to sing '*Norfolk's Wife*' with renewed gusto.

> '*Old Norfolk, he had a pretty wife,*
> *and Bessie was her name,*
> *they wed and lived in daily strife,*
> *Wi' both o' them tae blame.*
>
> *Dear Bessie did her heart give out,*
> *to any man would have her,*

and she would swive any lout,
and make his pintle purr...'

"Sing, you dirty mouthed bastards, sing," Suffolk tells himself "for it is all that is keeping you from destruction!"

*

"Are we seen?" Miriam asks, and the young squire leaps from his horse, and bows low.

"My Lady, a scout, English from his dress. He went off towards Norfolk's army like the devil is behind him. I doubt he saw more than a dust cloud, and lots of armour glinting in the sun."

"Mostly ladles and cooking pots worn on cook's heads," Miriam replies with a broad grin. "Then our army is known about, and Norfolk will have to stand his ground. I pray to every god listening that he decides to wait for our arrival."

"The Lord will see where righteousness lies, My Lady," the lad says, and clutches at the small cross hanging at his neck. John Smith is a Catholic by thought, and a Draper servant by trade. Miriam tolerates every religion, even the Moorish and Indian faiths, so he feels safe in her company. "With His help, we will win the day. He touches the old sword he has liberated from the Calais armoury, and adjusts the ancient steel helmet, which is a size too large. He has spent many hours in the practice yard, and can use a sword and knife to good effect, although he has never fought in anger.

"John, you shall make a fine soldier, but put some wadding in that helmet, lest it falls over your eyes at the wrong moment!" Miriam says, and the boy glows under her gentle scolding. To the east, she knows Captain Stubbs is coming towards her with his sailors and hired Genoese crossbowmen, but she hopes he will not be needed.

*

"Do we turn yet, General?" This is from Captain Jeremiah Cord, who is the temporary second in command, whilst John Beckshaw performs a more delicate task in the opposite direction. "I ask only for my own knowledge, for I would not question your mind in any way."

"Well put, Captain Cord," Will replies. He is dust covered from the hard cross country riding, and his throat aches for a drink. The water is rancid, and he has only a little diluted beer in his canteen, which he hopes to make last a while longer. "We are beyond where any man might set a scout, so it is time to make our swing about. We should come upon the enemy's rear in three of their leagues... about five miles or so... and hope to take them unawares. But our horses are near blown with the hard ride. I fear we must dismount, and lead them for the next five miles. Can we do it in time?"

"The men have all been taught to double march, sir," Cord replies, "but only over short distances. A mile or two, and they must rest a while."

"Then order a general dismount. Set the men off at the march for a half mile, then up it to the double. Wait until you see the first men flagging, and order a remount. We then canter for a while, to save the horses. After that, we dismount, and double march until we see the glint of French steel."

"The lads will perk up then, sir," Cord says. "It is an admirable plan, and will see us there speedily. May God grant us time before the battle starts. Will you drink with me?" Cord holds out a full canteen of sweet water. He has another on his saddle, and can spare the offer.

"Fresh water?" Will asks, as he gulps down a long mouthful. "How so?"

"A fellow in Calais, sir. He claims to be an apothecary, and he says boiled water is fever free, and sweet tasting. He charges a few pennies, and boils the rank water from the harbour, until it is clear and fresh. though I am sure he adds a little sugar to make it more drinkable."

"That is a brilliant trick that I must remember," Will says. "For sitting outside a castle without water, and a full moat before you is an agony. From now on I shall have cauldrons brought up, and boil all we need."

"That is for then, General… for now, drink, and let us hurry on. We have some damned Frenchies to kill!"

"If they do not see us coming," Will mutters to himself. It is a desperate plan, which relies on the French acting predictably. They must face forward, and wait for Norfolk to make the first move. As they outnumber the English, and are in a solid position, Will hopes they do not bother with a rearguard. He slips from his horse's back, and begins to lead it onwards. One by one, his men follow suit, and soon the Examiner column is marching towards their destiny.

The common troopers feel better for knowing that they now approach the massive French army, and they care not that they are outnumbered by some thirty to one. If the general says charge, they will charge, and be damned with the odds.

4   Fragments of a Battle

The English choir, some two thousand men wide, and six lines deep is in fine voice. Their choirmaster, and poet, Sir Thomas Wyatt is waving his arms, and directing them with the skill of a true musician. It helps that he knows when they stop singing, they must fight for their lives. So, he thinks, here is to any old thing I can think of.

> *"King John of old was a worthless soul,*
> *and his name shall stink afore him,*
> *Then Edward confessed and lost his whole*
> *to the pope who would then be-saint him."*

The long line of pikemen, knowing that their lusty singing will delay the oncoming charge, let rip with great spirit. They are professional soldiers, paid to fight, and if need be, to die. However, to die in a stupid fashion is not to their liking, and they all know that marching onto the maws of such huge cannon, loaded with chain shot as they are, is suicide. So, they sing, and hope for a reprieve.

Five hundred paces to their fore, the French gunners reply with a song they cannot understand, but it is accompanied with many Gallic gestures that attest to its fruity nature. Then, one of the French gunners, a huge Gascon, advances a hundred paces, as if offering single combat, and an English crossbowman hurries forward to the front line in case he can get in a clear shot.

The big man is being cheered by his own side, who see that the English are reluctant to charge home. At that moment the huge Gascon gunner drops his breeches, and displays his broad, very hairy arse to the enemy. It is the ultimate insult; a show of utter contempt. The English crossbow man settles his machine on the shoulder of a kneeling pikeman, aims, and fires. The steel tipped wooden bolt flies the three hundred paces in a moment, and embeds itself in the Gascon's left buttock. The big man leaps up, and pulls the offending bolt from his arse. He holds it up above his head, as if to say 'good shot', and then hobbles back to his own side, who are all hooting with laughter at his reversal of fortune.

Though he can ill afford it, Tom Wyatt scrapes ten shillings together from his light purse, and hands it to the man. "Here, take this fellow," he tells him. "On account. Another ten shillings when I have robbed a few French bodies!"

The singing comes to a halt during this interlude, and any lull might prompt the garrulous Duke of Norfolk to sound the advance. It is then that one of the pikemen… a sturdy looking Welshman… begins to sing a well loved hymn of praise. Even the French recognise the lilting tones of the twenty-third psalm.

*"The Lord's my shepherd, I shall not want.
He maketh me to lie in pastures green.*

He leadeth me ... the quiet waters by."

the Welshman sings, and soon several hundred join in the haunting refrain. It gives Tom Wyatt some respite from trying to dredge up old doggerel, but he cannot help but recall the lines that speak of 'walking through the valley of the shadow of death,' and he shudders.

"I will fear no evil: for thou art with me; thy rod and thy staff ... they comfort me." Jeremiah Cropper intones the words under his breath. "Surely goodness and mercy shall follow me all the days of my life, and I will dwell in the house of the Lord for ever."

Jeremiah Cropper, is a most unusual kind of parson, who since meeting Will Draper has been his personal chaplain. He is a dichotomy of a fellow in that he is both a man of God, and a drinker of the greatest great renown. He gives his sermons with an English bible in one hand, a bottle of rum in the other, and a sword tucked into his waistband.

But for all this he is a man of great character, who is devoted to God, and his master, Will Draper. Now he passes up and down the long lines, shriving any man who asks, and handing out comfort and support to the rest.

"Fear not, lads," he says. "For God is with us. Don't let your line waver, and stick it to those Frog bastards good and hard. They are the antichrist, and we are here to show them the light. So, consign their stinking souls to hell this day and make room for me in your company." He closes his bible, and slips it into the folds of his black garb. Then he draws a sword almost the length of his arm, and fits himself in the midst of the first rank. "Come on lads, another song. What about the one where the pope is caught swiving the choirmaster, and tries to hide up the soot filled chimney. What, you do not know it?"

"I know the one, good parson," Tom Wyatt says, as he comes up to inspect the ranks. "Pray retire to the rear. this is not your place."

> "*The poet and the drunken parson,*
> *go off to war one day,*
> *'to the rear' the poet says to the man,*
> *and this did the parson say,*
> *go swive yourself Tom Wyatt,*
>
> *for I can die as well as any here*
today," Cropper declaims. The fractured rhyme causes the men about him to laugh, and then cheer his noble sentiment. Then, as only such hard, yet sentimental military men can when facing death, they urge the parson to retire.

He refuses time and again, until they are almost pleading with him. A parson in the front line is just not the done thing. At last he submits, but only to moving back a row. He is cheered roundly, and the men begin the rude song about the pope and the choirmaster again with real fervour.

As they reach the final line about the serving wench who lights a fire beneath the cooking pot, and scalds his holy backside for him, the entire army finish with a great 'huff, huff, huff!' and cackle with glee. It is strange, but these men can cross themselves at one moment, and curse His Holiness in another.

"Tudor Rose, lads," Tom Wyatt commands, and they begin to sing of how 'Bluff King Hal's dad' did find his crown upon a white rose bush, whose petals are tinged with the red blood of his enemies. The song is wistful and lamenting, and mercifully, very, very long.

*

"Will they never stop?" Norfolk is tired of hearing about the seven deadly sins in bawdy song, and longs for it all to cease. The repetition of such sins reminds him that he is sixty nine, and has committed each one too often. He is closer to his end than any other man here today, and the thought makes him a little uneasy.

"Only at your order, father." Surrey, realising that the battle is still not underway, has recovered from his unaccountable 'stomach pains', and comes to see what is afoot. "They will sing songs all day if you let them. For Christ's sake, sound the advance, and let the tuneful bastards get a taste of some cannon fire. It will stir them into action quickly enough."

"Thousands of loyal troops are closing on us, as we speak," Norfolk explains, and mistakes Miriam's pot washers for battle hardened infantry. "They will be here within the hour."

"Then do not let them arrive before we start fighting, or their commander will say he won the day." Surrey is no strategist, but he is sly enough to see every advantage that can be milked from the situation. "Instead, join battle, take our casualties, and use his men to make the final push. Then he cannot say ought, other than he helped a great general complete a victory that was already almost won. You see what I mean, father?"

"Yes, I see. Clever lad, who put that idea into your head... some squire you overheard? For all that, I think it a wise move. Pray mount your horse, and ride down to Sir Thomas Wyatt. Mush Draper is in charge, I believe, but he is not a gentleman, and so cannot be spoken to on equal terms. Besides, rumour has it that he has run away. If not, keep away from him, for he is as like to rip out your guts if he gets you alone. Tell Wyatt that he is to sound the advance at once. All six lines, at fifty pace intervals. He is to force their cannon to fire, then overwhelm them with his numbers as they reload. If he complains about the chain shot, you must tell him that it is much overrated, and that I expect many of the third and fourth rank will survive to take the guns."

'Yes father, and then..."

"No sense in riding back. They need leaders, especially if Draper has run away with all of his best men. You might take command of the third rank, behind Mush Draper and the poet."

"But father, surely I am more useful by your side?" Surrey can feel the fear already, and his hands are shaking.

"Not at all. A good general should lead from the front. I an sixty-nine years old, and unable to keep up with you younger men, so you must fill my place for me. There must be a Howard in the fray, lest the king thinks us to be cowards. Now, get yourself off, and do your duty. I shall explain it to your mother, if necessary. If it is that you die this day, then do it with real panache, my boy."

"Sir, I am your heir," Surrey complains. "Would you die without a son to pass the dukedom on to?" It is a persuasive argument, but Tom Howard simply laughs.

"You think yourself the only son I have sired?" he says with a wink. "If need be, I will produce a wedding contract that predates the one I signed with your mother, and recognise which ever bastard I wish. Now, be off, and be a man, my son!"

"Yes father," Surrey replies, but he knows that at the first sign of cannon fire, he will fall to the ground, and hug it to himself like a willing girl to her lover. If he is to live long enough to inherit his father's title, he must play the coward with all of his might.

*

"Slow the pace," Tom Cromwell advises from the back of his horse. "We must not arrive too soon, or the ruse will be revealed. Let Norfolk think we are his saviours, and may God put it into his head to stand firm and wait for our arrival."

"He must, or the day is lost. Thousands dead without good cause." Miriam is concerned for her husband, who is risking his career on a dangerous ploy, but more so for her younger brother, Mush, who is foolish and brave in equal measure. He will stand in the place of greatest danger, and defy the odds. His friends Ibrahim, Rob Buffery, Edward Tunnock and the Spaniard, Alonso Gomez, are beside him, but they cannot stop chain shot at fifty yards.

"Then let us come to a halt here, and take some food and drink. Our arrival can only worsen their chances."

Miriam agrees, and the ramshackle force of old men, kitchen maids, cooks and servants comes to a halt. They have done their duty, and can boast that they were at the famous battle to come. Should they lose, it is a long way back to Calais, with a thousand French horsemen at your back.

"Will it work, master?" Miriam

asks of her old benefactor, and he shrugs, as if to deny the near infallibility she accredits him with.

"It is in the lap of the gods, my dear. Now, find a strong lad to help me from this blasted saddle, for I cannot do it alone. Since my death, I have become uncommon weak about the knees."

"I have a balm for your aching joints, master," Miriam replies. "Marion Towler tells me it is made with goose grease and the oil of mint leaves."

"Towler you say… then she has wed her forger at last?"

"Last week, in secret, and before he left to join Will."

"Forger to fighter?" Tom Cromwell frowns. "I must send them a splendid gift, but I shall wait until the battle is done. I do not wish to upset a widow, if that be the case."

"Will says he will keep him safe from harm." says Miriam.

"Let us hope he can perform that miracle twenty five thousand times over," Cromwell tells her, "and so save an entire army's life."

"Are we doomed to failure, Master Tom?"

"No, not if Suffolk is man enough to overrule Norfolk, and Will arrives in good time. We must hope and pray."

"I cannot bear it. Every time Will

leaves me, I know his life is at risk. He has escaped from ambushes, won against Italian bandits, and defeated foreign armies in France and Scotland… without more than one serious wound, when he was laid low by a Yorkshireman's musket ball. I fear for him, because I love him so much. He has a fortune, three wonderful children, and me. Why can he not keep to his own hearth for the next few years? We are both in our thirties now, and might expect some retirement."

"Not whilst Henry lives," Thomas Cromwell explains. "Will is his shadowy right hand man. He fears losing him more than anything. Your husband must serve him, or flee England for ever. His own sense of honour will not let that happen. Nor would mine have done, but I was drugged and stolen away from my fate. Now, I must live out my days as a retired Flemish merchant. Uncle to you, and your boisterous brood."

"You are unhappy with us, master?" Miriam asks.

"No, not unhappy," Cromwell replies, "but I would have it otherwise, if I could. My honour died when I did not."

"Hush, that is a morbid thought on the eve of battle, Master Tom. Let us speak of lighter things. The returns for the last pepper shipment came in yesterday."

"What, sold already?" Cromwell is

constantly thrilled at his Miriam's sharp nose for business. "How so?"

"The Venetians have a ship arriving tomorrow, laden with pepper and other spices, to try and break my English monopoly. It is not the Doge's doing, as it breaks our arrangement. He wrote to warn me, so I sold my stock on to some decent traders at a good price to them. When the renegade Venetian merchants arrive they will find the market flooded with cheap pepper, mace and ginger. They will have to sell at less than their cost price, or sail home as ruined men. My agents will buy up the cargo at a low price, and ensure they cannot find a return cargo. They will have to go home to explain how they made a huge loss on the voyage."

"Damn me, but that is a fine jest to play," Tom Cromwell tells her. "It's something I would have done in my earlier years. What of the new cargo?"

"I shall hold it in my warehouse, until the current produce is bought up by the people, then release it at the better price. I shall recoup my profits, and have given Venice's rogues a bloody nose."

"Doge Gritti was ever a friend, though he is long dead." Crowell recalls their adventures whilst fleeing from an avenging French army, intent on killing them both. "Who can ever replace so fine a man?"

"The new Doge, Pietro is a Lando. He is in his eightieth year now, and still as sharp as a knife blade. He was a dear friend of Andrea Gritti's, and sees us as his allies. We keep our word, and pay promptly, and in return he guarantees our monopoly of the Venetian spice route. Now, if only I can stop the Portuguese from trying to break my hold, things will go better for us. Can you not arrange a small fleet of warships to sink their merchantmen?"

"Alas not," Cromwell says, "but I hear that a roving band of piratical Barbary Coast fellows are raiding all around the Iberian peninsula. Let us hope they put into Lisbon Harbour, and burn a few ships."

'Not without a hefty bribe," Miriam says, and Thomas Cromwell, who has already sent a bankers draft to be collected on completion of the task, smiles beatifically. It is a small price to pay for so great a prize. He does not yet know that, by an ironic twist of fate, the pirate fleet sailed into the harbour at the same time as two English warships were paying a courtesy call to deliver a new ambassador to the Portuguese royal court.

After a few stout broadsides, the Barbary fleet sees all is lost and limps off, less five of their number, and the English ships shall chase them half way back to North Africa.

Thomas Cromwell saves a hundred

thousand Ducati in bribes, but Miriam's total monopoly will fail to materialise, and she will have to resort to another ploy. In the meantime, Crowell is oblivious of these events, and sits happily on a fallen tree stump to imbibe a glass of wine, and eat some of Miriam's small meat pies.

"Delectable, my dear," he says, to make small talk, and keep her mind from dwelling on how her own family are, once again, risking life and limb for Henry Tudor. Suddenly, in the far distance, they hear a roar, as if of thunder. It is the sound of twenty four thousand men giving vent to their rage, as they begin their advance onto a wall of cannon, loaded with chain shot. Miriam looks at Tom Cromwell, and they both shudder. Too late, they think, the word is given, and battle joined. Miriam mutters a short prayer in Hebrew.

"Amen," Tom Cromwell adds.

*

"Enough, you dogs!" Surrey reigns in his mount so hard that he slides from the saddle and lands in a heap on the dusty ground. The common soldiery laugh at this, until he leaps up screaming with rage.

"You are to advance at once, Wyatt," he cries, through tears of anger and frustration. "Now, laugh at that you stinking whore-son bastards!"

The ranks fall suddenly silent and men begin to check their weapons one last time, and some even cross themselves. The time of testing is on them once more, and for some it is to be a first blooding. They do not resent Surrey's cursing, for many of them are soldiers because they come from such low backgrounds, and seek to better their lots. The army welcomes bastards, for they make the hardest soldiers in a tough fight.

"Ibrahim, pray escort Lord Surrey to a place of honour amongst the men, and let him advance with us. Put him with Edwin Tunnock in the third line, so that he might survive the first cannonade. See how I love you, Harry? You shall have the honour of reaching their guns, if you are fast. Take the guns, and we take the day."

"Dear Christ, Tom… I do not think I can …"

"Stay so far back?" Wyatt says. "Then come and stand by me in the front rank, if you so insist."

"No, the third rank is honour enough for me, sir," Surrey says, hurriedly, and lets himself be led away. In truth, once the guns open up, the first four ranks will be slaughtered, and the rest left in confusion, ready to be swept aside by cavalry. Tom Wyatt knows this, but must follow his orders.

"Ready lads? Keep close order, and march at regulation pace. Once at the guns, go for their master gunners first. Then kill the rest. After that, you may break ranks and charge any supporting troops. If we get into difficulties, form a square. Pikes outside and muskets and crossbows inside. Give them bloody Hell!"

He raises his sword, and brings it down in a sharp cutting motion. The first line lurches into action at a steady regulation twenty steps a minute. The slow advance will ensure the line is not broken.

"On lads," Mush Draper urges his second line, and Ibrahim shoves Surrey forward in the third line, which is commanded by old Edwin Tunnock, who tells all who will listen that he has fought six battles in France over almost forty years, and lost every one of them.

It is, he thinks, about to be his seventh and last such defeat. The chain shot will flay though men like a knife through butter, and reach his own rank with ease. It is not a fine thought, but a reasonable one. They have delayed as long as they can, and that is all they can do. Now, they must fight, and they must die. He looks across at Norfolk's son, who is white with fright, and can scarcely hold his sword up straight. Ibrahim has him by the elbow, else he would fall to his knees.

"Take heart, lad," Tunnock says. "God only takes the brave. When the guns roar, kneel down low, and let the shot pass over you, then run at them like a demon.

they will think you are Beelzebub himself, and run from you. I promise."

"Truly?" Surrey asks

"My word as a gentleman," Edwin Tunnock replies. "I should know, boy. I have fought the French on six previous occasions, and I am still alive to tell of my many military adventures."

Then, quite suddenly the front line stops, and the effect ripples backwards to them. Something, it seems, has happened.

*

"Mount up, lads", Will Draper says, and five hundred men climb into the saddle. "Swords or lances, as you wish. We charge straight at the guns, and ignore the rest. Is that clear? We must take the guns before they start to fire, or see our comrades done to a foul death. Ready Captain Cord?"

"Ready as can be, sir."

Then please be so kind as to give the order. Your voice is stronger than mine own just now. I fear I am weak from thirst still, and it is so damned hot."

"An honour, general." Captain Jeremiah Cord pulls out the hug war axe he keeps hanging on his saddle's crup, and raises it above his head. "To Hell or victory, boys. Charge!" Two lines of men surge forward, down on to the unsuspecting French rear.

At the last moment those men who malinger in every army, and do their best to stay at the rear, see what is happening, and scream out a warning. It is too late, and the five hundred Examiners sweep through them with barely a   second glance. An unlucky few receive passing slashes or the thrust from a lance, but the rest escape injury, save in the crush to get clear.

Draper's disciplined troop surges on through the startled masses of infantry, who scatter in terror, and head for the unsuspecting cannoneers.   At the last moment the French manning the cannon see their danger, and throw up their arms in surrender, but war is a cruel game, and they are cut down where they stand.

At that moment TomWyatt breaks the rules, and orders a full charge. Pikes, musketry, infantrymen and crossbows all charge, and rush into the attack. They leap the cannon, and find the French in full flight. The Examiners are chasing them, cutting down any who seem ready to offer some resistance, but the main army is running for its life, and will not stop again until it reaches Paris.

Will Draper sees a magnificently arrayed gentleman standing, with his sword held out, hilt forward. It is their commander, and he offers his sword in the expectation of quarter, and immediate parole. Will begins to ride towards him, but an excited bunch of infantry fall on the startled man and beat him senseless.Then they rob him of everything he has, even his clothes, and leave him naked and battered on the ground. Will gallops over and details two of his own men to guard the mistreated and abused opposing general.

"See he is re-clothed, and tended to by our own physicians," he commands. "Then chain him up until my return." Next he rides off to see how the army has fared. All about him are dead Frenchmen, but in their hundreds, rather than their thousands. It is clear that they have little stomach for a hard fight.

He finds TomWyatt, who is grinning like a devil at him. The plan has worked, but only in the very nick of time. He has been counting the dead and thinks the French number six hundred dead at most, whilst he has lost eleven men dead, and as many more wounded.

"A good butcher's bill then," Will says. He does not know that a musket ball, fired in panic by a running Frenchman has found its mark. As he leaps up on one of the cannon, with a triumphant yell, a dear friend is hit in the head, and killed outright.

*

A squadron of French cavalry flee the carnage of defeat and circle out of danger. They come upon the makeshift 'army' led by Miriam, and realise that here is an easy victory, with plunder, slaughter and women to be had for the sake of one single charge. Their captain orders them into line, and then calls for a canter into the attack.

Miriam's squire, John Smith, already devoted to his mistress, canters to meet them, with his borrowed sword in hand. He has never fought a real life action, and knows only the skills of the tilt. He evades the thrust of a lance point, and lunges home into the enemy's chest. The man falls backwards with a crash of armour. The women's army give a great cheer, as the boy swerves aside from a second charge, and slashes down into an exposed thigh. he is just becoming confident in his prowess when a third Frenchman drives past his parry, and sinks his spear point into the boy's side. The force breaks the lance, and as the man gallops by, the squire sends him on his way with a vicious backhanded slash that opens the Frenchman's back almost to the spine. Then he slumps down to the ground and bleeds to death in moments.

The rest of the French are charging at the densely packed English women and servants, when a trumpet sounds. Colonel John Beckshaw leads a swift charge into the enemy flank, and though outnumbered two fold, soon has the French horse in disarray. He hacks his way through them, until he is between them and the ones he has come to protect. His horror at seeing his own wife

waving an axe and yelling bloody murder at the enemy is beyond measure.

"Pru, pray calm down, the day is ours," he cries over the noise of battle.

"They murdered poor John," she says.

"Poor John killed three of them," Beckshaw replies. "He fought and died like a man, my dear. You should exalt him, rather than grieve. His mother will be well cared for, will she not Mijnheer Cornelis?"

Tom Cromwell is loitering behind a horse, but is still seen by John Beckshaw. He comes forward and nods to the colonel.

"Good day sir." He smiles at the routed French cavalry, galloping away in all directions. Behind them they leave at least fifty dead and a dozen more are un-horsed, and wounded. "A fine day for a good battle. I have heard no cannon firing, so must assume that the Lord Templar's plan has worked, and the French are beaten?"

"Did you doubt it, sir. Will said you would be here, with Miriam. He claimed she could not keep away, and would try to join in. Though your ruse must have kept that damned fool Norfolk in check long enough. I reckon he thought you to be the king with a new army for him. The silly bugger."

"What are your orders?" Cromwell asks.

"To turn you about, and escort you

safely back to Calais. The rest of the army will follow on at its convenience."

"Then we do not march on Paris?" Miriam asks. In commerce, she is the best of the best, but her political awareness can sometimes become clouded.

"That was never the real plan, my dear," Tom Cromwell explains. "Henry does not wish to spend three or even four years outside that city's prodigious defences. The army is for Calais, from where it will raid south and east at will, until François sees sense and deeds over enough territory to make us go home. Brittany and Normandy, with the Loire, down to the river's northern bank will suffice."

"He will not give away so much," Miriam says. "That is half of his kingdom, and the best half at that."

"That is why we have an alternative plan," Cromwell says, with mounting slyness in his voice. "For what we really want is to enlarge the Calaisis area, and that means we must take Boulogne. The Duke of Suffolk is commanded to split away from Norfolk before reaching Calais town, and turn north. He and your husband will take the town, and make it into an English stronghold. Then we can offer good farmers and sheep herders free land to settle. In twenty years the entire west of the country will be English speaking, and shall pay their taxes to the English crown."

"I see." Miriam understands now that her husband, and an entire army is put at risk for nothing more than the gaining of a town, and all the thousands of fertile acres that lie between it and Calais. "Simple greed."

"No, my dear. I seek only to make us strong, and a larger French buffer state will do that. It will keep the French king at bay, and show the Spaniards that we are a major power, not to be trifled with."

"They will still want to destroy us," John Beckshaw says with the bluntness of a military man. "For we are unfettered protestants, and that is anathema to them."

"You think so?" Tom Cromwell shakes his head in deprecation. "Twenty years ago you could count the number of protestants in England on your fingers, now they number almost three million souls. Whilst the German states, though under the rule of the Holy Roman Empire, are three quarters Lutheran, or some other sort of schism that has sprung up. In the next ten years, all of Europe will convert, save Rome, and Spain."

"You think so?"

"I do, sir. Then it will be a Spanish army against a million soldiers from all over the continent. Each nation will defy the old church, and each nation will aid any attacked by the Catholic Spanish. At that time, the Empire will split into two…with two emperors, no doubt… and the north shall help us defeat the south."

"You can see so far ahead?" Miriam asks.

"It is pure summation, based on deductions, a few known facts, and how we place our bribes. Why pay a prince, when we can buy his bodyguard for a tenth of the amount? Such men hear all, and can pass it on for their fees. So yes, I can 'see' someway into the coming time."

"*He who is lost but not lost will lose another, then be lost again,*" Pru Beckshaw utters, with her eyes fluttering. Her husband dismounts and runs to her side, in case she falls as she comes out of the mild trance. She opens her eyes, and seems not to realise that she has spoken. All those about her try to recall the exact words, but there are conflicting versions already. Tom Cromwell keeps his peace, because he has every word imprinted on his mind, to digest at a later date.

"What of that, Master Tom?" says Miriam.

"I make nothing of it," Tom Cromwell replies, and is saved further explanation by the arrival of a horseman. It is none other than Alonso Gomez, the personal servant of Ambassador Chapuys, who has joined the English of his own free will.

"Gomez, how goes it?" Cromwell

calls, and the Spaniard gives a start of surprise.

"Señor is that you?" he says, hiding a smile. "I did not recognise you under that fulsome beard and balding pate. I took you for an impoverished Jewish uncle of the fine Lady Miriam."

"Oh, how you do jest," Tom Cromwell says, sourly. "We won?"

"Of course. Master Will appeared in their rear, and they fled, We caught and killed about seven or eight hundred of them, but they had wings on their heels. The battle field is strewn with abandoned muskets, pikes… even horses, enough horses to outfit an entire regiment. This fine beast is now mine, and I have a new musket slung at my back."

"Did we suffer many losses?"

"Not a dozen, sir, but one was most sad. He was killed even as the battle was won. He fell back into the arms of the drunken padre… Cropper, who closed his eyes for him and said the last words."

"Who, damn it?" Cromwell demands.

"The old man who has fought so many times before… Master *Ed-ween Turr-nock*."

"His seventh battle," Cromwell murmurs. "May he be at rest now, for never was a man driven so hard to give out justice, and fight the good fight."

"Edwin brought you from the dungeon, across his shoulders, with Ibrahim on the other side. Is the Moor safe?" Miriam asks of Gomez, who grins and nods his head.

"He was by your friend when a spent musket ball hit him in the head. The crazy bastard ran into a company of musketeers, and killed four in moments, and the rest ran for their lives."

"But he is safe?" Miriam asks again. She has a special need for the handsome Moor, and fears fate might remove him because of his wild adventuring. It is tragic that a friend is dead, but there are still new adventures to be completed.

"He is going around, gathering up horses, which he claims he is going to take around the world to far off Cathay. It seems that New Found Land lacks decent horse flesh. I told him not to be a damned fool… for the world is a great disc floating beneath the Heaven in a giant bowl of water. Go far enough in your little ship, and you will fall off the edge and into a watery grave."

"This world is round, my dear Alonso," Thomas Cromwell says softly, but with an insistence born out of the latest scientific discoveries. The Spaniard considers this for a moment, for Tom Cromwell has never lied to him once, and he loves him as much as he does Eustace

Chapuys.

"If you say it is round, then it is round," the Spaniard decides, "and I will kill any man who says otherwise to my face."

*

The king is late for the battle, of course. It seems that his barge, commanded by Sir Thomas Heneage has found its way up the wrong creek, and left His Majesty almost back at Ghent. As his leg is troubling him greatly, he must, at the last, take a well sprung carriage to the scene of the fight.

"Always late, damn it," he growls, as the four burly squires with him try to ease him from the coach and onto a seat within the royal pavilion, which is set up about a half mile back from the scene of battle. "Why am I doomed to turn up after the last arrow has been fired, or when the enemy bodies are to be counted?"

"Fate, sire," Sir Thomas Heneage says, in a subservient way. "The maps of this area are notoriously fickle, and even hardened seafarers can go astray." In fact, those close to the king all know that, come what may, Henry must be kept away from all danger. Since his desperately stupid charge at the 'Battle of the Spurs' his life is to be protected, but secretly, for if he should guess he is being herded like a sheep, the world would not be large enough for his courtiers to hide in.

"I smell the whiff of gunpowder, sir, and that means the fight is either underway, or recently finished. Which is it?"

"Over, I believe, Your Majesty," Eustace Chapuys tells him. "Though it must have been a speedy affair, for the sun is only now overhead."

"Sir Thomas is outside, sire. He comes with a first hand account for you." Heneage holds his breath, and hopes that Henry will allow him this escape, for the news is not what the king hopes for.

"Which blithering Sir Thomas, you spavined dolt?" Henry demands. "My court is overrun with them. It is the most common of names these last ten years."

"Sir Thomas Wyatt, Your Majesty," Heneage replies. "I dare say he has already composed the battle into a thirty stanza epic poem. The ordinary footmen, he claims, are already calling it the *'Second Battle of the Spurs'*."

"By God, then I am still remembered fondly for my charge," the king muses. "It is a good name for a battle. Show Tom Wyatt in at once, you damned fool; then fetch me fresh linen for my privy. I think you will be needed this night, for the oysters I had for dinner last evening are out of season, and do trouble my innards overmuch." He raises one buttock, and lets out a loud fart. "There, Master of the King's

Privy, did I not say your services will be needed?"

Heanage bows and goes to fetch Tom Wyatt, and he considers how much longer he can keep on doing his present task. Unfortunately, despite the honour of the position, the two hundred a year salary, and the chance to listen into all the best court gossip, few gentlemen offer themselves up for the post. If the passing of one's days, waiting for the king to have a bowel movement is not an arduous task, it is certainly an odorous and onerous one.

Washing and cleaning His Majesty's broad arse is bad enough, but since he has taken to eating food secretly, behind Queen Katheryn's back, his diet has become almost intolerable. Oysters in a month without an 'r' in it, thick slices of warmed over pork from the kitchen stores, and endless pies, smuggled into the royal bedchamber by the agents of the Draper Company all contribute to a very lively time in the royal privy.

"Your Highness... I fear we could not wait another moment," Tom Wyatt says, as soon as he enters. "I begged Lord Norfolk to wait but another half hour, but he refused, and his reasons were seemingly sound. It appears that Lady Miriam and her entourage were approaching, and he mistook them for another armed force. To wait would be a disaster, he reasoned, and sounded the advance onto the French cannon… all fifty of them."

"Dear Christ, is the man raving mad?" the king rants. "Pikes against chain shot? Did we fare badly then?"

"No, sire, for at the very moment the order was uttered, General Will Draper made his sudden appearance in the enemy's rear. He had fooled them into thinking he was running away, but circled about, and so took them from the back. It will make a saucy poem, I think, with much play on 'rears' being swived by English lances, but that is for another day. Suffice it to say, the field is ours, and the French are in utter rout. We took their commander, a French duke, captive, and put an end to over five hundred of their troops."

"Five hundred, out of twenty five thousand?" Henry frowns at this. "Should *we* not have killed them in their thousands, my dear poet?"

"Sire, they ran too fast. It is a French virtue, when confronted by stout Englishmen." Tom Wyatt edges around the fact that Norfolk's troops refused to go any further, once the cannon were taken. The bounty, fifty pounds a gun, is too much to lose, and they would not leave them alone and undefended. "The men are already calling it the 'Second Battle of the Spurs', and with good reason."

The men, mostly under thirty, have

never heard of Henry's famous battle, and have had to be told what it was all about. They scoff at fat old Henry charging on a horse, but accept the name. They do not care if it be called 'the Battle of the Moon', just as long as they get a fair share of the spoils.

"Yes, that gratifies me, Tom," says the king, "and I will reward the survivors. How many of our fine fellows did we lose?"

"Twelve, sire," the poet admits. "Six men fell in the charge, and were trampled to death by their own comrades. It is usual in such fights. Then another four or five stopped to plunder too soon, and were cut down by the fleeing enemy. Captain Edwin Tunnock was killed taking a gun. A spent musket ball hit him in the forehead, and killed him at once."

"I know that name," Henry says.

"He has done Your Majesty some services in the past. You might recall the matter of the forged golden A*ngels*?"

"Yes, of course; he was a most loyal fellow." Henry tugs at his straggling reddish beard. "Family?"

"None, sire," Wyatt replies.

"Then see he is buried in a decent church, as befits his standing in my court. The crown will pay for a stone plaque, denoting his time on this earth."

"Too generous, sire," Tom Wyatt tells the king. In fact, Tunnock's body is to be placed in a vault within the church at Calais. His friends will give him a wake that shall shake the world, with wine and food flowing for all who knew him. "I shall see to it all."

"Good man. So, dear Cousin François is in full retreat?" the king asks. "Back to Paris, I should think, like the cur he is."

"Yes, he fell for your ruse, sire." The poet presses home that which Tom Cromwell says is already placed in the king's mind. "Charles Brandon and his six thousand foot are marching on Boulogne, this very afternoon. As soon as he is re-equipped with new lances, and swords, General Draper will follow him south with his full six hundred Examiner horse."

"Boulogne?" Henry knows this is an important thing he is being told, but cannot recall exactly what is going on. "Yes, that is so. Remind me, how does … *Mijnheer Cornelis* see things?"

"As you do, sire," the poet responds. "A quick siege of the town will give us a swathe of land from the Calaisis, all the way to the smaller, unwalled towns beyond Boulogne. Some eighty miles of coast, extending inland for twenty five miles, towards Lille and Amiens. That is one million, two hundred and eighty acres of fine farming land, sire."

"And the plunder?" Henry asks.

There must be plunder after a battle is won. "How much does the royal treasury get from this?"

"With the ransom raised from the Duc de Ponet, and the sale of some two hundred horses we took, I believe you might see about about fifty thousand in French coin."

"And in pounds?" Henry asks.

"About eighteen thousand pounds, sire," the poet replies. "Though the French ordinance is worth the battle alone. Fifty new cannon is a great prize." It is an unpalatable fact that the war is costing about three thousand pounds a day, and the treasury is already about fifteen thousand out of purse. "Though *Mijnheer Cornelis* did mention your clever plan to me, which will turn us a tidy profit."

"He did?" Damn these potions, the king thinks, for he cannot recall events from one day to the next these days, and this is something he cannot begin to imagine. "Does he have another idea?"

"No, sire, he still thinks that your idea to sell the captured land to those gentlemen amongst your court who have money, but no land, is sound. Without a few acres, and a fine manor house, what import is there to the knighthood?"

"Yes, that's the way forward," Henry replies, already convinced it is his own idea. Do we have figures?"

"After Boulogne falls, we shall have a little over two thousand square miles of new land, Your Majesty. You need only break it up into manageable parcels, or estates, and sell them at a very fair price. In this way you will have a standing army living in your new French dominion. About six hundred estates, each armed and ready to fight for their king."

"Yes, I knew it was a fine idea," the king agrees. "Six hundred noblemen, each with a mesne of ten or twelve dependant soldiers. Six thousand men on François's very doorstep. But what about Paris?"

"Boulogne first, sire," Tom Wyatt says with a shrewd smile. "For …

> '*did not we tup old François's rear,*
> *and send him back to Paris?*
> *Let him rot behind his walls,*
> *whilst Boulogne we do harass*?'

"Damn my soul, Tom… but how do you do it? Sometimes, I must sit for hours, thinking up such a coupling."

"Merest doggrel, sire," Tom Wyatt replies. Though the words have just sprung into his mind. "To write such fine poetry as yours, I would need an age."

"Of course you would, my boy. I know I am the better poet, but you are the quicker one." Henry farts again, but even louder. "I will come to Boulogne, my dearest poet, but for now… pray send

Master Heneage in, with his cleansing linen cloths, for I do fear an avalanche is about to descend, and his help is much needed!"

5   **Boulogne**

Contrary to what the more optimistic of the Duke of Suffolk's troopers believe, Boulogne is not waiting to be plucked like ripe fruit at all. In fact, the town's burgesses have locked the gates, and ordered every available able bodied man to the walls. The duke arrives, just in time, to be greeted by a raucous chorus of catcalls in a mixture of French, Breton, and even some Scots. One, a huge Highlander, bellows out an insult directly at the duke.

"Saucy devils," Charles Brandon says to one of his captains of horse. "To say such a thing, when they have never even met my mother. Pickets every hundred paces, Captain Maltravers, and rustle up a few crossbowmen to keep their heads down."

"Yes, My Lord," Tobias Maltravers replies, smartly. Until a few days ago, he has never left England, and this will be the greatest adventure of his life. As a gentleman farmer on Lord Suffolk's land, he is usually content counting his well fed sheep, and dispensing local justice as a sitting magistrate. "Are we to attack today?"

The duke looks at his man as if to see if he is jesting, then realises that he is in deadly earnest. It is one thing to be brave, but foolhardiness cannot be countenanced. He points to several black silhouettes that can just be made out on the nearest battlement.

"Four cannon, Tobias," Charles Brandon explains to the eager horseman. "Not very big, but enough to cause us some loss. Then there is a three hundred yard stretch of open ground to cover. We have six thousand men, and it will take half of those in casualties to breach the outer wall. No… pickets, and then we wait for the king to arrive with our very own cannon."

"General Draper's men cannot be far behind us, sir," Maltravers says. "I shall have the men start to pitch the tents and dig privy trenches."

"That's the spirit, old fellow," Suffolk replies, as he dismounts. "We must settle down, and wait for these damned froggies to see good sense. Once they start to go hungry we can name our own terms."

*

The king is inordinately pleased with himself for masterminding the siege of Boulogne, and he quite forgets that the idea has been foisted on him for these many months past. He is to get his wish at last… one final, magnificent, campaign against the old enemy.

"We must invest all three landward sides of the town," he tells his comrades clustered around the hastily erected map table. Pebbles hold down each corner of the plans, and prove to be proof against the gentle mid morning sea breeze. "Though I must have my cannon concentrated against the main gate. If I decide to storm the place, we must be able to knock our way inside… what?"

All heads nod, but even Rafe Sadler knows that Henry's military ideas come from the time of the old Romans, when a Caesar might think of losing twenty thousand men in a frontal assault. If it comes to a fight, wiser heads will prevail, and casualties will be kept to a more civilised level.

"The garrison are a mixture of French regular troops, and a company of Scots and Welsh mercenaries," Will Draper reports. "Tough opposition, I fear."

"These Frenchies are not very brave," the king continues, as if his general has not spoken a word. "They will try to escape, if they can… by sea I should think." He pauses then, as if the notion has just struck him. What was the point of storming the damned place, he thinks, if they just sail off from the harbour? "We must blockade the port at once. I want a couple of my warships to sail from Gravesend this very day."

"Excellent idea, Hal," says Will, but a squadron is already off the coast, and has been for a week or more. It is all part of the forward planning that a king sees no need for, as his 'iron will' should be enough to make it all happen. "Perhaps they might wish to parley with us?"

"Parley with me?" The king smirks and shakes his head. "I am Henry Tudor. They will submit, or fight. What is there to parley about?"

"The town would be better for being handed over without damage, sire," Rafe Sadler offers, and Henry snorts with derisive laughter.

"A Privy Councillor's lame suggestion. Both Will and I know that it ain't a war without plenty of blood and thunder. No, we tell them to yield, then blow down their gates. That'll show them."

"As Your Majesty wishes," Rafe replies. "I thought only of the affect on crown revenue." The mention of money is a masterstroke, and pulls the king up short. "A ruined town must be re-built before it can be any worth to you, sire."

"Sir Rafe has a valid point," Sir Thomas Wriothesley says. He has been a quiet onlooker until now, but Will Draper demands his support over the pointless sacking of a town with a warning glance. "I fear these frogs will wish to become loyal subjects of yours, sire."

"I suppose we need not inflict too much damage on them," Henry says. "Are the revenues all that interesting, Sadler?"

"The port levies, import taxes, and liens on the town's merchants will pay for the war inside a year, sire." It is the clinching argument, and the king is suddenly for sparing the town from the worst excesses.

"Offer terms, General Draper!" he declares and hobbles off to his private pavilion, still a little upset at not leading a charge against the foe. "I must write to the queen, and inform her of events. Rizz, see that ink is found!"

*

"Another important missive from the king?" Tom Seymour asks as a messenger places the parchment onto the silver tray at the queen's elbow. Katheryn is entertaining the two Seymour brothers to afternoon wine and sweet, honied, cakes, whilst Princess Mary, now a squat ungainly young woman, sits by the fireplace with her needlepoint. At her feet, a red haired Elizabeth amuses herself with a deck of cards given to her by 'Uncle Wyatt' on one of his irregular visits to the Palace of Enfield.

"Of course it is, you dandiprat," Ned sneers at his brother. "It has his seal."

"Dandiprat?" Tom's voice rises at the casually thrown out insult. "Rather that than a… a *risible* coxcomb."

"Risible? Why, you stinking…"

"Enough, boys." Queen Kathryn's weary voice cuts across their sibling dislike of one another. She is the friend of both, and once thought to marry Tom Seymour, before duty thrust her into the king's path. "It is most likely a despatch from the ongoing siege of Boulogne. His Majesty's news is always welcome to me."

"It is God's judgement for raising his hand against Cousin François and his 'most Catholic realm," Mary says, and Elizabeth makes a rude farting sound with her lips.

"The king should hang them all," the child says. "Uncle Wyatt says they are all stinking heretics."

"Hush, child," the queen says to her step daughter. "They are misguided, and should have accepted the king's offer of quarter. The Lord Templar made the most reasonable terms."

"Oh, he did that," Ned says and both brothers laugh. The story is famous. Having negotiated for several days, Draper and Rafe Sadler came up with an amicable peace. It remained only for Henry to ride up to the gates and accept the surrender.

"The king could not resist gilding the lily, and gave an impromptu speech of how he had once before vanquished a French army 'single handed'. The burgesses, who were lining the parapet over the main gate promptly dropped their breeches and showed Henry their hairy gallic buttocks!"

"God's will," Mary repeats, and the two men grin at her bloody minded

Catholicism. At least, they think to themselves, such papist views will never taint the English throne, for their little nephew, Edward, is in thriving good health.

"The king writes that he grows impatient, and demands General Draper acts. I fear it is going to be a grim and bloody business. Still, the sooner it is done, the sooner His Majesty can come home and start to run the kingdom again."

Since being in France, Henry leaves the day to day running of affairs in Katheryn's hands, and she is a most capable administrator in his absence. In most matters, Dick Cromwell, still unwell, and not the man he once was, is happy to advise, and Lady Miriam is able to help with financial matters. During her husband's time in France, Katheryn has successfully dealt with the new wool tariffs, and subdued a minor border incident with the ever troublesome Douglas clan.

"I should be there," Ned says. "The king has need of good men about him."

"And you know of one?" Tom Seymour snipes. "At least I have done service with the Magyars against the damned infidels. When did you ever draw your sword and wave it at a Turcoman?"

Queen Katheryn shakes her head in despair at the brotherly dislike. It does not bear well for the time when they must act as co-regents for the young king Edward.

*

"They actually showed me their arses, Will!" The king, a full week on, still cannot believe the effrontery of the French townsfolk. "Now they must pay for the insult. I want their walls down, and our soldiers running through their streets. No more delays. I *command* it!"

Will Draper bows and sets off to find Mush, who is drilling a company of musketry in sight of the town's main gate. His brother in law sees his approach, and delegates the drilling to Ibrahim, who is thoroughly enjoying the way the men keep bumping into one another.

"Good day, My Lord Templar," he says with an exaggerated sweeping bow. "How went your council of war with His Majesty?"

"He still fumes over being shown a few French arses," Will replies. "Why could he not have just kept quiet, and let them give in?"

"Alonso Gomez says the good burgesses of Boulogne were more than happy to surrender," Mush tells him. "They do not care who rules them, just as long as their taxes don't rise too much. Alonso also says that the foreign mercenaries, a hundred Scots, and a handful of Welsh, have not been paid for three months. They are unlikely to fight against us, our Spaniard says."

"Gomez says a lot," Will muses. "Has he gained second sight of late?"

"Of course not," Mush says with a chuckle at so silly a notion. "He has a lady friend in the harbour, and sees her most nights." For a moment Will is speechless at this revelation, then he regains his composure.

"Gomez can get into the town?" he asks, hardly able to credit his own hearing.

"No, of course he cannot," Mush replies. "He goes down the coast, about a quarter mile, and hires a small rowing boat from one of the local fishermen. He rows into the harbour at dusk, ties up at a spare jetty, and visits his lady. There is a low, gated inner wall, with a couple of guarded ways up to the town and the fortress."

"But he has never tried to enter the town?"

"His woman is probably a harbour-side fishwife," Mush replies. "Why bother?"

"Because we might just be able to land a small party of men, and open up the town from within." Will sees how, though dangerous, such a ruse could work quite well.

"And ruin the king's fun?" Mush is no fool, and he knows that Henry will not accept so bloodless a victory. "Gomez has already thought it out, and even has a map of the way through the narrow byways, but the king will not be cheated of his victory. He craves glory above all else."

"Then we must not let him realise he is being cheated," Will decides. "Henry wants Boulogne to fall at once… nothing more. It does not have to be a bloody slaughter."

"You have a plan?"

"Can you and Gomez get into the town at sunset?" Will asks.

"We can take two boats into the harbour," Mush replies. "Alonso, Rob Buffery, me, Tom Wyatt and another four should suffice."

"Not our poet," Will tells Mush. "He is our best ordinance man, and the king will listen to his advice. You must be at the main gate, and ready to throw it open at the right moment. Can you do it?"

"Why not?" Mush replies. Anything is better than all this interminable drilling up and down!"

*

Mijnheer Tomas Cornelis is weary. After the various arrangements to prepare for the coming English occupation; the bribes, the negotiations and the threats, he is finally back at the Palais de Juis in Antwerp. In a following carriage are Miriam and her companions, whilst a dozen Examiner troopers ride as escort. Now, as they trundle into the great house's courtyard once more, Tom Cromwell can revert to his true self.

"Shall I rouse the servants, Master Tom?"

"No, leave them be, Kel," he replies. "I am sure your good wife will be awake. There is a candle at the window, see? I imagine Maisie will be arranging something for us even as we enter. It is good to be home again." Kel Kelton nods his agreement, but he knows that this cosy picture is not all that his master seems to think it is. There are at least four armed men within the Palais de Juis, to protect the children, and keep the big house safe from intruders. Cromwell enjoys the fiction that Antwerp is so much safer than London, and who is Kel to have him think otherwise?

"There will be a cold table, and cool Venetian wine to sup," Kel surmises. "With all your plans working so well, you deserve a rest, master. We are none of us so young anymore."

"I will rest easier once Boulogne is actually under our flag," Cromwell worries. "With thirty thousand French troops wandering aimlessly about the country, it only needs a good general to cause us grief. Though I doubt they have a competent enough fellow to hand."

"They are fit only for fighting Lombards and Romans," Kel says. He jumps from the carriage, and helps his master down, as Lady Miriam and her friends begin to debark from the following coach. "I doubt they will find the courage to take us on again."

The front door opens, and Maisie Kelton is there, a candelabra held aloft. She curtseys to her master and hustles him inside. It is a cold night, and Tom Cromwell's ageing bones must find a chair close to the roaring fire.

"Are you born addled, Kel?" the woman asks. "Master Tom should have a blanket on such a night. Now, get inside, and see the fire is well banked."

"Yes, my love." Kel, who has killed more men than he cares to remember in his time goes in mortal fear of upsetting his wife, who he still adores now, as when they first met. "Shall I send some servants out for the baggage?"

"No. Leave it until later. Set a boy to watch no one steals a bag." Maisie turns to Tom Cromwell with a sharp look on her face. "You have a visitor waiting on you, sir. That Señor Chapuys is here on what he calls 'state business'. I put him in your library with a tray, and bade him wait."

"Really, Maisie!" Cromwell goes to make his way inside. "Eustace is a friend, and you must not treat him like some courtier, looking for favours." He pushes open the library door and sees that the little Savoyard diplomat is dozing in a chair by the glowing fire. His once dark and curly hair now shows signs of greying and, in repose, his friend's face is etched deep with the lines of fast advancing middle age. A glowing ember falls in the grate with a gentle hiss, and the ambassador pulls himself up into a sitting position with a start.

"Thomas… here at last," he says, and rubs at his eyes. "I have news… and it is not the best kind. I fear that the emperor has remembered me at last."

"What do you mean?" says Cromwell, but in his heart he can already make a shrewd guess. "You are a loyal servant of Emperor Charles, and he must hold you in the highest regards."

"He does," Chapuys replies. "So high that he wishes me to go to Bourburg and act as a negotiator for the coming peace talks. The emperor thinks the French will ask for terms the moment Boulogne is taken,"

"Then, surely, you will return to us?" Tom Cromwell asks, with sudden hope.

"No. I am advised that I should consider retirement to Savoy, or some other Imperial state." The little man is obviously distraught at the news, and finds it hard to impart the news without a tear in his eye.

"Are you rich enough to retire?" Cromwell asks a question that only a true friend can ask. "I know you must have pensions from the emperor, and Henry settled a thousand marks a year on you upon retirement, but that is hardly enough to keep a reasonable house running, these days."

"Calm yourself, old friend. These last three years, I have been most prudent. An uncle left me the income from his estate at Annecy, and I have been granted several ecclesiastical sinecures, in Toledo, Osma and Málaga by a grateful pope. I have also increased my wealth over the years through prudent investments in Antwerp."

"I cannot imagine life without you around me," Tom Cromwell confesses, and they hug. All thought of sleep is gone now, and the two old comrades will spend the hours until dawn drinking wine, and talking over old times. The library door opens, and Miriam is there with a tray of cakes.

"Maisie tells me the emperor has no more use for you, Eustace," she says, consolingly. "Might you now consider coming into my employ?"

"The emperor's advisors will never countenance such an arrangement, my dear, generous girl," Chapuys replies. "They would think it treasonable… and I cannot say they are wrong."

"Then retire to the nearest Imperial city." Tom Cromwell tells his friend. "Or to Ghent. I know it is full of protestants, but it still bows respectfully to the Holy Roman Empire. It is a pretty place, and there are some comfortable country estates to be had around the city."

"I have considered such a thing," Eustace Chapuys replies, "but the risks are too great. If we are within easy travel, I would constantly be drawn into your many plots, Thomas. If one was to be against the emperor... then where will I be?"

"Not so," Miriam says, brightly, "for Master Tom is retiring... for good. No more intrigues, no more plots, and no more answering to the king." Cromwell is taken aback by Miriam's presumption, but nods his head in confirmation. If it will keep his friend close, he will wash his hands of all future political activity, and concentrate on helping Miriam with her vast, expanding trade house.

"That cannot be," Chapuys says. "Your king is a bully, and a tyrant. He will not allow you to leave him, now he knows you still live."

"Henry is caught in his own trap," Miriam explains. "He cannot threaten a dead man... and the world knows that Thomas Cromwell lost his head in the Tower of London. If Master Tom should then be found alive... well, it would make the king out to be either a complete fool, or a wicked liar. Imagine what Emperor Charles might think of a ruler who condones such behaviour. Deceit, lies, and corruption abound. All vital parts of a strong king, but only if not displayed in public. No diplomat could ever trust his word again. No, Henry must accept the master's resignation, and let the world think he died on the block."

"You have it all worked out, my girl," says Cromwell. "When were you going to inform me of my impending retirement?"

"Do not scold me," Miriam replies. "Running around after the king is wearing you out. You sit up into the small hours, working by candlelight, and live for the next despatch from London. Well, enough, I say." She puts her hands on her hips, and tosses back her mane of black hair. "Rafe can do as well as you now, and once Richard gets over his latest gloomy malaise, he can help. Then there is that awful Rizz fellow. He is a slimy toad, but loyal to my husband out of sheer fear."

"There is also Sir Richard Rich, Uncle Norfolk and Stephen Gardiner," Chapuys puts in. "I think they would not wish the Austin Friars set to triumph, and rule the king. Your idea is noble, but flawed, my dear."

"I think not," Miriam Draper replies, rather heatedly. She is the owner of a dozen merchant ships, fifty cogs, valuable spice routes, fifteen grand houses, and a half mile of the Thames river frontage, on either bank. She is not to be gainsaid in this.

"Richard Rich has but one ambition… to be Lord Chancellor of England. We must see that he is offered the position, and make it clear that it is within our gift. Rafe can see to that, and there will be no real power attached to the position by then."

"Yes… possible… just possible," Cromwell mutters. He likes the idea of Rich getting his cherished post, only to find himself isolated, and politically castrated.

"The Duke of Norfolk is seventy soon," Miriam continues. "His days as a powerful man are done. Besides, his lands are mortgaged, and he owes yearly interest that is more than his net income. He must sell off land, but which bank might allow him to do that… other than the Galti Banking House? As the master owns a quarter of the bank, and the Draper Company, half… we can do as we please."

"Poor *Norfook*," Chapuys says. "How will he get by?"

"We can leave him with Arundel," Cromwell tells his friend.

"Why?" Miriam asks. The old duke has caused her family much pain in his time, and she is all for leaving him to rot in a farm labourer's cottage on a shilling a week.

"Because, if you take too much of a man's dignity, he will turn about, and he will fight," Cromwell says. "Besides, Surrey will inherit one day soon. He is another viper."

"I shall ask Alonso Gomez to call on him," Miriam says, with cold blooded intent. "Then the dukedom will be available for Henry to hand out again. Perhaps he might look to your nephew?"

"We are not of such noble blood, my dear," Thomas Cromwell tells her. "It will go to the Duke of Cumberland's boy, or even Chester's poor excuse of a son, I think."

"Then we have Bishop Stephen Gardiner," Miriam concludes. "I can always have him…"

"Stephen was once a very good friend," Cromwell says. "No more death, my girl, lest you come to enjoy it too much."

"I was only going to suggest we give him Canterbury, once the archbishop dies," Miriam explains. "Tom Cranmer is venerable, and ancient, and he cannot last much longer."

"Yes, that will work." Cromwell reaches for his quill, and starts to make notes. Chapuys sits quietly by the fire and contemplates how, in the last few minutes, the future of a great realm has been decided. It seems that he must live in Ghent, whether he wishes to or not, for Miriam must have it so. He smiles, for the prospect is not so very displeasing. He loves her and the three children with the passion of a favourite uncle. Besides, he muses, Ostrich feathers are far cheaper in Ghent than they are in Savoy.

*

Boulogne is still defiant, but in that curious and amiable way that only the French can achieve. At noon, each day, a few of the inhabitants, usually one of the burghers and several rich merchants come out of the small postern gate, and setup a picnic beneath the walls. It is the civilised way, they explain, when they invite some of the English to join them.

At first, Henry is for rushing them and teaching them a lesson, but Mush and Rafe prevail on him to forebear. Why not share a luncheon with these men, and see what can be found out? The king blusters, then agrees to let Rafe and a couple of Will Draper's best men attend. Soon, it is an accepted part of the daily siege, and for an hour or two, the rancour is forgotten.

"How was lunch?" Will asks Mush after a week of amiable picnics. "Was the wine acceptable?"

"Very good," Mush replies. "The food is quite remarkable too. They do not seem to be staving just yet."

"Nor will they," says Will. "For each night fishing boats slip into the harbour, right under the noses of our warships. They bring in fresh fish for the market, flour, salt and game. While we sit out here in the mud and rain, they dine on hare casseroles and goose livers."

"Yes, they do this thing with them," Mush says, with some enthusiasm. "Then they spread it onto this marvellous, crusty bread and…"

"Enough!" Will snaps. "It has to stop. If we do not take the place soon, the king will order a general bombardment until the wall comes down, then send in every man we have."

"They will just withdraw into the fortress on the mount," Mush replies. He may like his lunch with them, but he is always alert to anything they might let slip, and he knows they intend holding out until Henry grants them safety and other privileges. The king's demand for an unconditional surrender does not sit well with the wealthy French merchants who usually run Boulogne.

"I know." Will takes a deep breath, and explains what he is going to do. Spoken aloud, the simple plan to infiltrate the town, and open the gate from within sounds clear enough, but it tastes of a kind of treachery that he is not happy with. "I want you to join Alonso Gomez and the others tonight. If all goes well, we might gain a victory without having to slaughter hundreds of innocent people."

"I do not care for it,"Mush tells his brother in law. "It smacks of something

Richard Rich might do, were he clever enough. Though it would save lives… providing our men do not decide to sack the town and put it to the torch. They have been stuck outside for weeks, and their tempers are short."

"The army will be stood down, and busy cooking their evening meals around the camp fires. I will have Captain Cord, and a hundred picked men, horsed and armed. As the gate opens, Jeremiah will gallop in, and seize control of the outer walls. If he is successful, he will ride on up to the fortress, and try to catch the guards unawares. Do we have a plan, Mush, or must I ask lesser men to help me?"

"No, we have a plan," Mush says. "But Henry will be furious at us not fighting."

"I am going to have our biggest cannon drawn up to face the wall to the left of the gate, and ask the king to take command of the first action. He can stand well behind the big gun, in full armour, and wave a sword about.

"The moment you hear the cannon roar, throw open the gates. The town is ours, and I shall inform the king that, as at the famous Battle of the Spurs, the enemy caved in the moment they knew he was coming. He is so addled with poppy juice and pain that he will see himself as a great victor."

"You seem to have it all in hand, Will," Mush agrees. "I shall find Alonso Gomez."

*

"You want me to command the bombardment of the town?" Henry frowns at Rafe Sadler's sudden change of heart. From wishing to wait and see, he is now eager for the fray. "And it is to commence this very evening?"

"Will Draper assures me that it is the best time to start." Rafe, after years serving the king, is a practiced diplomat, and he can lie without fault, if it is for England's sake. "He says it will unnerve the townsfolk as they sit down for their evening meal. A single, huge cannon belching fire and brimstone at their wall, then silence. We can take our ease over a late supper, whilst the French cower under their tables, wondering when the next cannon will fire."

"I see. We let them worry all night, then storm the damned place on the morn?" Henry likes the idea, and lets himself be convinced with ease. "I shall wear my best armour, of course. And Tom Wyatt must instruct me as to how I might give the best command. I favour holding up a drawn sword, and then lowering it with a magnificent flourish. What say you?"

"A magnificent idea, sire," Rafe replies. "Let us make our preparations." He prays that Will's ruse comes off, for if it fails, the king is intent on a full bombardment, and then storming the walls with long ladders. "Will you command the attack on the gate, or lead the men up the scaling ladders, sire?"

"Eh, what's that?" Henry considers both options, and does not see merit in either.

"If you wish to scale the long ladders, you must foreswear weighty armour, and climb in nought but a leather jerkin and hose… because of the heaviness of it, you see."

"What, no armour?" Henry feels a twinge of horror at the idea of climbing a frail ladder. "How might my leg stand up to the climb?"

"Fear not, sire," Rafe says, straight faced. "Old soldiers tell me that the sheer weight of men pushing behind gets you up and over the walls. Though two thirds of those on the ladders die, the survivors have the honour of fighting their way down to the gate, and holding it, until we can break in from without."

"Two thirds, you say?"

"At least, and I shall be right behind you, Your Majesty," Rafe Sadler says. "Imagine the pride my children will feel, knowing that I died by my king's side… or straddling his murdered body with mine own."

"Died… oh, well… yes," Henry's

mind is beginning to clear, and he foresees a way out of his predicament. "England must not lose its best ministers, and I must forbid your involvement. If you do it because I am there, then I too must sacrifice my royal desires for my royal duties. On the morrow, I will accept a lesser command, and order those who will storm the gate from behind. In this way, I will be ready to lead my horse soldiers into the town, and take full possession."

"A splendid idea, sire." Rafe smiles at a happy thought. "Then you can still wear full armour, and so impress the foe with your martial splendour."

"Exactly!" Henry thinks this to be a much better plan, and he looks forward to the morrow. "Full armour… that's the thing.I have the most splendid new suit… of Italian design, and as magnificent as anything ever made."

"You are the bravest man I have ever known," Rafe says. "Even Richard the Lionhearted never rode into an enemy castle in his best armour, for fear of every arrow being aimed solely at him. England will salute you, sire, to a man…whether you be alive afterwards, or riddled with crossbow bolts and archers shafts."

"Quite," Henry says, uneasily. He will not sleep a wink, as he worries about so evil a death, but Rafe is unperturbed. He knows that no such thing will come to pass, and that Boulogne will soon be an English town. With luck it might be done without bloodshed… not even Henry's!

*

"Marie?" The hoarse whisper sounds like a gunshot in the deserted harbour side. Gomez crouches behind some creels and a heap of recently mended fishing nets, with Mush, Rob Buffery and three of Will's toughest Examiners. "Are you there, my sweet?" Mush marvels at how good the Spanish cutthroat's French is, but wishes he could keep his whisper down to less than a shout.

"Alonso?" The woman replies from the darkness. "Forgive me… but he knows about us, and I could not help it." There is a sudden movement in the shadows, and Marie's cuckolded husband appears, with his two brothers, and each has a knife in his hand. Gomez slips a hand to his dagger, but Mush stays the movement.

"No bloodshed, my friend, he whispers, and beckons to Rob Buffery. The burley retired soldier moves forward, followed by the Examiner troopers, and Marie's husband is transfixed. For a moment, he thinks these must be other lovers of his woman, and he wonders at how quickly the odds are stacked against him.

One of the brothers makes as if to put up a fight, but Rob Buffery cracks him on the head with the heavy wooden staff he is armed with, and the man collapses in a heap. The husband and the remaining brother are quickly tied up and gagged, as is Marie.

"Forgive me, my petal, but this is business," Gomez tells the woman. "I shall come back for you, and steal you a way from this indolent life." Marie is alarmed now, for her husband is a very rich and generous man, and she does not relish losing it all for a life following the English army across all France.

"Come on," Mush urges, and the six men begin to make their way through the streets of the harbour. Soon they come to the low wall... no more than the height of a tall man, that is there to ensure any imports and exports are taxed at one of the small toll gates.

The gate they find is padlocked, but a blow from Rob Buffery's cudgel soon springs it open. Mush removes the chain and eases the gate back. It screeches, and sounds like a demon to their tense ears. They pause, and listen. No sound comes from the town, save a dog yapping in the distance. It can smell trouble, but no one cares, and its annoyed master soon kicks it into silence.

Their main fear is that the poor map they have will not suffice to guide them to the main gate, but they see, above the roof tops, a crenellated length of wall that shows them the way. Mush leads them on until they cross a small town square. Every one is inside, settling down for their evening repast, save one man, who owns the tavern to their left. The man, a huge brute of a fellow knows he will get no custom until after dinner, but he is still busy setting up a few tables outside, where the older men like to sit and exchange gossip.

The tavern keeper glances up as the six foreigners pass on the far side of the square, and gives them a wave. Sailors from a merchant ship, perhaps, he thinks, looking for a drink?

"*Bonsoir, mes amis,*" he calls. "*Ca va?*"

"*Ca va, bien,*" Alonso Gomez replies, and shrugs to show that they cannot stop for a jug of wine. They hurry on, and the tavern keeper consoles himself with the thought that they must return the same way, and might then be thirstier.

Mush Draper slips down a street that is almost narrow enough to be an alley, and emerges into an open space. In front, guarded by one sleeping townsman, is the main gate. It is a solid enough thing, all huge oak planks, crossed by iron for strength, but only kept closed by a single crossbeam.

"See to the guard," Mush whispers, and Rob Buffery nods. He strolls across to where the man is dozing on a stool, and taps him on the head. The Frenchman slumps to the ground, and the English raiding party move forward to take down the heavy locking bar.

*

"At your command, sire?" Tom Wyatt is standing by the big gun, which he has only three quarter charged with black powder. It will make a lot of noise, and belch smoke, but the heavy ball will have little force behind it. They do not want to damage the town at all, and there will be nothing more than a loud crash, and some masonry dust to clog the eyes.

"Very well, sir," Henry calls. He is fully fifty paces behind the huge cannon, for fear of it exploding. "Am I far enough… I mean properly positioned?"

"Perfect, sire," Wyatt replies and subdues a grin. "If you will?" The king sees that the moment is on him. His army are eating, unaware of the fact that their monarch is about to launch the attack, single handed, once more. He raises the sword, and sweeps it down with such force that its tip buries itself several inches into the soft ground.

"Touch," the poet orders, and his gunner places a smouldering fuse into the cone of gunpowder wedged into the firing hole. There is a soft hiss, a spark of light, and then a deafening roar. The heavy cannon ball hurtles out, and strikes the outer wall about a quarter way up.

To Tom Wyatt's dismay, and the shame of some poor French builders, the wall trembles, and a crack appears from top to bottom. A moment later, and a twelve foot section of the wall crumbles, and falls outwards to shower the poet, and even the far off king, with dust and debris. At the same moment, the gates open, and Captain Jeremiah Cord and his cavalry troop gallop through them.

"God's sainted teeth!" Henry says, through his visor, which has fallen over his eyes, obscuring his vision. "What is happening?" I hear horses. Are we undone? Must we flee?" Tom Wyatt reaches the king then, and prises open his heavy visor.

"Your Majesty," he declares, "the wall is breached, and the town is ours!"

"What?" Henry tries to move in the heavy armour, and only manages to do so when a couple of squires run up and assist him. He sees the open gate, and the crumbled wall, and beams with satisfaction at his own skill. "They surrender?"

"The gate is open, sire, and your Examiners are in the town. It is only a matter of time, and Boulogne will be yours."

"Yes, just as I planned," Henry crows. "If you fellows had listened to me a month ago, I would be back in England now as ruler of France. Save that piece I generously leave to François... if he can stop the Emperor Charles from taking it."

"Shall we dine, sire, whilst your troops secure Boulogne?" the poet asks, and the pair make for the king's pavilion. Henry understands that he must share his men's camp rations as closely as he can, so they will make do with some hare soup, a platter of steamed river trout, roast lamb in mint and vinegar sauce, roast beef with a mustard dressing, a couple of dozen fresh water oysters, a game pie, some marchpane fancies, and a light custard tart or two.

"Damn me, but the men must eat well enough, he muses, as they sit down to dinner. "Do they enjoy oysters, Tom?"

"No, sire. Their tastes are simple, and they prefer to eat boiled beef and hard biscuits, soaked in wine." This will make a fine doggerel poem, the poet thinks to himself. The king and the soldier's dinner, he thinks. "Other than that, and the rich sauces which sour their common stomachs, they eat the same this evening."

"Jolly good," Henry says. "Pass the cheese, and some of those devilishly good pickled eggs."

"At your service, sire," the poet says, and he cannot help but run some words together in his head, concerning the events of the day.

'Dear Hal did make the trumpet call,
that like Jericho did the walls make fall,

and the gate opens to the royal winner,
who now sits, and eats a hearty dinner'

He considers the doggerel rhyme for a moment, and thinks it quite the worst he has ever composed. It shall be consigned to the scrap heap of poor verse that he fears grows ever more prolific with each passing year.

6   Glittering Prizes

The French are a phlegmatic breed

when it comes to losing battles. On either side of the *Blessed Jean D'Arc,* they have lost wars to England, the Holy Roman Empire, the Moors, Switzerland, and almost every other country in Europe. So it no surprise to find that they have now lost the siege of Boulogne, without even knowing it was truly underway.

The cannon's roar, and unfortunate collapse of a badly built wall brings every townsman out into the streets, where they find heavily armed cavalry at each corner. After passing a few comments with their neighbours, one man takes it upon himself to approach the man who seems to be in charge.

"Pardon, M'sieu," the merchant asks, "but have we lost?"

"I regret so, my friend," Mush replies. "Unless you mean to fortify your fortress and make a stand? In which case we must order up our best cannon, and reduce it to rubble."

"The fortress is damp and empty, sir," the Frenchman says with a Gallic shrug. "What will happen now?"

"Nothing," Mush tells him. "On the morrow, go about your usual business, as both harbour and town will be free to trade. Only now, you are all the subjects of King Henry of England."

"Fair enough,"the merchant says, then thinks of something else. "What about your army? Will they not want to rape all our women, and then pillage?"

"An English town?" Mush says. "Have no fear, sir. The army, with the exception of a thousand men to garrison the town, will march to Calais on the morrow."

"Forgive me asking about the pillage and rape, sir, but my wife wanted to know. Though I doubt she would be the first to be troubled by unruly soldiers, lest they have very poor eyesight, or simpler tastes."

"Your wife will not be bothered, sir," Mush replies, and the two men smile at the rude jest.

"Then we will cause your men no trouble, sir," the burgess replies. "We want only to live out quiet lives."

Jeremiah Cord is busy placing his men and he forbids them the offer of free drinks from the tavern keeper in the square. He knows that even the most disciplined of troopers can soon become unruly when filled with strong red wine.

"All in order, My Lord," he says to Will Draper when he rides through the wide flung gates. By his side is the king, who smiles from the back of his huge warhorse, and dispenses small waves to the astonished townsfolk. In all their lives they have never even seen their own king, and this is probably the greatest event that will ever happen to most of them.

"They cheer me, Will!" he says

with childlike pleasure. "Do they hate François so?"

"His tax collectors make him unpopular, sire," Rafe says from the other side of the king. "They go unchecked, and often take more than they are entitled to by law. It does not happen in your own realm, thanks to the wise laws put in place by Thomas Cromwell, at your urging. The king sets the rate, and your collectors never overstep their legal authority."

"Good fellows," Henry says. "But how do we know they do not, Rafe?"

"Our agents watch them, and if they overburden the people, and keep the profit, Your Majesty has them hanged."

"Of course. A salutary solution. The rope deters many a scoundrel… for they do not repeat the offence… what?"

He chuckles at his own jest, and lets his squire lead his mount into the main square. He is of a mind to make another grand speech, but recalls that these French are a crude lot, not above giving offence to their betters. Instead, he waves a little more. It grows dark, and Henry recalls that, because of his daring exploit in taking the town almost single handed, he has not had any decent supper, other than the scant soldiers repast he shared with Tom Wyatt earlier. "Food?" he grumbles, and Will Draper beckons to Jeremiah Cord.

"Captain, ready the finest house in

Boulogne for its new king, and see that a fine supper is arranged. Tell the people that we will pay for everything we take with good English silver."

Inside the hour, Henry is ensconced within the mayor's house, and seated at a long banqueting table. He is flanked by Rafe Sadler, Will, Mush, and Tom Wyatt. The other places are filled with some English officers, and the Duke of Suffolk, who arrives just as the first course is served. He is amazed at the sudden victory, and can scarce understand how it came about so abruptly.

"Really, Hal," he says, "I go out on one patrol, and you capture the damned place without me!"

"Poor Charles," the king boasts. "You are always second to me in all things. I took it into my head to be done with the matter, and went to it with my cannon. Bless me if the whole wall did not tumble down, and the gates spring open. I charged into the town, with Will's troopers a little behind, and they all fell to their knees and surrendered."

"A fine engagement, old friend," Suffolk says, but he can smell the mendacity like the aroma of rotten fish. "What were you thinking of, My Lord Templar… letting Hal be so reckless?"

"You know His Majesty when his mind is set," Will replies, and gives the duke a private smile. "Mere stone walls are no barrier."

"Just so," the king says. By the time he returns to London this ridiculous fable will be lodged in his mind like it is the greatest truth. "Ah, the food!"

Will is not hungry, but the steady flow of courses, prepared by the French kitchens are staggering in both volume, and quality. He watches Henry devour a soup made of wild mushrooms and sour cream, roasted wood pigeons in a berry sauce, thin slices of mutton in hot cider, broiled trout, and a great haunch of venison in a rich juniper gravy. It is only when the fancy cakes arrive that he wonders if he might have been advised to safeguard against poison,

As the food is almost gone, and no one is yet showing signs of ill health, he decides that the newly conquered town really do want nothing but peace. He contents himself with a piece of cheese and some bread, and slips away to see that all is in order outside. The gates are closed again, and Alonso Gomez sits by them, playing dice with Rob Buffery and some of the French fishermen fro the harbour.

"A good days work, Alonso," he says in passing, and the Spaniard just shrugs.

"Lor' save us, General Will," Rob Buffery exclaims. "You should have seen us all jump when that stretch of wall came down. Old Alonso here crossed himself, and started to pray, as if Old Hob was after his heathen soul!"

"You ignorant pig," Gomez curses. "I was merely giving thanks to God for his intercession. Is that not so, Pierre?"

"*Mais oui, M'sieu Gomez*," Pierre confirms. "Once I knew my wife was cuckolding me with you, I also gave thanks to God. Under the circumstances, she could not be angry with me at taking a lover of my own, but a week earlier."

"Perhaps not, but as it is her own sister, I wonder," Gomez replies, and slaps the man on his shoulder. "Have you untied her yet, my friend?"

"Soon," Pierre says, and the two men smile at the idea of it. Will grins at this show of good humour between erstwhile enemies, and goes about his inspection. On the morrow, he will ask Suffolk to pick four hundred men to garrison the town, and then move the army back to Calais. With luck, he will be back home within the week.

The king will linger, of course, if only to taunt the French king over his recent defeats. Rafe will stay by his side, and see that when the prizes are awarded, the Austin Friars men amongst the troops are taken care of. The booty from the battle, together with the bond to be paid by the town of Boulogne will amount to a sizeable sum, and the land alone is enough to furnish an estate for every gentleman who dared cross the Channel with their king.

Each man of noble rank will receive several hundred acres of lush French countryside, to hold for his liege, and every foot soldier should see a bounty of ten or fifteen shillings in his purse. As for Henry, he can now, without fear of being ridiculed, call himself King of all England, Ireland, and France.

*

The Calais road is a well worn one, and Will, together with his entire Examiner regiment, are on it by daybreak. Every man is eager to be back in England, and they soon began to sing. The song acts as a rhythm for the march, and the ground seems to be eaten up at speed. After 'Down Amongst the Oak Trees', they start up with 'She did smile upon me', a tale of love found, lost and found again.

It is almost noon when John Beckshaw, the colonel of the regiment, indicates that they should take their ease, and eat. Each trooper has a flask of wine, bread, cheese, and cured bacon in his saddle bag, and they fall to, readily. Will notices that John is doing his job well, and guards are positioned on each flank, and to both front and rear of the column.

It is unlikely that they will come under attack, but somewhere in the vast, rolling lands beyond, a huge French army is waiting, and he has no wish to fight another twenty-five thousand of the enemy again at such short notice. Off to his right flank, a pistol shot rings out. Will sees that the outrider, on a low hill about a quarter mile away is waving to their rear.

Will looks, and sees two tiny figures in the distance, galloping towards the column. They close fast, and he sees that it is Mush and Tom Wyatt, riding as if the devil were on their backs. For a moment, he wonders if Boulogne has been retaken, then dismisses the notion. The gates are secure, and the breach in the wall is blocked with four of the king's best cannon.

"Slow down, lads," Will calls, as he gallops out to meet them. "What is amiss?" Mush cannot speak, for he is consumed with anger, and it is left to Tom Wyatt to explain.

"Dear God, Will... I can hardly believe it, save I saw it happen with my own eyes," the poet tells him. "After you left, Henry came out of the mayor's house and called for a troop of crossbowmen to attend him. Then he gathered every citizen in the town together, in the square. He lined them up, and went along choosing certain men. He recognised six as those who bared their arses at him the other week, and picked another four for good measure. Then he had them put in fetters, and hanged from the battlements... innocent men, without even a trial."

"It makes me sick to the stomach," Mush snarls. "I shall not serve that disgusting dog one more day. To exact such revenge for so small a matter is obscene. Then the fat bastard gave them a speech. He told them that they were now his vassals, and subject to his will. He even said he would close their churches down, and bring in 'honest' English parsons to teach them how to be civilised."

"Dear Christ," Will groans. "Last night the people cared not who rules, as long as they are fairly treated... now they will hate us with every breath they take. The man is a monstrous imbecile. Did not Suffolk try to stop him... or even Rafe?"

"The king asked Suffolk to inspect the harbour defences, and take along Rafe to assess any work that might need to be done. He had a free hand to do as he wished... and he chose to do bloody murder. It was planned, not a sudden whim, and for that neither of us can serve him again."

"How can you avoid it?" Will asks. "Henry is the king. There is nowhere to hide. If he thinks you revile him so, he will find cause to end you both too."

"I am finally for the Holy Land," Mush says. "I shall not set foot in England again… as long as he breathes."

"I am for Venice," the poet says. "I finally have a mind to write down all my poetry, and the city on the water appeals to my romantic soul."

"What about Isabella and your daughter?" Will asks. It is a pointless question. Mush's wife and child live in the Palais de Juis, and are safe from any outside harm. They will be content to wait for him, even if it takes a year.

"I leave them in my sister's care," Mush tells his brother in law. "Are you still going to serve him?"

"What else can I do?" Will replies, crossly. He sees how his hands are tied by past loyalties and oaths. "Miriam's business is strong, but it cannot sustain itself without the English holdings. I must remain loyal to the monarchy, for her dear sake, even if I loathe him."

The two men see the sense in this, but neither are for being dissuaded. After ensuring they have plenty of money readily available, he shakes each of them by the hand. As they spur their horse into a gallop, he watches them go, and wonders if they will ever all meet up again.

Friends are worth more than jewels, and he has just lost two because of a king's vile actions. He must continue to serve Henry, he thinks, but never again with the same vigour.

*

Rafe Sadler sits bolt upright in his bed, with his eyes wide open. It is like this now ,ever since he saw the barbaric way Henry treated his French captives. The men, whose only crime was to insult the king's dignity, had been dragged up to the battlements and stood with a noose about their necks. then the soldiers had simply eased them over the side, until they dangled. Each man took an age to die, twisting, kicking and choking slowly.

The townsfolk had stood in mute horror, as their fellow citizens died, and then turned away from the terrible spectacle. Henry then harangued them in a loud, bullying voice, but by the time he had finished his mad rant, the square was empty.

Since then Rafe would wake up in a cold sweat. It was not the fact of the murders, which he finds bad enough, it is that they were done without pity, by a man who thought it the right way for a king to behave. From that day on, Henry would become ever more wicked, and no one would be safe from his wilder caprices.

"What is it, dearest?" his wife Ellen asks, as she lights a bedside candle. Despite the six children, and the length of their marriage, she still insists on sharing his bed each night. "You are troubled."

"Boulogne," Rafe says, simply, and it is enough to tell her everything. If Henry can be so vile, she reasons, then his closest advisors are in constant danger over every act they perform, or piece of advice they give. "Leave him. Go back to your law practice, darling."

"He would see it for what it is," Rafe replies. "A repudiation of his gross behaviour. How long then before he decides I too am disloyal?"

"We could go to live in the Flemish lands, or even further away from his vindictiveness."

"And lose our fortune?" Rafe asks. "I am worth more than I care to admit… all honestly earned…but it is invested in property all across London, and land in Wiltshire. Besides, the children must be English, and not some wandering band of stateless orphans."

"Then what can you do?" Ellen, as faithful a woman as ever lived, will abide by his decision, and stay by his side.

"Carry on as usual, I suppose" Rafe tells her. "As long as we are careful, and give him no cause for suspicion, the king will leave us alone to fulfil our duties."

"I pray you are right, dearest husband," Ellen says, and she blows out the bedside candle. "Or that the Almighty takes him before he …"

"Hush, woman… that is treason!"

"Sleep, husband," Ellen says into the darkness, but her mind completes the sentence. With Henry dead, things would be so much better for everyone.

*

Will Draper watches as his men are disembarked, and sees to it that his sergeants account for each man, his equipment, and any stray booty that may have come their way. The order, from the king, is that all proceeds from the French expedition are to be gathered up, and shared out 'each to his needs'.

It is this last phrase that concerns the King's Examiner, for it smacks of lawyers, and sounds like something that Richard Rich might suggest. Whilst most of Henry's court followed him to France, Rich remained behind to advise the queen on any legal matters that arose. Now this, the collection, and redistribution of plunder.

Once Boulogne was taken Will and several other regiments belonging to Suffolk, had made their way back to Calais, and extracted what they could from the houses of those French nobles who had opposed them, and were now cowering in Paris. The gold and jewellery, left in place, because the French did not think they could lose, is easy pickings, and must come to many thousands of pounds.

"Good day, Will." The Duke of Suffolk seldom oversees such menial tasks, but today he is eager to speak with the Examiner's general. "I see your fellows have done well, as have mine. What make you of this nonsense about collecting the loot together?"

"I suspect Sir Richard Rich is behind the order," Will replies. "As Attorney General, he claims he has the right to ensure a legally acceptable distribution."

"You mean he and Hal are stealing it from us?" Suffolk says. "My boys will expect at least three or four pounds a head for the sergeants, and two for the foot soldiers. I smell trouble ahead."

"As do I," says Will, "but I am damned if I can do anything about it. I might speak with Miriam, and see if we can pay the King's Examiner's bounty ourselves, if they are cheated."

"Well enough for you, old fellow… with only eight hundred troopers to pay, but I have twelve thousand men, and they are not as disciplined as your boys!" Suffolk thinks how his yeomen will think of him if the promised rewards do not arrive, and he sees that fields are going to remain untilled, sheep unshorn, and rebellious workers will complain all across his county.

Then he recalls that once his men are paid off, and back on the land he is, as their lord, due a nice windfall tax on their earnings. He thinks of the thousands he is going to lose, and he groans in dismay.

*

Arturo Galti of the famous

Lombard banking house is in London to negotiate the purchase of war bounty. The equable little Lombard is staying at Draper House, and has been for two weeks. One might smile at his certainty that England will win, but it is a close secret that his brother, Luigi, is living in Paris on the same mission. Whomsoever emerges as the victor, the House of Galti will be there.

Lady Miriam Draper is ever the ideal hostess, but today she has to use all of her willpower to keep from slapping the scrawny little man who is just entering her house.

"Sir Richard Rich," Maisie says, with such contempt that the Attorney General gives her a cold stare. Maisie stares back, and it is Rich who must look away first.

"Sir Richard," Miriam says, with a forced smile. "Welcome to Draper House. Signor Galti is in the great hall. Pray do come this way." She introduces the two men, and withdraws. Rich crosses to the huge banqueting table and opens up the two thin ledgers he has brought with him.

"These are a complete inventory of the recent treasure taken in the French war," Rich tells the Lombard. "Might you care to run your eye over them?"

"*Si.*"

"They are most accurate, I assure you."

"*Si.*"

"You do speak English... don't you?"

"*Si.*" The Lombard smiles at him, and Rich thinks he is being made fun of, but then Galti crosses to the ledgers, and sits to read them. He nods at the first page, makes a tutting noise about the fourth, and then settles into a deep silence. Long minutes pass until Rich thinks the banker is asleep, then he sits up with a start and gives the Attorney General a long, baleful look.

"Well?" Rich asks.

"Where do you get these fanciful valuations from, sir?" The Lombard stabs a finger at the top item, and reads aloud. "One gold bracelet, inset with six garnets, weight three ounces... valued at sixty five English pounds... yes? Richard Rich expects some bargaining, but the Lombard's almost sneering words take him aback.

"Fanciful, Signor Galti?" he says. "Each item has been valued by our own Guild of Goldsmiths, and the separate jewels by the king's own jewellers. I assure you that the bracelet you speak of would fetch such a sum on the open market."

"A month ago, I would have agreed," Galti replies. "Since then, you English have conducted a very successful war, and gathered in a vast amount of treasure. You list hundreds of items of precious jewellery, all stolen from private homes… homes of French nobles, and honest gentlemen."

"The spoils of war are not stolen, sir," Rich says in his best lawyer's voice. "Right of arms bestows new legal ownership on any booty, and it can be disposed of as the victor sees fit."

"Quite so, but consider this, Sir Richard, if you will. A man comes to you, and offers a bracelet for sixty five pounds. It is just what you want, and the workmanship is quite excellent. So, you offer to pay him. Then another nine men come forward with very similar pieces, and each one offers to sell their own bracelets to you. As a shrewd man, what do you do?" Rich holds his tongue, and the Lombard grins at him. "You say you will choose the one that is offered at the lowest price, of course. So these men must reduce their asking price, until it is as low as they can afford, and then, you buy."

"Your point, sir?" Richard Rich knows when he is being manipulated, but must hear the nasty little foreigner out. If Galti tries to cheat him, he will look to sell elsewhere.

"My point, Sir Richard, is this. The market for such fine jewellery is limited to a few very rich gentlemen, the nobility, or the great rulers of Europe. If I try to sell so many beautiful things at once, the market will be glutted, and prices will tumble. Why would a duke pay a thousand, when he can choose from a hundred things and offer much less?"

"Then buy it, and keep most of it back," Rich says.

"An excellent idea. I can pay you the seventy-five thousand pounds you want, and store nine tenths of it in my vault for years. But wait… will that not tie up my money for all that time? Treasure in a vault does not earn interest, my dear sir."

"You rogue!" The words are out before the Attorney General can stop them, and Arturo Galti's eyes flash in anger. He stands, and starts to move towards the door. Then he pauses, and looks back, scornfully, at Rich.

'If you say this to me in Lombardy, I would slit your throat, Signor… for honour's sake. But I see you have no honour, dog, so I bid you good day."

"Wait, sir… I spoke in haste," Rich says. He has been called worse things by the king, and some others, and his skin is thick. "Of course we do not expect you to lose out by our transaction, Signor Galti. I understand that your bank cannot realise a profit at once, and am prepared to accept a lower valuation."

"Twenty thousand."

"What!" Rich is dumbfounded at the nerve of the man. Had the king simply taken his usual portion of spoils it would come to no more. "That is out of the question. The king would never…"

"The king will be happy with it," Arturo Galti snaps. "Years ago, when he saw fit to drive all the Lombard bankers from England, he would have been happy with ten thousand. Take it or leave it, for it is no matter to me."

"There are other bankers," Rich replies.

"Like the Jewish banking houses in France?" the Lombard says with a wry smile on his face. "They will not offend King François for a king who would have them executed for coming to England. Or do you mean the Francapaldi Bankers in Venice? They might be able to take the goods, but they will have the same problem as I do. A pretty woman wants a necklace, not a score of them. Twenty thousand… a bank draft now… or I must take my leave of England."

Richard Rich sees he is caught between the king's urgent need for money, and the market value of the booty. He knows that it cannot all be sold at once, for fear of depressing the market, but he was willing to let himself be beaten down to thirty-five thousand This would allow him to pay the king his due, and keep a nice profit for himself. Now, all his hard work will be for nothing. The Lombard's hand is on the handle of the door.

"Wait, sir," Rich says, " for I think we can do business."

"A most wise decision, Sir Richard," Galti tells him. "I shall arrange for payment the moment the goods are in my warehouse in Stepney. Should you ever feel the need to visit Lombardy, pray remember that your earlier insult is still to be avenged. Set one foot on my territory, and I will kill you. Good day."

*

"You offered to cut his throat?" Miriam laughs at the idea, and pours Arturo Galti out another glass of wine.

'He called me a rogue."

"But Arturo, my dearest old friend… you are a rogue," Miriam says. "Here, let me cut you some more of the game pie."

"These 'pie' we do not have in Lombardy," the banker tells her. "They are delicious. As is all this fine food. I think your Attorney General will have no appetite though. I thought he would rage more, but he saw it was futile. I should have offered ten thousand less, Lady Miriam."

"No, that would have meant Henry being short changed, and that is a dangerous thing to do to the king. This way, he has his usual cut, and cannot complain. It is only Rich who loses out. You have heard from your brother Luigi?"

"I have. He is lodged at the French

royal court, which is currently residing in Paris. It seems that King François has the city locked up tight, and fears the English army will arrive at any moment."

"Luigi has made all the arrangements?" Miriam asks. She knows how efficient the banker brothers are, yet still likes to keep her eye on the small details.

"Last week. The French nobility want their treasures back, and will pay a ransom of sixty-five thousand pounds. Once I am reimbursed of my outlay to Rich, the profit can be used to pay your army's bounty."

"Excellent, Arturo," says Miriam. "The king is satisfied, the army is satisfied, and my husband owes me a favour. When he told me of how Rich was robbing the men who fought by his side, he was almost distraught with rage. Had I not come up with this scheme, he might well have sought Rich out, challenged him to a duel, and killed him."

"Then even Rich has profited," the Lombard says. "For this way, he gets to live to breath for another day!"

Miriam is pleased at the day's business, and takes quiet pride in the fact that she is able to do what no man can. The Draper Company is hers, and she owns a large part of the Galti Bank of Lombard. With planning, she thinks, wars can be won and lost by the influence of her wealth. It is Draper wealth that helps support Henry's desire to wage war, and Draper arms that keep the king safe from his own follies. She and her husband, she thinks, are two sides of the same coin.

"You must have your commission, Arturo," she says, and the Lombard waves the very idea away.

"I am rich enough, thanks to you, my dear lady," he says. "Though there is a favour I might ask."

"Then ask."

"We Lombards are still banned from England, and my fellow bankers tire of having to use middle men every time one of your gentry needs a loan.'

"I will speak to Will. He may be able to influence the king. If not, Rafe Sadler will help us."

"You own him?" Galti asks, and Miriam laughs at so typical a Lombard thought.

"No… he is a friend… a good friend," she says. He will not refuse me."

To a Lombard Italian, 'good friend' is a euphemism for 'lover', and he nods his misunderstanding. General Draper must be a tolerant man, he thinks, to allow so beautiful a wife to take lovers, and then boast openly about her many 'good friends'. These English are a strange race, he concludes, and they have no idea about the niceties of 'amour'. Still, she says that the man, Sadler, will oblige her, and that is good enough for him.

*

"No, Lady Miriam, I must refuse you." Rafe Sadler can see the surprise in her eyes, and he hurries on to explain. "To approach the king just now, and suggest favourable treatment of the Lombards would be disastrous to my career. Since the terrible incident in Boulogne, the king realises that there is a feeling of disquiet, even in his own court. He regrets his actions, but cannot accept any blame. Henry reasons that he was driven to the act by others; namely the very Frenchmen he hanged."

"That is madness."

"Yes, but it is a king's madness," Rafe replies. "It is the fault of those damned foreigners, you see? Now, he thinks of any man not English as an enemy."

"Then he blames the world, rather than himself," Miriam says with a sigh. "If you mention the Lombards, he is just as likely to extend the proscription."

"Just so." Rafe is relieved that she understands. "Perhaps in a few months…?"

"It is strange, is it not, that there are no English bankers," Miriam muses.

"Apart from the Draper Company, no one else can raise the capital," Rafe explains. He is on safe ground now, and enjoys passing on his knowledge to an old friend. "To run a bank, one must have money. So much money that you are not affected by the odd bad debt, or failed venture. One lost cargo might leave a bank five thousand out of pocket. So, you must raise a fund of… oh, say a hundred thousand pounds. Then you must know how to lend wisely."

"I see." Miriam knows all of this, but encourages him to continue.

"Many merchants, and even some gentlemen, have the ability, but lack enough capital," Rafe says. "Even a rich merchant would be hard pressed to find fifty thousand pounds, and few would risk their entire fortune on such a dangerous venture."

"Why not form an association of merchants?" Miriam asks. "They can each invest a portion, as do Venetian and Lombard banks, and take a share of the profits?"

"Trust," Rafe replies. "Each thinks the others to be scoundrels. They cannot get along." Miriam sighs at the stupidity of otherwise clever men, and thinks for a moment. The answer, when it comes, is obvious, and will make sure that London has a bank to rival even her own in Lombardy.

"Get together the eleven most likely men," she advises, and invite them to Draper House for dinner. I shall be the twelfth partner, and match whatever they think able to put in. I know these men, and each one can find ten thousand pounds in ready money. We shall buy a suitable building, and have it converted into a counting house, with a strong vault."

"They will baulk at the cost," Rafe replies.

"No, they will not. For I shall fund the purchase and conversion, and thus own the building. It can be rented back to them for a small consideration."

"They will all wish to be in business with you," Rafe says, "but that does nothing to stop them distrusting one another."

"Inform them that I guarantee the good faith of each of the twelve partners," Miriam says with a wry smile. "If any of them should misbehave, I will send my brother along to discuss matters with them."

"Ah, the thinly veiled threat," says Rafe. "You have learnt well from Master Tom. No merchant in his right mind would antagonise Mush, for his reputation for evening up old scores is renowned."

"Good, then it is settled. Once the bank is running, I will give it as much business as it needs to stay afloat. Once the Antwerp and Ghent merchants know I use it, they will follow suit for all their English transactions."

"Does this wonderful edifice have

a name?" Rafe asks. He is already calculating how much legal work such an institution may generate, and what it is worth to him and his law practice.

"Something grand," Miriam tells him. "I want it to sound as if it will last for a thousand years."

"The Mercantile Bank of London?" Rafe suggests.

"Dull."

"The London Bank of Commerce?" Rafe is not over imaginative if it does not concern the law, and he flounders for an idea. Miriam just shakes her head, then claps her hands in glee.

"I have it," she says. "The Merchant Venturers Bank. It sounds exotic, and just a little exciting. Customers will expect us to be more daring in our way of business."

"Oh dear, daring?" Rafe foresees a few problems with 'daring'. "That will not suit the other partners, I fear."

"Do not tell them." Miriam refills their glasses.

"Oh, I fear to say it, but there is a major problem with your idea, madam."

"What is that?" Miriam asks.

"Mush is not able to threaten anyone… at least, not in London. He is half way across the continent, and intent on riding to the Holy Land. He will be in Jerusalem, fighting infidels."

"Both he and Tom Wyatt are aboard one of my ships already," Miriam says, as she displays the breadth of her ring of spies. "They sail from Genoa, and will be here in ten days time. Jerusalem must wait."

"But Mush was so intent on his pilgrimage," says Rafe. "How comes it that they are returning to England?"

"We can thank Tom Wyatt for it," Miriam explains. "It seems he paid out most of his new wealth to a Genoese merchant, who deeded over to him a grand palazzo he owned in Venice. Our poet took his deed, and decided to visit his new home in Venice at once. His idea was to live there, and put down on paper all his poetry. I have the rights to publish, of course, and will do so, one fine day."

"Then he should be in Venice," Rafe replies. "Writing his stanzas beside a pretty canal."

"Indeed. Unfortunately, the Genoese 'merchant' thought they were both going to the Holy Land first, and would not be back for a year or two. In short, the 'palazzo' did not exist, and the entire deal was nothing but a tawdry fraud."

"Even a child might think to check, before paying over many thousands of pounds for a Venetian great house," Rafe says, smugly. "So, Will and Mush went to Venice, to take a look at Tom's new home?"

"They did. Once the fraud was

rebealed, they went to the Doge for help. He had an arrest warrant issued against the rogue, but the fellow was in Genoa, of course, and not subject to Venetian laws."

"Let me guess what came next," Rafe says. "Mush and the poet decide to enforce the warrant anyway, no matter where the fellow lives."

"Just so. Unfortunately, the scoundrel was the black sheep of the Barlotti family. Despite being the bane of his father's life, he could not be abandoned to his fate. When the rogue ran to the family, and begged for their help, they were honour bound to give him their full support."

"An unwise move, I fear," says Rafe. "Things must end bloodily."

"You know my brother too well," Miriam says. "Gino Barlotti arranged to meet Tom Wyatt on the island of San Michele, in the lagoon. My agents knew of this, and warned Wyatt and Mush that it was, in all probability, a trap."

"So they went anyway?"

"Of course. My agent in Venice is a sixty year old apothecary, and his wife is in her fifties, so there was no help there. Tom Wyatt offered Barlotti his life, if he returned the money, in full, and the fool refused. Instead, he whistled up a dozen cousins and brothers to enforce his demand that Wyatt and Mush leave Genoa at once, without a penny recompense."

"Hardly a reasonable negotiation then," Rafe murmurs.

"Mush pointed out that Barlotti was now on Venetian soil, and subject to the Doge's warrant. They refused to surrender, and even offered Mush violence."

"Oh dear."

"Gino Barlotti lost two brothers, and three of his cousins before the rest fled to a waiting boat. The fraudster was taken to the mainland, where the Doge tried him, and ordered the money repaid. The fool declined to reimburse Tom Wyatt, and claimed the gold was already spent on paying off a gambling debt. Tom asked that he was allowed to punish the man himself, and the Doge agreed. To kill a Barlotti meant blood feud ... or vendetta, and he had no wish to incur one upon himself and his own family."

"Wise man. I hope Wyatt did not overstep the bounds," Rafe says. "After all, it was only money. Besides, they both know about vendettas. Mush swore one against the Sardinian brotherhood, and killed them to the last man."

"Mush explained all this to Tom Wyatt, before the poet took Barlotti to Genoa, and hanged him from the yardarm of one of *my* ships. Now the entire Barlotti clan swear vendetta, and he can do nothing but return home. Fortunately, Mush is with him."

"Good news for you," Rafe says. "I think Mush will make a good guard against your new banking partners stepping out of line."

"Yes, fate can be so perverse at times, and so helpful at others," Miriam replies. "Now, listen carefully, and this is what we shall do…"

7   A Rogues Charter

The royal court moves about the

country, at the king's whim. This month, the court is being held within Hampton Court Palace. The grand hall is packed with gentlemen eager to secure the king's good will. To do this, they flatter nobles, offer small bribes to servants, and try to get into the inner court at every opportunity. The lot of sorting out the tumult falls onto the harassed shoulders of Charles Brandon, the Duke of Suffolk.

"Gentlemen, you must really behave yourselves," he shouts, over the hubbub of quarrelsome arrivals. "The king is not responsible for the division and apportionment of the new lands in English France. The Privy Council are in charge of the entire business."

"Then how can we press our claims?" one young rake calls out. He is a second son, and due nothing on his father's death. With a few hundred pounds borrowed or saved, he hopes to become a lord of the manor in France.

"I do not know, fellow…and a 'Your Lordship' will not go amiss." Someone makes a rude noise, and the packed chamber erupts with laughter. It is clear that even a peer of the realm will struggle with this crowd. Then, as if by divine intervention, Will Draper is there, shouldering his way through the throng. He is a pace ahead of Rob Buffery and Jeremiah Cord, both of whom tower over the mob.

"Good Day to you, My Lord," Will says in his best formal voice. "What is amiss?" Suffolk explains in a few moments, and the Examiner General turns to face the crowd. "Gentlemen, you must put your requests in writing. Find a parson if you cannot read and write, and he will compose the letter for you, for a couple of shillings for his rum. I see that your presence here is now not needed. Please clear the chamber, and good luck with your bids for land in France."

"We will be cheated," a voice calls from the back. "The Attorney General will keep the best for himself."

"Bloody scoundrel!"

"Weasel!"

"Piss o' wind perjurer!"

The insults fly out, and Will lets them vent their anger. It amuses him to know how poorly the minor gentry think of Attorney General Rich. Then he holds up a hand for silence.

"You know me, gentlemen, and you know I am a man of honour." There are no dissenting voices now. "I shall speak with the king, and see that everything is done fairly. Now please, go back to your homes, or I shall have to send Captain Cord and Master Buffery amongst you with their staves."

The crowd begins to break up, and

Suffolk pats Will on the back. He appreciates that his friend has averted a very nasty incident, and says so."

"This is all Richard Rich's doing," he says. "The swine seeks to have the list oversubscribed, so that he might inflate the price he asks. What decent man can stomach such a vile rogue?"

"Henry," Will says. "They are ever in one another's company now. It is as if the king wants to make his own guilt diminish by surrounding himself with scoundrels."

"Just so. I called in yesterday, and Hal was playing dice with that murderous ruffian who works for Chapuys."

"No longer. Eustace is recalled, and must serve out his years in Europe," says Will. "Alonso Gomez is now in the employ of my wife."

"Yes... your sweet Miriam... she is well?"

"Yes, she thrives."

"Quite. I was wondering if she knew how it came about that my troops received their bounty. I know that the turd that is Richard Rich was most furious, and that the king was perfectly content with his share. I do not understand the finances at all... damn it, I am a duke... but I know the smell of a Miriam Draper deal. Do I owe her my thanks?"

"She simply arranged for the sale of the loot, and the distribution of the bounty. Your men were content, I trust?"

"Indeed. They will return to their farms, content in the knowledge that next year's rent and taxes are already in their possession," Suffolk says. "I myself am content with my share, which is enough to reduce my gambling debts, and pay off the interest on my various loans for a few months."

"Then we are all happy," Will says. "Might I go into the inner court, and wait for Henry to finish with the lizard?" At that moment the doors are opened inwards, and Sir Richard Rich appears, with two clerks in tow. He cannot walk past either Will or Suffolk, without acknowledging them. Each man is of a nobler rank, and Rich must abide by the rules of the court.

"My Lord Suffolk... Lord Templar," he mutters, and bows.

"Ah, Rich," Will Draper says, "the king is free then?"

"He is, My Lord, but his temper is not at its best," Rich replies. "He tried to stand with his staff this morning, and the old wound opened up again."

"I must rely on His Majesty's innate love of his friends," says Will.

"Besides," the Duke of Suffolk says, tartly, "if he can stomach the likes of you, he can certainly tolerate us for a short while!"

Rich must bow again, and suffer

knowing that even the guards are sniggering at him behind their hands. One day, he thinks, I will get even with every one of them who ever thought evil of him.

*

"You must rest, my love." Queen Katheryn stands behind the court physician as he kneels by the king's chair. She can see where the ulcer is oozing out its poison, and she wonders at how her husband can stand such pain. "Doctor Dreyfus will ease the hurt."

Dreyfus, who is half French and half Spanish, would as soon cut off the offending leg, but to suggest such a thing will bring instant ruin down on him. Instead, he lies with practiced smoothness.

"The wound looks worse than it is, Madam," he reports. "It must be bathed with warm milk, mixed with the white of an egg. This will seal the wound, and allow it time to heal. Then, bed rest… and no more walking, even with a staff."

"Bloody quack," Henry growls. "I know the damned thing is not healing, but the pain is almost too great, even for me. Make the pain go, or get out of my sight!"

"My dearest Hal!" Suffolk bustles into the inner chamber with his hearty face on. "See I have the Lord Templar with me."

"Who?" Henry asks.

"Will Draper, sire," Will says. "I came as soon as I heard of your misfortune.

Is the pain great?"

"Does a whore raise her... oh, begging your pardon, my dear." Henry blushes, but Katheryn just smiles at him. She has heard worse during her previous marriages and does not offend easily. "Yes, it damned well does."

"Then I bring good news, Hal," Will tells the king. "It seems that the supply of poppy juice from Cathay has resumed, and I have purchased the first phial to arrive in England."

"What?" Henry struggles up into a more erect posture. "You have it with you?" Will holds up the flask, perhaps no bigger than a glass of wine, but the contents are enough to ease the king's pain for two months... or kill ten grown men.

"Let me prepare you a draft at once, Your Majesty." Doctor Dreyfus stands, and holds out his hand for the precious fluid, but the king raises the silver topped walking stick he keeps by his side and fetches the unsuspecting fellow a sharp crack across the side of his shoulder. The doctor yelps, and skips out of range of a second swipe aimed at his head.

"You damned charlatan," Henry cries, as he shakes in anger and pain. "Away and minister to some ailing herd of cattle, you... you... swine. Better still, get out of my realm, and back to stinking France."

"Sire, I am English," says Dreyfus.

"No longer, you rogue. Where is dear Alonso?" To Will's surprise, Alonso Gomez appears from the folds of a wall hanging, and comes to the king's side. Even more shocking is that the man has a brace of ornately handled throwing knives stuck in his broad belt. In the presence of the king, this is supposed to mean death.

'What is it, My Lord?" the Spaniard asks.

"Take this offal out and put him on the next boat to France. If he refuses… you may cut his throat."

Doctor Dreyfus, who is a weak, constantly frightened, little man feints in terror, and slides down to the ground. Gomez hoists him up, slings him over his shoulder, and leaves the chamber. Will Draper tries to hide his astonishment at this little pantomime, but Henry sees the look on his face, and seeks to justify himself.

"Good man, Alonso," he says. "He tells me he is the son of a Malabar pirate king, who fell on hard times. He was, until recently, in the pay of that froggy fellow, Chapuys. Damn me if he hasn't run off somewhere. Chapuys, not Alonso. Now he plays dice with me… and damned me if he isn't a hundred to the good just now!"

"He is a very fine fellow, Hal," Will agrees. "Now, drink this down, and it will ease the pain." The potion is taken, and in moments the king is dozing fitfully.

Queen Kathryn touches Will by the sleeve, and draws him off to one side. Two of her ladies in waiting are in a far corner of the chamber, to attest that the Queen is never compromised by being left alone with a young man. Heanage, the king's Master of the Privy is also lurking about, but he does not count, as he is older, and quite unmanly in his ways.

"Lord Templar," she mutters to Will, "can I speak to you frankly?" Will sighs inwardly. In truth, she should not, for what she says might compromise him, and his duty to the king.

"If you wish, Your Majesty," he replies.

"This wound… can it ever be healed?"

"I am no physician, madam," says Will, "but the general opinion is not. It runs deep, and never has enough time for the flesh to bind. Besides, you must have noticed the excretions?"

"Yes, it is foul smelling." Kathryn shakes her head in pity, and drops her voice to little more than a whisper. "I pray morning and night for the king's recovery, but I fear the time when he is no longer there to guide and protect us."

"As do I, madam." Will can say no other, but he is uncomfortable with how this conversation is progressing. "We must trust in…"

"God, My Lord Templar?" Kathryn chuckles, and her ladies look over, disapprovingly. "I believe poor King François does that, and look how that is turning out for him. No, I would rather trust in men of integrity, sir, and you I number amongst that rare breed."

"I shall always be happy to advise Your Majesty," Will says. "Though only if it is on a matter I have knowledge of."

"You will understand the meaning of *primogeniture*, I trust?" Kathryn asks, and Will almost winces. This, if it becomes common knowledge, is as near to high treason as can be. If it were any other woman, even his beloved Miriam, he would tell her to hold her tongue, or expect a sound thrashing. Instead, he must answer in a civil manner.

"I do."

"And you agree with it?"

"I do, madam," Will replies, on safer ground now, providing she speaks in a general manner, and does not specifically refer to the royal succession.

"Then you will support Prince Edward?" the queen asks, and Will's blood runs cold. To answer 'no' is treason, and to answer 'yes' is to enter into a conspiracy against the living king. Everyone knows that by the laws of *primogeniture* the eldest living son inherits everything; titles, lands, endowments, and debts. Thus, Edward must follow Henry, but it is treason to speak of it, for it imagines the king's death.

"I believe that the French adhere to the custom of *primogeniture,* madam," Will tells her, and he sees a way out of his predicament. "François will rule until he dies, and then his oldest boy will rule. I believe that is the answer you seek, madam?"

"Then you would…"

"Your Majesty!" Will looks her in the eyes, and she holds her tongue. "Were I to have the great misfortune of being a french nobleman, and François died, I would support his heir with all my heart. To do other would be dishonourable. However, this is not a suitable topic for conversation, for even royal walls may have ears."

"Of course. Let us change the subject, my dear sir," the queen agrees. "I hear that Uncle Norfolk is in a black mood again. Do you know why?"

Thank God, Will thinks, she wishes to gossip, and that is not treasonable, as long as it is not about Henry in a disrespectful way.

"I do, madam," he replies. "It seems that when Lord Suffolk and I went off to capture Boulogne, he decided to march his own forces off on a rampage into Picardy. He set off with ten thousand foot, and two thousand heavy cavalry, and began to ravage the lands around Amiens."

"Very war-like," Kathryn muses. "I take it things did not prove to be to his liking?"

"It is always prudent to ensure a good line of supply," Will explains. "Norfolk left it to his son, Surrey, who passed the task on to some drinking friend of his. In short, the food ran out after three days, and the French withdrew, burning everything behind them. The duke found himself trying to plunder an empty countryside. Even the rats were gone, it seems."

"The foolish old man."

"Just so. On the fourth day, he decided to withdraw his army to Calais... as were his original orders... and found himself harried from the rear by several thousand French cavalry. He was forced to march day and night, for fear of halting and the main French army putting in an appearance."

"His poor men." Kathryn dislikes waste, and losing soldiers without good reason is a crime in her eyes. "How they must have suffered."

"Oh, no, they reached the *Calaisis* intact, save for the usual few hundred deserters," Will tells the queen. "Norfolk is in a dark mood because his idiot son had made a rousing speech at the outset, promising his troops a generous bounty. There was no plunder, but Norfolk's captains pointed out that a promise is a promise, and the men expected some silver for their purses."

"Ho! That accounts for his mood," Kathryn says. "How did he get out of that?"

"He didn't. He refused, and the troops refused to come on parade. Then he promised to pay them something, once back in England. His men then threw down their pikes, and swore to stay in France, and find a new lord. He was forced to pay them ten shillings each... three months wages... just to get the men aboard the waiting cogs. It cost him almost seven thousand pounds, which he borrowed from a Lombard banking house. The Galti brothers must have the promissory notes of half the great men in England by now." Will sees that she is diverted by the anecdote, and wonders if he should tell her the rumours about Sir Richard Rich's latest quarrel with his blunt talking brother in law, but thinks it too rude for a queen's ear. Then she shatters his growing calm.

"I know that Norfolk and his son are both scoundrels, but they still hold great power in England. Do you think *they* will support Prince Edward?"

"Madam, I must take my leave. I hoped to speak with the king, but he is too tired, and should be left to sleep."

"Is it about this distribution of the new French land?" Queen Kathryn knows all about it, because Tom Seymour speaks of nothing else of late when he visits to see his little nephew, Prince Edward. "Might I not be able to help you with it?"

"There are a thousand applied, and only four hundred estates created," Will tells her. "I hoped only to influence the king in his choices of men to fill the places."

"I see, you seek to place men of honour, men who are friends," Kathryn says, but is surprised at Will's response.

"Good God, no!" he says. "My advice would be to offer the new estates to the worst men in the kingdom… the rogues who cheat, those younger brothers who dun their fathers and seek easy recompense for their misfortune, men of low morals, or those who are just out and out scoundrels."

"You jest, surely?" Kathryn thinks this is too strange for words, but the Seymours are hoping for a generous grant of French land to increase their worth.

"No, madam, I do not," Will tells her in a serious, insistent voice. "Four hundred estates carved out of the soft underbelly of France will take some handling. Let the rogues go to it, and see what they can do. The French cannot attack them, without risking the English armies at Calais and Boulogne falling on them, but if we withdraw from either place, and bring home even more soldiers, François will grow bolder, and seek to invade the new territory. If he does, and we are all back in England, the new landowners will have to face the French. In short, let the greedy take the land, and pay the king for it, then watch as the French come back."

"You cannot think Henry will abandon his new lands," the queen says.

"Why not? If he decides that supporting Boulogne is too costly, he might sell the town back to France. François would pay a hundred thousand to be rid of the garrison in Boulogne. With the town back in French hands, the new estate owners will be cut off from England. The French will eat these new lords up, one at a time, and the land will become France once more."

"That is a cynical viewpoint, My Lord," Kathryn says. "What if we keep Boulogne?"

"We will not," Will says, and the queen senses the honesty of what he says. Henry will sell out his people for a hundred thousand pounds, and leave them to be driven off, or even killed. She shivers at the thought.

"I think you might be right," she says. "Perhaps you might consider drawing up a list of all those who we can do without in England?"

Will Draper takes a scroll from inside his cloak, and hands it to the queen.

"Four hundred names, madam," he

says. "I trust this rogue's charter will reach your husband?"

"It will, sir," Kathryn says. "I shall place it before him as soon as he wakes up." She exchanges a few banal sentences with him for the benefit of her nosey ladies in waiting, as she walks him to the chamber's door, and resolves to write to Tom Seymour at once. This new investment is unsound, she will tell him, and hope he does not ignore her advice. One day, when she is widowed once more, he says he will marry her, and she does not want a penniless lover, no matter how good he is, in her bed.

*

The expansive *Palais de Louvre* is, François thinks, far too large, even for a royal palace. One day, it should be converted to some other use. Now, he sits on the royal throne, and waits for the presentation of a messenger from his floundering army. To right, and left, worried courtiers wonder what is happening beyond the walls of Paris. Many have estates in the newly occupied land, and wonder if they will ever see them again.

"No matter what," François muses aloud, "our walls are impregnable. Fat Henry will grow thin waiting for us to surrender. What say you, Cordelier?"

"Your Majesty sums up the situation admirably, as usual," the courtier replies. "All the food for a hundred leagues is in our storehouses, and the English must eat grass…like the sheep they are so fond of." This last makes the king grin and nod his head. He is a short, rather ugly man, with an overly large nose, and blackened teeth in his mouth. Only the eyes seem normal, unless you dare look too closely. Look into them, and you will find pure cunning looking back.

"Yes… eat grass. It is all they are fit for," the king sneers, and ignores the fact that he is cowering in his Parisian fortress after losing yet another battle to the 'unfit' English army. "They took Boulogne by trickery and deceit. Paris is not so foolish. How goes my command regarding the common herd?"

"Your soldiers are already sweeping through the city streets," Cordelier replies. "The old, the beggars, and the useless are being expelled, and told to travel east. They are told they might return after Paris is safe, but that is something Your Majesty can decide upon at some later date."

"Why do the Scots not invade England whilst their army is in my country?" François asks. He thinks that the 'Auld Alliance' with England's northern neighbours should compel the Scots into some sort of action.

"If you recall, sire, we were committed to an attack on Venice last year, and could not support their war against Henry. They lost, and seem disinclined to enter the field again."

"Cowards," the French king snaps. "I will not yield another acre of our sacred French soil to those perfidious dogs." It is then that the great doors at the end of the gallery open, and an elegant young man swishes in, strides up to the throne, and bows low.

"Your Majesty," the young man says, "may I name myself as the Chevalier Didier de Poitiers, a captain to the esteemed…"

"What is it?" François shouts, and the man steps back as if slapped.

"Victory, sire," he says. "The English army is in full retreat. That was two days ago, and they are now either locked up in Calais, or back in England, licking their wounds."

"You see?" the king says, standing up and striking a royal pose. "I have triumphed over Henry once more!"

"Congratulations, sire," says Cordelier. Like his English counterpart, François considers ever success to be his, just as every failure must be laid at other doors. "Shall I order the news to be declared throughout the city?"

"Let us wait until the useless and infirm have left first," François says with callous economy. "It will ease the cost of keeping them, and having them cluttering up the streets with their pathetic begging."

"A wonderful idea, sire. Are we to compose a rude letter to King Henry, deriding his pathetic attempt at trying to best you?"

"Yes, see to it. Make sure I am very witty, and he is ridiculed to the point of utter humiliation." Then it occurs to King François that the messenger has rather cleverly avoided any mention of a crushing military victory. He crooks a finger and beckons the man nearer to the throne. "Chevalier, how many Englishmen did my army kill?"

"They could not face us, sire."

"Where was this battle?" François demands, and the chevalier goes down on one knee, with his head bowed.

"Sire. They would not stand and fight. We did try, honestly, but the perfidious *Norfook* ran away from our forces."

"Then they retreated?"

"Well… yes."

"In good order?"

"We took some prisoners, Your Majesty," the young chevalier replies. "A hundred of them."

"Deserters?" François guesses, shrewdly. "You found them wandering about the countryside?" The chevalier holds his tongue. He is only here because his captain dislikes him, and someone has to give the news to the king. "Bah! No wonder we never win any wars. Get out of my sight... all of you!"

The throne room clears rapidly, as François' courtiers sense one of his rages coming on. Unlike the English king, the French monarch has no constraints. He is the law, the jury, and the judge in all things, and his will is everything.

Cordelier, braver than the rest, hangs back to ask what is to be done with the English deserters. He owns a share in some mines in the Dolomites, and free labour would be most welcome.

"Shall I have the English prisoners sent to work in our quarries and mines, Your Majesty?" he asks, ingenuously. If François guesses what is going on, he will expect a hefty cut of the profits.

"Yes... no... that is, I have a notion to play a jest on my cousin Henry of England. Do you recall how my ancestor, the Dauphin, did bait the fifth Henry with a chest full of tennis balls?"

"I do, sire." Cordelier groans inwardly. The tennis balls were meant to insult the young English king by saying he was fit only for playing childish games. The jest was a fine one, of course, until Henry V crossed the Channel with his army and laid waste to half of France, before finally crushing the Dauphin's knights at

Agincourt. "All France laughed at its droll and insulting way."

"Then I shall bait this Henry too," François says, and his mind is set upon it. Cordelier bows to his king's wishes, and asks for the details of his clever jest. As the king explains, the hairs on Cordelier's neck stand up in horror. Then he smiles, for even in this, he can see a profit for himself.

*

Alonso Gomez is adept at many things, from the ability to cheat at dice and cards, to picking locks, spying, and murder. Now, by chance, he is learning a new skill… how to be a courtier. The king's mistrust of even his oldest friends leaves him with few people he can pass the time of day with, and he finds the Spaniard's irreverent ways refreshing.

Rafe Sadler is still amongst the favoured few, and he stands by the dice table now and watches as Alonso Gomez rolls another winning hand. The king winces and shakes his head in despair.

"Impossible… you rogue… how do you do it?" he asks.

"I cheat, Your Majesty," Gomez replies with a saucy grin. "Did you not know?"

"Ha!" Henry slaps a hand down onto his good thigh. "You jest well, my dear Corsair, but in truth, what lucky charm do you own that gives you such constant good fortune?"

"Your Majesty means my lucky fairy?" Gomez says without a smile. "She is my most treasured possession."

"A fairy you say?" Henry grins and wags a finger at the Spaniard, as if to say 'grass may be green, but not I'. "Then pray let us see this marvellous creature."

In answer, Gomez slips a hand into the front of his doublet, and produces a tiny wooden box. It is no more than an ebony veneered thing that might be used to keep a valued ring in. He places it on the table, and lets the king see its lid is held in place with two tiny brass hinges, and a hasp and staple made of some silver metal.

"Sylvia lives within," he says.

"Who is Sylvia?" Henry asks.

"My fairy. I simply touch the box, and she makes sure I never lose." Gomez does not leave it there. He places a finger on the lid of the box, and picks up two of the dice from the table. "If you would give me a number, sire?"

"A number? Oh, yes. Splendid… a magical demonstration, Sadler. What about that?"

"Perhaps Sylvia might join us for dinner later, sire?" Rafe replies, and glances over at Tom Wyatt and Mush, who are almost doubled over with constrained laughter. This will end badly, he thinks.

"Don't be silly, man," Henry

scolds. "Fairies do not eat as we human kind do. Do they, Gomez?"

"They live under toadstools, drink thunder storms, and fart rainbows, sire," Gomez replies. "A number, if you will?"

"Twenty," Henry says, and Gomez blinks in incredulity.

"Sire… I have but two dice to throw. Might it not be better if you chose a total nearer the twelve?"

"Oh, of course. I was not thinking straight for a moment. This poppy potion does make me a little… where was I?"

"A number, sire," Gomez reminds him.

"Nine." Henry watches in rapt awe as the Spaniard taps the box, as if to awaken the fairy within. Then Gomez blows on the dice, rolls, and throws a nine. "Damn me, but that is amazing. Again, but this time, throw me a seven."

"Seven… listen well, Sylvia," Gomez mutters, and throws a seven. Henry is beside himself with astonishment, and he reels off number after number. Each time, Gomez obliges with the right result.

"You see this, Sadler?" Henry says, his face flushed from the excitement of the event. "What say you now to magickery and the otherworld of creatures unseen?"

"They are unseen because they do not exist, Your Majesty," Rafe replies, without thinking.

"Doubting Thomas," Henry snaps at his advisor. "He denied Our Lord until he saw with his own eyes. Now we can see this with ours. Gomez asks and…" As he speaks, the Spaniard flips open the box and tips it up for them to see that it is quite empty.

"It seems Sylvia the Fairy is not in, sire." Rafc hcars the scorn in his own voice and winces at how it must sound to the king. Henry, however, is far too astounded to take any offence at him. Instead he grips Gomez by the wrist and pulls him close, so that their noses are almost touching. It is only the smell of raw garlic on the Spaniard's breath that makes the king relax his grip.

"You lied?" he asks.

"Yes, Your Majesty," Gomez says with a malicious little smile playing about his lips. "I lied to you, and you believed me. But only because you would not believe the truth I offered to you."

"But you threw every number I named, without one mistake," Henry says.

"Because I cheated," Alonso Gomez tells the king. "I told you I did. See?" At this, he picks up the dice and rolls double six over and over.

"No one ever lies to me," Henry says, with a dangerous quaver in his voice.

"Not so, sire." Rafe Sadler risks interrupting this volatile conversation with the truth. "The French ambassador lies to you every time he pays court, as do Scots lords, self seeking courtiers, and even certain high ranking nobility."

"You mean Norfolk?" Henry considers this for a moment, and sees that there is a professional lie, and a private one. An ambassador lies for his master's ends, and it is done in a business-like way, but men like Norfolk lie to ruin others, or gain power. "The old man is still trying to advise me. I should do something about him… and soon. Do you lie to me, Rafe… or does dear Charles?"

"The Duke of Suffolk is a loyal friend, sire," Rafe replies, "as is your own poet. Wyatt is as honest as can be, because his art demands it of him, and Suffolk is flattered by your friendship, and speaks as he thinks, or so I suspect. As for me… yes, I lie to you sometimes. I tell you the doctor insists on bed rest, because I know you are overworking, or agree with you about a fine cut of meat… even if I only find it fair. As for my advice… I give it straight to you as I see it, and let you think as you will."

"Well said, dear friend," says Henry. Then he catches himself up, and turns on Gomez. "If not by magic or sorcery, then how do you do this?"

Alonso Gomez scoops up all six dice and places them on the palm of his left hand. He raises the hand to eye level and invites the king to examine the ivory cubes.

"These are my own dice," the Spaniard explains. "They were made for me by a very clever fellow in Toledo… a man who was half Moor, half Venetian, and half Spanish."

"Three halves?" Henry asks.

"*Si, Jefe*," Gomez replies, without a blink of the eye. "He was a very large man, and could easily contain these three halves. They say that he could walk through a crowd, and come out a rich man, so clever are his hands at lifting purses.

"He is known in Madrid and Paris as the King of Vagabonds, or the Prince of Thieves. It was quite by chance that I came upon the fellow. I had upset a certain churchman, and his minions were after my blood. I hid here and there for brief times, but always was only just ahead of my pursuers. The city gates were watched, and I was trapped."

"My goodness. It is as if I am there with you, my dear Alonso," Henry gasps. "What then?"

"I went into the sewers… great tunnels built by the old Romans… and tried to find my way out of the city. It was there I came upon the secret lair of the King of Vagabonds. At first, his men were for cutting my throat, but my ready wit impressed the Vagabond King, and he befriended me. After a while, he led me out to the outside world, and saw I had enough money to see me safe out of Spain."

"Stout fellow," Henry says. "He acted as a real king should... as I would act."

"Just so, sire," Gomez continues. He is as ready to hear how the story ends as is the king, for he is making it up as he speaks. "He pressed these dice into my hands... for I had seen him use them, and knew their secret... and bade me good luck. Since then, whenever I was hungry, or in need of money, I would take out my dice."

"Tell me the secret of the dice," Henry begs, and Gomez moves his hand closer to Henry's eyes.

"Look closely, sire. Each cube has a tiny shaving off one corner, and this makes them fall in certain ways. If you know how to read these small things, you can hold them in such a way and roll them either from high, or low, to land as you wish. It takes practice, but a good dicer will soon learn."

"You mean I could do it?" Henry is fascinated now, and forgets all about who is lying to whom, or who has cheated him for these last weeks.

"Why not?" Gomez can see no reason why the king cannot be taught his secrets, but there is always a price to be met. "Though it can only work with these dice. I suppose I could lend them to you, sire, or…"

"I must have them," Henry insists. "Name a price, and it is done… within reason."

"I usually pick up about fifteen shillings a week dicing with your soldiers, and as much again from your courtiers," Gomez says. "Say seventy pounds a year?"

"Three hundred, and that includes your showing me how to hold the things," Henry says. "See to it, Rafe. Now, everyone out. *Señor* Gomez and I have a lesson to be learned. Come and sit with me, my wily corsair. Why do you call me 'Heffy'?"

"*Jefe*… it is a great lord," Gomez replies, as he draws up a padded stool and gathers up the dice. "I think we must start with one pair, and add more as we progress, and your skills grow, sire."

"I prefer '*Jefe*', you scoundrel," the king laughs. "Now, show me how to cheat with these magic dice!"

Rafe Sadler moves to the outer court, with Tom Wyatt, who is still grinning at what has just occurred. Alonso Gomez, who still considers both Tom Cromwell and Eustace Chapuys to be his masters has alerted the king to the fact that Norfolk, and more recently Surrey, are lying to him. In the king's present state of mind, that will bode nothing but evil for Norfolk and his son.

"Neatly done, Rafe," the poet says.

"I do not know what you mean," Rafe Sadler responds. "Dicing is not my game."

"No, but I see now how things are going," Wyatt replies. "Henry grows ever more wary of those around him. He has even stopped asking advice from Richard Cromwell and Charles Brandon. This leaves Henry in a dilemma, for he cannot reason, or come up with any ideas of his own, and he must feed off what others say."

"Fanciful rubbish," says Rafe. "You would do well to keep such thoughts to yourself, and this is a wild fancy."

"Of course it is. You would never dream of placing some scoundrel close to Henry, a scoundrel who might voice ideas that are those of another man." Robin Askey grins, and makes his way out into the rose garden. Rafe Sadler follows him out into the fresh air, and catches at his sleeve.

"The king met Alonso Gomez at some dinner or other, and found him to be amusing. I can hardly be blamed if the king then listens to whatever the damned fellow says. Can I help it if he arouses the king's suspicions against some, and praises others?"

"Then it is Norfolk's time?" The poet recalls all the past skirmishes between the Howard family and Austin Friars, and how the old duke has come close to ruining them all on several occasions. Now, in the twilight of his life, he still wishes to interfere with how the kingdom is run. "Removing him will not really help, if the son assumes his father's dukedom."

"Yes, we know." Rafe Sadler needs to say no more. If Norfolk is to fall, then so must the son. "It will take delicate planning. Norfolk is still the first noble in the land, and his ten thousand armed yeomen are a strong card he has in his hand."

"Then you must separate them from their master," the poet advises, and Rafe Sadler just smiles at him. Austin Friars may no longer be a great house, but the spirit lives on, and there are many who serve the cause, and who think of themselves as Austin Friars men, who have never sat around the old house's famous breakfast table.

"Our people are working it," he tells Tom Wyatt. "If your help is required, I will call on you."

"You know I am eager to help," the poet says. "You speak of subtlety and guile… both of which I lack, but should you need a man who can extemporise a poetic slander, or who can use a sword, then here I am."

"We never doubted it, old friend," Rafe says. "Though I am sorry that poor Gomez must lose his loaded dice to Henry for a few hundred pounds."

"Oh, do not sorrow overmuch,"

Tom Wyatt replies, hardly able to contain his laughter. "To my certain knowledge, Alonso has sold sets of those dice to at least four lords. I believe that Warwick, Cumberland, Chester and Cornwall each paid over a hundred a piece. He even charged me twenty pounds. Our Spanish cutthroat is becoming a very rich man."

"He is. I act for him, and he has a sort of animal cunning when it comes to investment. He had me buy a tenth share in one of Lady Miriam's ships on a voyage to Tangiers. You recall what happened to the *Far Rover,* do you not?"

"Yes, she ran into a Barbary pirate ship on its way back from raiding the Spanish coast," the poet replies. "Did not Miriam's ship outgun them, and send the pirates to the bottom of the sea?"

"Yes, but before she sank, our boys boarded her, and the pirate cargo was taken aboard the Far Rover. The plunder from their raid amounted to a little over seventeen thousand pounds. Along with the profit from the usual cargo, Alonso's tenth share came to three thousand pounds, for a hundred pound investment."

"Lucky man." Tom Wyatt cannot make money, and when he does, it seems to vanish without any real effort.

"The man is worth thousands, and I do not understand why he does not simply go off and enjoy his wealth. Still, he is devoted to our cause, and I cannot deny he is a far better man to have as a friend, than as an enemy," Askey says.

"I shall immortalise him in verse," Wyatt jests. "Perhaps I might call it 'The King's Spaniard?"

"Really, Tom," Rafe Sadler speaks, as friends often do, without thinking. "Your poetry, for all its prettiness, will go to the grave with you. For I have never met a lazier fellow at putting it down on paper. Why, I doubt you have even made a will."

"Can I leave my debts to someone then?" the poet replies, with a broad grin on his face, but the words have struck home. Tom Wyatt will die, and posterity will know nothing of his talent. In that moment, he resolves to set himself the task of putting his words down, so that future men might be able to judge his worth.

"Bequeath them to Norfolk," Rafe says. "For it will be just one more weight we mean to hang about his neck. Now, will you stroll with me down to Draper House for lunch... and you too, Robin?"

"I am not expected," the poet says, but in truth it is because he is unshaven, and still in the same clothes he put on two weeks before. Since coming back from Genoa, he has run through his share of the loot in an orgy of self indulgence, and is back to his usual state; tired, dishevelled, and penniless.

"An invitation is not required," Rafe says to the poet. "The kitchen is warm, and the food plentiful for any who are Austin Friars men. Lady Miriam is a generous hostess, and will not turn you away because you look like a vagabond!"

"And I, Master Rafe?" Robin asks of the older man. "Why is so lowly a fellow as a king's squire invited to dine with such exalted company?"

"You keep more noble company than we poor folk," Rafe replies. "I hear you lend money to Harry Howard?"

"The Earl of Surrey often borrows small sums from his friends," Robin says, "and Master Cromwell bade me become such when he first hired me... for a shilling... which he pressed into my hand and said would keep me 'honest'. I pass on whatever he says, unless it is outrageous."

"How so?" Rafe asks.

"Like a wild claim he made the other night, whilst drunk." Robin shakes his head. "You know I am loyal, but the plot he spoke of was too shocking for words. I should have said..."

"You cannot know the worth of everything," Rafe tells him. "Come, and dine, whilst you unburden yourself with this latest tale of Howard family deceit. You too Tom... for Miriam will not allow you to slink away because of a rough chin, or a creased doublet."

"Very well," the poet replies, and launches into a merry verse.

> "*The heart is greater for being fed,*
> *With such love as are romantic sighs,*
> *But better by far to my empty head,*
> *Is when I'm stuff'd with hot meat pies.*"

"Shall we ever hear a decent rhyme from your lips, Master poet?" Mush moans, and they all laugh. "You spout such tedious offal thcsc days, Tom."

"Tedious?" The poet staggers, as if struck with an arrow, then he bows to his friends. "Am I to be ever so badly misunderstood?"

"Then write it all down," Rafe says.

"On my death bed," Wyatt promises. "For I owe five hundred pounds for a book of poetry I never delivered. Let my last words be my epithet… and truly, I die for my art!"

8   The Great Insult

Of all his estates, Tom Howard, the

elderly Duke of Norfolk, enjoys Arundel the most. It is a comfortable, modern sort of a house, with a fine stables, and enough deer to hunt every day of the year. It is also near London, and boasts the most obliging female staff outside a good city bawdy house. These days, Norfolk contents himself with these home comforts, and often lays abed til noon, with a warm woman, and a cold bottle of wine.

Today, however, he is up and dressed, for he is expecting a visit from his son. This would not normally elicit so joyful a response, as Norfolk loathes young Surrey, but today is different. Surrey is coming to tell him how they have faired in the execution of their latest plot.

"Where is that damned moron?" he demands of his steward, who can only shrug for an answer. Then he recalls the heavy rain that fell during the night.

"Perhaps the roads are too muddy, sir?" the man offers, and he receives a sharp slap to the side of the head for his trouble.

"Yes, the roads are muddy, you bloody fool. Anyone can see that, but it is no reason to stay my son's progress. Have a couple of grooms saddle horses, and go to find him. If the little bastard is swiving away in some low bawd's hovel, I will hang him up by his balls." Just then a group of horsemen come into sight, and ride straight for the house. The duke grins and claps his hands. It is the idiot son, and six of his equally brainless friends.

"You are late, you little swine." Norfolk glowers at the other riders, who are mostly the second sons of debt ridden nobles, who will inherit nothing. "I suppose your little playmates are here to freely sup my wine, and eat my food for the nonce?"

"They are my closest friends and advisors, sir," the Earl of Surrey says, as he dismounts. "They are the very men who have helped us triumph as we have this day."

"Triumph?" The Duke of Norfolk can hardly contain his joy. "Then some are chosen?"

"No, sir," Surrey replies, with a smug smile. "All are chosen. I could not believe our good fortune. Though I had these stout fellows apply for a land grant, I dared not think that more than one or two would succeed, but each one is picked, and we are all made men, father. Those fools never guessed that these six men were our creatures, and that the land grants are now ours, and a valuable part of the Norfolk estates."

"You have the deeds?" Norfolk asks. His son is a scatter brained dolt at times, and must be checked at every step.

"Yes, six deeds, all with the royal seal on them. All we need do now is buy these deeds from these men. Let each have the promised hundred pounds, and they will be on their way, leaving us with a French estate that is as large as Wales, but ten times richer in every way."

"Then let these good fellows dismount, and come into the hall. I shall have wine and some cold cuts brought, whilst we deal with the business." The duke frowns at having to part with six hundred pounds he can ill afford, but consoles himself with the vast wealth to come.

Later, when only he and his son remain, the old duke considers how to administer his new found realm, and he can do little more than grin at his sudden good fortune.

"With our lands here, and these new holdings, I will rule a land that is equal in size to Henry's precious England. My soldiers will number twenty, or even thirty thousand, and my new French domain is rich with strong castles for them to hold for us. The king will have to treat us as equals... not vassals."

"Henry will really hate us for this day's work," Surrey says. "I wonder what he might do?"

"Do?" Norfolk laughs at this. "Why, nothing, for he would have to raise an army to dislodge us, and that is fraught with danger. He might lose, and that would be the end of things for him. No, he will swallow it, and return to calling me Uncle

Norfolk again. He will place me at his side, and hope that we accept this secondary roll."

"And will we?"

"Of course, you pillocking great fool," Norfolk snaps. "It is all I ever wanted. Me by the king's side, advising him... and that bastard Draper ruined. If I am to be Henry's man, then Draper cannot stay at court. I shall have Henry send him somewhere unpleasant. Did he not once fight in Ireland?"

"He was a common soldier, or so the rumours go." Surrey knows everything about Will Draper, because he hates him so. "And a priest killer."

"Then we shall make him General of the King's army in Ireland, and insist he conquers the rest of the place outside of the Dublin Pale. That will keep him quiet for a few years, no doubt."

"Henry is sick," Surrey says. "Jack Hartley, one of the king's squires, says the doctors are scared to treat him for fear of him dying on them."

"He will creak on for now," Norfolk says. "In the meantime, we should become better friends to the Seymour brothers. When Edward ascends the throne, we must be in his good books."

"He is a boy," Surrey scoffs. "He will do as he is told. I suppose that means us having to put up with Ned Seymour in council."

"Unless he is disgraced," Norfolk says with a sly smile. "I wager his accounts at the admiralty are not in order."

"Really father?" Surrey thinks it best not to ask how the duke is so sure. "If he falls from favour, I suppose you would become the new king's foremost advisor."

"With Suffolk," says Norfolk, "but he is no match for me."

"Then, when you die, I will…"

"Still be an idiot." Norfolk despairs of his son and heir ever being anything more than a fool, and he dearly wishes he had other sons to choose from. "You must surround yourself with clever, immoral men, and keep your opinions to yourself, my boy. That is the only way you will survive these turbulent times… for your wits are insufficient for the task fate will allot you."

"Oh, I think I shall do nicely, father," Surrey replies with a smug little smile. After all, had not Miriam Draper's strange friend predicted how he would 'be raised up, above his father'? "Besides, if I am the Duke of Norfolk, you will have gone onto your celestial seat. I dare say God has a place for you in His Privy Council!"

"You wish me dead, you spavined little turd?" Norfolk snaps, and his son grins and shakes his head.

"Not I father… not for now. It will

take two of us to run these new lands, once the wealth starts to roll in, and I shall trust no one, save you."

"Wisdom in a fool," Norfolk says, and goes to find the six hundred in gold he needs to complete the task.

*

Kel Kelton's cross Channel messenger service has eased somewhat since the recent foray into France. Thomas Cromwell seems to find everything less urgent now, and asks for nothing more than a weekly update on the English court's affairs. So it is odd that Kel arrives at the *Palace de Juis* two days ahead of his usual visit.

"What is this, Kel?" Cromwell asks, as the young man comes into his study. "Has some great disaster befallen England?" He smiles at his own flippancy, and pours them both a liberal helping of wine. Kelton gulps down his, and wipes a hand across his mouth.

"The king is taken to his bed, sir, and there are rumours that he is close to death." Kel sees that his master is visibly shaken by this news, so presses on. "Only his doctors, the queen, and the Archbishop of Canterbury are allowed into his chamber."

"It is too soon," Cromwell says. "Norfolk is still to be removed, and the Seymours are still to be brought into our circle. We must step up our efforts, before Henry dies and leaves us in limbo."

"Can you not enlist your son, Gregory, into our band?" Kel asks. "After all, he is married to Jane Seymour's sister, and thus an in-law to both the Seymours, and the king."

"Gregory does not know I am still alive," Tom Cromwell replies. "Besides, he is a gentleman these days, and I would prefer to leave him be. Let him lead a normal life, rather than wallow in the depravity of court politics. No, I must find another way to make the Seymour brothers into allies."

"As you wish, master." Kel moves on to the next item of news, which he hopes will make his master smile. "Rafe Sadler has been busy selling off the parcels of land in France to any low scoundrel he can find. Every corrupt courtier can apply, and each is judged by his complete lack of worth."

"A cruel jest," Tom Cromwell muses. He is sure the king will not hold his French conquests beyond the next fighting season, and any man fool enough to buy land in so parlous a situation deserves what he gets. "Though it will fill the treasury coffers up again, and that is never a bad thing."

"Better yet, one man has used agents to subvert the auction, and he has gained six entire French counties, for as long as he is able to hold them."

"Who would be such a fool?" Cromwell asks. "Do we know?"

"Of course, master. Your agents know everything," says Kel Kelton. In fact, the information is known only because Robin Askey has passed on Surrey's drunken boasts. "It is Norfolk."

"Splendid. Then the old dog still fancies he has a bite." Cromwell ponders this news for a moment, then understands the motive. "The old duke seeks to enlarge his lands, until he rivals the king. Then he will seek to raise soldiers in his new French holdings and create a vast army."

"Then he is becoming an addle pate," Kel responds. "His French lands are just that… French. I doubt they would take kindly to an Englishman's rule and they will not fight under his banner."

"Yes, and that aside, Boulogne safeguards the land we have taken. Once Henry decides to sell the town back to François, all these new lords will be kicked out by the rightful owners."

"*If* the king sells," says Kel.

"Oh, he'll sell," Cromwell avows. "He loves money far more than some little town across the Channel, and François will offer a fair price to get his country back."

"Then the war was for nothing?" Even Kel, who likes a good fight, sees how Henry will make it all a cruel sham. "Men died to enrich the king?"

"Yes, Henry will make money," Cromwell says, "but so will most of the men who fought. Each one received his bounty, and you profited from selling your beef carcasses to the army."

"My Scottish cattle were ready for market," Kel says, defensively. "Was it my fault that the army quartermaster offered the best price?"

"I do not blame you," Cromwell replies. "Why, even the Draper Company benefitted. As for Antwerp and the other cities to the north, they picked up the traders that would usually go to France. All are content, save a few casualties."

"Like Edwin Tunnock?"

"I liked Edwin. He was a born soldier of fortune, and could not settle down to a peaceful life. He was a spy for Cardinal Wolsey, and then an assassin, bent on revenge for ten years. Finally, he came to us, and sought out the most dangerous missions he could find. The man was destined to die with a sword in his hand. I did not kill him."

"I did not mean to accuse you, master," Kelton argues, "but show up the guilty."

"Hush, lad," Thomas Cromwell says. "We are all guilty of something. Henry's England is more content now than ever before. Surely we can allow the man one little war?"

*

Queen Kathryn sits by her husband's side, and places a fresh poultice on his ulcerated leg. It is not the task for a queen, but she is the only one Henry does not curse, or try to hit out at. He groans, then takes her small hand in his huge one.

"My dearest wife," he says. "It was a good day when I wed you, and I do not regret a thing. You are faithful, and tender towards me. Can any man want more?"

"You honour me, sire," Kathryn replies. She sees that Henry has something on his mind. "Though I must say that you seem to be fighting with some faraway thoughts these days. Can I not help unburden you of these vexing things?"

"You know me too well, my dear." Henry furrows his brow, and decides to accept Katheryn's offer. "In truth, my mind will often linger over things best left alone. I think about the Aragon woman, and how I did treat her. Then I see the Boleyn girl's face, and it smiles at me, as if hiding a secret. Worse are the dreams. I see men I have broken, and whom I will meet with again in the next life. What do you say to that, My Lady?"

"You treated Catherine of Aragon well," the queen tells him. "I was at court then, with my first husband, and we all saw the agonies she put you through. As for

Anne Boleyn... what can her shade reproach you for? She was an adulteress, and even took her pleasure with her own brother. Put her from your mind. As for all these faceless spectres that crowd into your dreams... eat less cheese before bedtime, and take a glass of mulled wine with a drop of poppy juice in it."

"You speak honestly, my dear, but God can see into mens hearts, and I fear he will see my darkest secret. I have no wish to go to purgatory."

"Sire," Rafe Sadler is standing to one side, as if he might be a casual onlooker, but he hears every word, and evaluates them. He is the king's advisor, and must be aware of his moods, and the workings of his mind if he is to be of any use. "Your fears are unfounded. The English Bible contains no reference to Purgatory. It is a Papist nonsense, dreamed up to dun the poor out of their coppers, and fleece the credulous rich. Your Majesty shall go straight to Heaven, and sit by His right hand. For you are anointed by God, not the Bishop of Rome."

"Yes, that is so. No Purgatory," Henry brightens up. "Then I shall go with good grace. What of my last will and testament, Rafe?"

"It is still locked up in my law office's vault, sire," Rafe Sadler replies. "It needs only those parts left blank to be filled in. You are yet to make specific requests, and you do not mention an heir."

"It is bad luck to speak too quickly," the king says, and closes his eyes. "Boast about some title, and the gods are as likely to trip you up. I shall make such dispositions anon, when I confess to Canterbury, and the new fellow, who dogs his heels like a puppy."

"Sir Anthony Denny, sire?"

"What, I knighted him?" Henry asks of the new lawyer in court.

"Last month, Your Majesty… at the archbishop's request. He thought the man's legal work for the church to be quite meritorious. It is Denny who will be scribe when you are ready to speak."

"A vulture hovering above a falcon," Henry mutters, sullenly, and the queen makes a disapproving clucking noise in her throat.

"Your Majesty is recovering his health," Queen Kathryn says. "Let all talk of wills be banished for now. The world knows you favour Edward, and that is enough." 'Yes, do not ponder too deeply,' she thinks. If Edward is king, then a Seymour will be Regent of England, and great men will have to accept the new order.

"You speak good sense, as usual, my dear," Henry says, "and the subject is closed. Is there any other business today, my dear Sadler?"

"There are no petitions, sire," Rafe reports. "I think that news of your ill health has made men think twice before bothering their king. Though the French king has sent you a present, and a letter."

"A gift?" Henry smiles at this. "What is it?"

"A fine cedar wood chest, sire. It is inlaid with precious nacre and jewels upon its lid. There is a jewelled key with the letter, which asks that you open the gift by your own royal hand."

"What is within?" Henry asks, and Rafe confesses he does not know. The letter is polite, and stops just short of admitting defeat. François hopes that they might become friends again one day, and he looks forward to that time. Under such circumstances, it is only proper for the French king to send a lavish gift as a token of his esteem.

'*I count the days, dear cousin*,' the letter says, '*and hope you do too. To this end, I send a gift that will help you count off those future days*.'

"Damn me, is it a clock?" Henry asks. The Swiss are making the most magnificent time pieces these days, and a fine example can cost upwards of two thousand pounds. "A magnificent timepiece would sit well within my private chamber."

"Perhaps Your Majesty might use the key, and put us all out of our misery.

The chest is heavy, and I too was inclined to think of some golden ornament, or clever machine."

"Yes, Hal, my love," the queen urges. "See how even my own ladies strain to see what the French king has sent you. Pray let me help you to put in the key." The king smiles, and lets Kathryn guide his hand. The key turns once, and then again, and the lock springs open. Henry throws open the lid, and reels back in horror. Kathryn closes her eyes, and someone else screams. The magnificent cedar wood chest is full to the brim with fingers.

*

Tom Wyatt, the new resident poet at Draper House cannot stop laughing. Mush thinks he might have an apoplexy if he does not cease.

"It is not that funny," he says, and shakes the poet by his shoulder. "Henry was absolutely furious, and the queen was quite distraught. Rafe Sadler closed the chest at once, and ordered two guards to take it away. Then he sent for Will and asked him to look into the horrible affair."

"Yes, of course he must. He is the Examiner in Chief, and he never fails the king, who *counts* on him. Though I must wonder at the subtle nature of the Frog King François. 'Something to help you count', he says, and fingers are many a man's first resort. I see the jest, but where is the threat?"

"What do you mean?" Mush asks.

"François writes to Henry, and uses these fingers to shock him, but where is the threat? François does not utter a threat of more war, or of violence against Henry's person. A child might think up such a silly thing, were it not so gruesome. It does not make sense to me."

"Perhaps Will can see what it all means," Mush says. "At least, this shows that we are still in the king's favour. In moments of anxiety, he always turns to we Austin Friars men."

"Then I hope Will succeeds, for Henry thinks him to be a miracle worker." Tom Wyatt thinks for a moment. "Now I must think up words to rhyme off against 'fingers'!"

*

Marion Giles stands at the oak table in her apothecaries chamber, and starts to count the rows of fingers before her. There are exactly eight hundred of them, and each one is starting to decay. Will Draper has begged her to look at the fingers and give him something to help his floundering investigation.

She frowns at how long it has taken Will to ask her to examine the gruesome haul. It is a while now since the chest's first opening. Two days is a long time when it comes to the dead. Still, there may yet be much to find out. As she begins to lay out the severed fingers she sends her new husband to fetch her a dozen large specimen jars, each half filled with strong malt vinegar. In this way, Marion hopes to preserve the fingers from further rot. The vinegar will pickle them, and give her time to reach her conclusions.

To give him his due, Will Draper leaves it for a full day and a half before demanding answers.

"What can you tell me, my dear Marion?" he asks, and the apothecary draws his attention to several jars standing on a high shelf.

"There are eight hundred of them," she tells Will. "They are all human."

"I knew that," Will grumbles. "Tell me something I do not know."

"There are no thumbs," says Marion. "I do not know why. Then I examine the fingers and they speak to me. The skin is rough, and there are callouses on many of them. The fingers are not those you might find on noble hands. I must explain   myself better. The fingers' callouses are consistent with the men they come from having done heavy labouring, but the index and middle fingers are even more calloused. Each one has been cut off cleanly, not lost in a fight, or torn off in some wicked accident. I am sorry that I cannot offer you   a solution to this puzzle,

Will, but those are the facts."

"Thank you, Marion, but I am sure the answer is already known to me." Will stares at the large jars, and their macabre contents. "I know now where these poor things come from, but I am unsure as to the meaning of the gift."

"You can recognise the source of the fingers?" Marion asks.

"When the Duke of Norfolk ran away in France, an entire company of his men… archers… deserted. I suppose they thought to enlist with François, or become wandering outlaws. I believe those men are the owners of the fingers, because of the calloused fingers. The first and middle fingers are usually used to draw back a bowstring." Will tries to force his thoughts to a conclusion, but he lacks enough information. Was it François' idea of a jest, or something more sinister? What has become of the men, and why are there no thumbs in the macabre offering? "Further than that conclusion, I cannot say, and we may never discover the whole truth."

"Will Henry accept that?" Marion asks. "He was shaken by the gift, and now he will want to strike back at his French cousin."

"I can only tell him what I know," says Will. "The rest is down to him. I pray he lets the matter drop, for we still have several hundred French hostages awaiting ransom."

"You think the king will resort to maiming them, just to anger François?"

"Why not?" Will is under no illusions as to the moral character of the king these days. "He hangs innocent men without qualms."

"Can you not have Richard Cromwell reason with the king?" Marion asks. "Henry listens to him more than most.

"You are out of touch, Marion," the Examiner replies. "Richard refuses to go to court these days, and swears he is about to die at any moment."

"I did not know he was ill," Marion tells Will. "Can I not visit him and try to find a cure?"

"He is not ill," Will says. "He simply does not wish to live. When Lady Jane was executed, the light seems to have left his soul."

"Ah, love. There is no known cure for that malady, save the passing of time. Though I might yet make him up a tonic to revitalise his weary soul."

"Please do," says Will, "for he sinks lower with every passing day. Can a man really die of a broken heart?"

"He can," Marion replies. "If the love is true, then the loss of it can make a man sick unto death."

"God preserve my friend," Will says. "In the meantime, I must go to the king with the half of a story I know, and hope he does not go into a rage. He must take the thing as it is meant… a cruel, yet childish insult."

"Yes, it is a wicked thing to do for a jest," Marion tells her friend, "but again I ask you… why are there no thumbs?"

*

"You think François means to insult me with this hateful gift?" Henry asks his Chief Examiner. "Yet he does not wish to make war?"

"Just so, sire," Will explains. "We have a good friend at the French court just now, and he writes to say what he knows. It seems François was angry at the Duke of Norfolk's retreat being virtually unchallenged, and sought to poke fun at you from the safety of Paris."

"But why send me fingers?" Henry asks. "I fail to see where the insult lies."

"He implies that Your Majesty is slow witted, and must count on his fingers. The extra ones are to make the jest more pointed."

"That is a poor sort of a jest," Henry decides.

""It is French humour sire, and it does not travel well," Will replies. "Though the cost of making his little jest is sickening. The fingers are most likely those of common English soldiers, taken prisoner in the recent war."

"I see. Then he seeks to dun me in another way too, for the maiming of such prisoners is barbaric. Do we not always release our prisoners, once a ransom is paid?"

"That is the accepted practice, amongst civilised men, Your Majesty," Will says. "It seems that François is changing the rules of engagement."

"Be damned if he shall," Henry growls. "I want something done about it, my Lord Templar, and I want it done quickly."

"Might I beg a few more days, sire," Will asks. "Once my agents have all reported in, I will be in a stronger place to suggest a suitable retribution."

"A week… no more," Henry says. "Now, let us pass the time with a little dicing."

"Alas, sire, I am constrained from accepting by my urgent duties, but I am sure that Sir Mush and Tom Wyatt will oblige. They are in the outer court just now."

"Ah, the monkey and the poet," Henry chuckles. "Yes, send them in, and we shall dice. I wager I will soon clean out their purses."

Will Draper bows and takes his leave. Once in the outer court, he beckons Mush and Tom Wyatt over to him. They come, expecting to be enrolled in some wily plot, or tasked to take up arms against some new foe.

"I have a dangerous mission for you both," Will tells them, with a wry smile playing about his lips. "You are to entertain His Majesty for a couple of hours. He wishes to dice with you, and from the look in his eyes, I guess he wishes to use Gomez's loaded dice. So here, take this purse of silver, and let him win until it is empty."

"And what shall you be up to while we are busy being cheated by our own king?" Tom Wyatt asks.

"Our hero scorns to throw the dice
whilst o'er spies reports he lingers,
the French king's jest is n'er so nice,
and Will must count his blest fingers."

"Dear Sainted Christ on His Cross," Mush says with fervour. "I would rather dice with the devil than listen to your lame poetry, Wyatt. Here, take half of this silver, and let us go like lambs to the slaughter."

The pair, who are fast becoming inseparable friends, know that Henry possesses a set of Alonso Gomez's loaded dice, and hope that they are allowed to escape without losing too much. Will smiles at the pair, and thinks on how he will use this time saved from the king's maunderings to try and discover what is really going on.

It is one thing to send something gruesome to an enemy, as did many a Roman general, but quite another to use fingers, rather than a severed head, and even stranger… why were there no thumbs?

*

Thomas Cranmer, the Archbishop of Canterbury, is a survivor in a world where even the greatest of men can fall at the whim of a king. The secret of his rise to his present position lies in his dogged devotion to the king. No matter what, bc it a quick divorce, a queen's death, or even some wicked lie, Cranmer always sides with Henry. This policy has stood him in good stead until now, and his help in condemning Anne Boleyn, betraying Catherine Howard, and helping to be rid of Anne of Cleves, endears him to the king.

Now, Henry summons him. Not with a flowery invitation, but by the arrival of Sir John Russell and an escort of grim looking cavalry. The Archbishop of Canterbury stands in the nave of his great church and awaits their coming. As they dismount, and form into a twin column of heavily armed men, Cranmer can only think back to the days of Thomas Becket, the martyred archbishop, who had been hacked to death on this same sacred ground.

"If it is the will of God," he mutters to himself, "then I am ready to accept my end… but I pray that it is not God's will just yet… for I am a poor sort to die for his beliefs."

"Praying, My Lord Archbishop?"

John Russell says, with a broad grin on his face. "Say one for me too, if you can. I am a poor soul, much in need of some heavenly guidance."

"You are armed, sir," Cranmer says. "This is holy ground, and a man should face God unarmed."

"Forgive me, Uncle Thomas," Russell says, and rests his hand on the hilt of his sword. "But I am on royal duty, and must go armed, as must my men."

"You call me 'uncle' sir?" Cranmer is confused by both the friendly banter, and the odd way of addressing him.

"I do, My Lord," Russell replies. "You must remember my mother, Alice Wise? She was once a lady in your mother's household. When she married, you did lend your worthy name to her first born, as his godfather."

"Oh, then I understand," Cranmer says, somewhat relieved. "I have at least thirty godchildren, and can scarce recall them all. My secretary has their birthdates and sees that a purse of silver is delivered to them each year. So, you are Anne Wise's boy… how is she?"

"Dead," Russell says. "Some years ago now. I believe it was of a twisted middle, but I was in Flanders at the time."

"Poor woman. I shall pray for her."

"Thank you, sir," Russell says, not unmoved by the archbishops sincerity. He smiles at the recollection of the purse, always with five shillings in it, coming to him on each birthday. "Now please come with me. The king demands your immediate presence."

"Am I under arrest?" Cranmer asks,

"No, sir," Russell tells him. "I am to takc you to Whitehall, not the Tower of London. I believe the king is in need of your advice, and there is no malice in him for you."

"Yes, the king loves me," the archbishop concurs. "In private he often calls me Thomas, and has me call him Hal in return. I wonder what it is that demands a troop of soldiers to fetch me?"

"I cannot say for sure, but when he gave me my orders, he was examining a copy of the new English bible."

"Oh, dear," Cranmer groans. "Perhaps he is having second thoughts, and wishes to return to the Latin version."

"I doubt it, sir," Russell says, as he guides the archbishop to his coach. "The king loves being the supreme head of his own church, and he will not give that up for Rome's sake."

"Then he is displeased with my preface," Tom Cranmer decides. The new edition of the bible bears a long preamble, in which Cranmer sets out his vision for the future of the Church of England. In a moment of evangelical madness, the archbishop made much of things that may anger the more noble of the book's readers. "I disparage the Spanish way of Catholicism, and make my views on purgatory and the selling of church offices clear."

"All will become clear, sir," Russell says. "If we travel without halting, we may make London before dusk. You can get a good night's sleep, and attend court on the morrow."

"Sleep?" Cranmer shakes his head. "Sleep is for the innocent, John. When a man takes on high office, he loses the right to sleep soundly. My mind fills with thoughts of what my office drives me to, and an unquiet mind seldom finds rest. Do you sleep well, my boy?"

"I do, sir, but I am seldom sober," Russell says, with candour. "I find that a good wine, or even some black rum does the trick. You might try it."

"A drunken archbishop?" Cranmer takes his seat in the coach and pulls a woollen blanket over his legs. "I doubt my congregation would approve." The mere thought of drinking himself into a stupor is wickedly appealing, and he wonders if it will help him forget his past misdeeds. His betrayal of Catherine Howard, and the easy way he let friends, who would not recant their catholicism, go to the stake haunt his every waking moment, and crowd into his drams when he sleeps, so that he wakes up in a cold sweat. So, yes, he must consider the merits of strong drink to keep his demons at bay.

*

"Sire, the Archbishop of Canterbury is waiting in the outer court," Sir John Russell tells the king. Henry is still in his privy chamber, seated on the oval wooden seat that conceals the stone trough below. Thanks to Lady Miriam Draper, the king's private latrine is of the very latest Venetian design. The stone trough is linked to a wide lead pipe, that drains into a deep tank buried below the king's rose garden.

Henry is constipated, and he struggles to relieve himself. Sir Thomas Heanage, his Master of the Privy, stands close by, with a jug of warm water, and a pile of linen towels. He looks up at Russell, and groans.

"Damn me, Russell, but this turd is not for shifting," he complains. "What does he want?"

"You sent for him, sire," John Russell says.

"I did?" Henry frowns and thinks hard. He is not fond of having clerics about the royal court, and cannot understand why he would invite one to attend on him now. "Do you know why?"

"No, Your Majesty." John Russell

has been the king's man for ten years now, and he owes his longevity of tenure to always keeping out of the politics around the throne. He loves the Austin Friars way more than the Norfolk idea of running England, but tries to keep neutral. "Perhaps you wish to consult him on a point of canon law?"

"God above, no," Henry says. "I have enough trouble with these hard nosed bastards who still wish me to remain on friendly terms with the Church of Rome. They scheme and plot to good effect, and they do not like... ah... that is it. I remember now why I want to see dear old Cranmer. Let me finish here, and I will see him in the throne room. Stay close, and after I am done with him, you are to execute some warrants for me. Take as many men as you see fit, and round up those who would do harm to my church."

"As you command, sire." Russell withdraws, and leaves the king to his ablutions. The new 'water closet' is a fine contraption, he thinks, but it is too complicated to ever catch on. Each one must have a servant flush it clear with a bucket of water, and how many gentlemen can afford to keep their own private privy attendant? No, he will stick to the old way, and relieve himself behind a bush, in the open air, as God intended it to be.

Then he considers the king's

words, and sees that poor Tom Cranmer is in for a bad time of it. Henry will confront him, and then have the archbishop and his followers arrested. He considers warning his godfather, but what good would it do? It is impossible to escape, for every hand will be against him, and every port watched. Then he would be in trouble for helping an enemy of the king. John Russell shudders, and thanks God that he is only a messenger.

*

Tom Cranmer waits in the outer court, and finds himself to be rather popular. Several gentlemen wish to greet him, and offer him a kind word. That these gentlemen believe him to be a close friend of the king, and therefore worth cultivating, does not cross his mind. He smiles, and blesses them, each in turn, until Sir John Russell appears, and leads him into the inner court.

"In a moment the king's squire will come and take you into the throne room, sir." Russell is unhappy at his part in these proceedings, and wishes he could do something to save the old man. "The king wishes to speak with you… and he bids me wait, so that certain warrants can be served. I am sorry, sir, but there is nothing I can do for you now."

"Ah, I see. Even the great Cardinal Wolsey fell from grace, so why should I be any different?" The archbishop takes a deep breath. He is not a brave man, but he must accept the king's will, and hope his end is swift and painless. "Can you get a message to my wife, John? She is in Canterbury, with the children. Tell her that the time is upon us, and she must leave for Antwerp this very day."

"Will she believe me?" Russell asks.

"Yes, for she has been waiting for this moment for years," Cranmer says. "My wealth is lodged with Miriam Draper's banking house, and she will see my family do not suffer for my transgressions."

"I shall do as you ask, sir, but what is it that brings you down so low?" Russell cannot understand how so great a man can fall so quickly.

"Perhaps my writings on religion have upset the wrong people," Cranmer says. "Or the king thinks me guilty of simony… though I have never sold a church office, or taken money from rich men to ease their way into Heaven. It might simply be that he thinks me too powerful within his precious church."

"My Lord Archbishop!" The young Robin Askey, a replacement for the late Thomas Culpeper, bows in a most revering manner. "His Majesty bids me fetch you into is presence." The young man gestures towards the open door, and ushers the elderly archbishop into the lion's den.

Henry is looking flushed and he is seated on his throne, with his injured leg up on a well padded stool. He holds his arms out wide, as if ready to hug Tom Cranmer to death.

"My dear, dear Archbishop Cranmer... Tom... come closer, so that I might converse with you without shouting."

"As you command, sire," Cranmer says, and moves to within an arm's length of the throne. The squire fusses about and plumps up the cushion beneath Henry's leg.

"Enough, young Rolly," the king says. "Your devotion is quite admirable, but I must speak to Cranmer in private... so piss off." The squire bows, and scurries away. "Now, Tom... to business. You know, of course, that you are under investigation?"

"No, sire," Cranmer splutters. "I had no idea that any such thing was afoot. Have I so offended you?"

"Offended me?" Henry looks aggrieved at this. "The investigators have spoken to many of your closest friends, and it has even questioned your own clergy in London and in Canterbury. Has no one warned you?"

"No, sire. Not a single word." Cranmer sees that his friends have shunned him, fearing that they might be condemned with him if they speak out. "I have no idea what I have done wrong."

"Upon its completion, the report

was handed to me, along with a letter signed by many leading clergy," Henry tells Cranmer. "In particular, Germain Gardiner, the Bishop of Winchester's nephew, who makes some very serious allegations, concerning your doctrines."

"I know the fellow, Your Majesty," Cranmer says. "He is a conservative, who advocates we remain close to Rome. Though he does not scorn your Church of England, he wishes it to temper some of the reforms I have suggested."

"The report is here," Henry holds out a thick sheaf of papers. "It condemns you, sir, in no uncertain terms. It says you wish to remove Latin from our church offices, and that you wish all future church documents to be written in English."

"Is that so bad a thing, sire?" Cranmer asks. "Is it not better that every man can read what your church says and does? Must we submit to these people's wish to still curry favour with the corrupt Bishop of Rome?"

"Germain Gardiner concludes that your actions are nothing short of treasonable, Cranmer. You must see that I have no choice in the matter. There must be an immediate investigation, and some swift justice dispensed. You agree?"

"I cannot disagree with my sovereign lord," Cranmer says, glumly. He sees his end is coming with a whimper, and that a few jealous men will bring him down because he is too liberal.

"Then that is that," Henry says, happily. "You must head up the enquiry, Archbishop Cranmer, and see that the signatories to this spurious document are arrested, and brought to heel."

"Sire… you want…"

"I want these stick in the mud Catholic lovers arrested," Henry replies. "I want them in the Tower, as soon as can be, and I want you to wheedle out any clergy who still wish to undermine my new church. In particular, I want this Germain Gardiner tried for… well, for something. Speak with Rafe Sadler, or Barnaby Fowler, for they have the finest lawyer's minds in England."

"As you command, sire. I am grateful for your support in this matter." Cranmer can feel his heart hammering in his chest, and he offers up a silent prayer for his deliverance from his enemies.

"You are my man, Cranmer," the king tells him. "I am not about to be lectured to, by a bunch of Roman arse kissers. Gardiner and his followers must receive a fair trial, and a swift end."

"Your Majesty, must we resolve the matter so bloodily? This document is signed by twenty names or more."

"Oh, you are far too tolerant, Thomas," Henry grumbles. "Though you are a man of God, and must always seek a saintly course. Very well, then. Pick out two ring leaders, and lock them up for a few years. Frighten the rest into swearing loyalty to the Church of England, and warn them that I will boil alive any of them who ever oppose my will again. As for Germain Gardiner… he must die."

"Bishop Stephen Gardiner will object," Thomas Cranmer says. "He has some sympathy for his nephew's cause."

"Stephen Gardiner will hold his tongue," the king replies. "Rafe Sadler tells me that he is being investigated by the Attorney General's Office over the misuse of church funds. It seems that Gardiner and Richard Rich are no longer friends."

"Then I will do as you bid, sire," Cranmer says, with joy in his heart. "This will send out a clear message to the Bishop of Rome, telling him that our Church of England refutes him and his corrupt doctrines. It will also annoy King François."

"Excellent." Henry is pleased that his dear old friend understands. As king, he must not allow anyone to present him with an un-looked for report, *demanding* he do what *they* bid of him. He is the absolute monarch, and any challenge must be crushed. Germaine Gardiner will hang because he demanded, rather than suggested. "You know, Thomas, old friend, if those fools had worded it differently, I might well have supported them."

"Then I thank God that your well known good sense prevailed, sire," Cranmer tells the king. "I am your greatest ally, and my support for you will never waver. Together, we will make England into the world leader of protestant reform, and Your Majesty into the figurehead of the new religion all across Europe."

"Quite so, Thomas," Henry says. "Now, you must join me for dinner. I wish to discuss a new preface for my English Bible."

"My pleasure, Hal." Thomas Cranmer sighs, and wonders if he might escape before the drunken roistering begins. Then he recalls that, but an hour before, he was expecting to be condemned, and executed. 'Surely,' he thinks, 'I can put up with a few ribald songs, and saucy jests in return?'

"Yes, the one you have written does not mention me enough. I am the king, and that must be made plain, as must my supreme right to rule over the Church of England." Henry smiles at his own sense of power. "The preface must be dedicated to me, with my full titles."

"Henry, King of England, and Defender of the Faith?" Cranmer suggests, and the two men cackle together. The archbishop will have his new bible, all six thousand copies, put in every pulpit, and further, he will use his new power to route out all who would oppose him.

The worst must die, of course, but many more will have a taste of the Tower to keep them in line. If they insist on keeping to their catholic ways, he will send them to the scaffold, or the pyre. Those who defy the king will forfeit their lands, their wealth, and their lives.

9   Dark Voyager

Ibrahim ben Rachid thinks he is about thirty three years of age, but he cannot be completely sure, as his birth is shrouded in some mystery. As a young boy, in Spain, he was often lodged with many different families, whilst his father travelled. Ibrahim liked to think of him as a man of mystery; a man who dealt in danger, and intrigue.

Ali Ahmed Rachid was, in fact, a horse trader, petty spy and informer, who made a precarious living by selling gossip to anyone who was interested. By the time he was rich enough to take an interest in his son, Ibrahim was too wild to tame. The father frowned at his son's general bad behaviour, and decided to buy him a commission in the Spanish army.

"I made a very poor soldier," he says to Mush, who is there to wave him off on his great adventure. "I shall make an even worse sailor. Your sister's trust in me is entirely misplaced."

"Miriam has faith in you," Mush tells his friend. "She believes you to be the only man in England who can find a new way to reach Cathay. If you sail around the world, you will find the new rout, and we will all become fabulously wealthy."

"She must not trust me."

"She calls it women's intuition," Mush replies. "Besides, Pru Beckshaw came up with one of her mysterious predictions, and she is never wrong."

"Dear Pru… what did she see?"

"An '*ebony lord who will sail*

away', and '*a great, landless king who will bow before him*'."

"A landless king?" Ibrahim shrugs his shoulders. That he is meant by the 'ebony' lord is clear, but what king can be king without any land to rule? "Perhaps, in far Cathay or India, men can fly like birds, and this king is master of the air?"

"You think so?" Mush says, then he grins at how easily he falls for such a silly jest. "It must mean you will meet up with a king who has been dispossessed of his realm. You might win it back for him, and gain his favour. The King of Cathay might bend the knee to you."

"Or I find a new way to sail to the East, and the infidels murder me and all my crew," Ibrahim says, and he draws a finger across his throat. "Tell Miriam that I am not to be trusted. Tell her that I have no faith in this expedition, and I will let her down."

"You waste your breath, my friend," Mush Draper tells the Moor. "You command four of the best merchantmen that the Draper Company owns, each with a dozen large cannon aboard. Your crews are all seasoned sailing men, and each ship has a half company of soldiers, and those women who wish to escape London for a new life. That is eight hundred men… good men, and enough firepower to drive off any who might wish to oppose your progress."

"Please, warn dearest Miriam

against me, and advise her to find another admiral for her mad expedition," the Moor insists, but Mush just grins and urges his friend up the gangplank.

"The tide is favourable," Mush tells him. "You will make it to the New Found Land by November. Spend three months building forts, and subduing the natives. Establish a colony, and have your men marry the women. I shall set out once the weather is right in April, with more troops, carpenters, artisans, farmers, and womenfolk. Once I arrive, you will be free to lead an expedition into the wilderness."

"And never be seen again."

"Nonsense. Miriam and her wisest people think you will march about two hundred miles, then come to the far shore. The carpenters and shipwrights, who I will deliver, can soon build you a couple of sturdy ships. Then you can sail across the far ocean, find India or Cathay, and establish the Draper Company in their lands."

"Easy," Ibrahim says. 'The whole idea is crazy', he thinks. Even if the wilderness is only a couple of hundred miles wide, it might be nothing but dense forest, or filled with thousands of hostile natives. Then he wonders at how easily he is supposed to construct a new fleet. He might be able to build a passable merchantman or two, but what does he do for sails… or cannon? Must he drag hundreds of yards of canvas and a few heavy cannon across the new world? No, it is madness, He has one last try. "Mush, are we friends?"

"Of course."

"Do you believe I love you like a brother?"

"Yes. We have saved each other's lives, and I know our bond is stronger than a blood tie," Mush tells him. "Now, let me be gone, and set yourself to marshalling your fleet."

"If you love me, Mush, then listen to me," the Moor says, earnestly. "I am not the man for this task. I pray you go to Miriam, and tell her that I must not be trusted. Tell her that I swear this to be true, and she must abandon all hope of me finding her new world for her. Will you do this for me?"

"And have her scoff at me?" Mush says. "My sister prides herself on her ability to pick the right people to work for her. She takes a man who should hang, and turns him into a hard working chandler, or turns a loose woman into an accountant, and she is *never* wrong. Even when she is wrong, she is never wrong. Miriam and the king share this trait, and she will not accept your claims. She trusts you, and that alone will make you act as she wishes."

"May Allah and all the other gods

bear witness," Ibrahim cries. "I swear, on my family's honour, that I must not be trusted. Relieve me of this task, Mush, and I will be your servant for ever more."

"Good day to you, Admiral Rachid," Mush tells the frustrated Moor. "May the tides be in your favour."

"You are a damned fool," Ibrahim curses. "I have done my best, and now, you must take the consequences. I sail as soon as the tide turns.

*

The four sleek merchantmen slip out of the harbour with the high tide, and make sail to the south west. They keep in tight formation, and a few hours into their epic voyage, the admiral's ship hoists up some signal flags. They are to come about onto a more southerly tack. Over the next couple of hours, Ibrahim has a series of flags run up, each unveiling his new instructions. They are no longer sailing to the New Found Land, and Lady Miriam's fresh orders, unveiled by the Moor, reveal a new plan. They are to make for the North African coast, and the fortified city of Tangiers. There is nothing in writing, but Ibrahim knows that, at sea, the master's word is sacred law enforced, ifneed be, at the end of a rope.

"Damn you, Mush," the Moor says into the face of a gentle rain that is starting to fall, "did I not beg you to mistrust me?"

*

The letter is sent by the fastest courier from the coast. The King's Post Rider knows who Will Draper is, and that he should receive a generous purse if he gallops throughout the night. He arrives at Draper House on the last day of September, and receives a couple of golden angels for his trouble.

Will Draper retires to his study, and slits it open with great expectations. He reads it through, twice, and curses. Rather than solve his investigation, it seeks to add another layer to the mystery, and make life just that much more dangerous. It says:

> *My dear Will,*
> *Greetings from Paris. I am loathe to write to you with such unhappy news, but I can only impart that truth which I can establish beyond reproach. I am residing, at the moment, within the magnificent Hôtel de Ville, as the honoured guest of His Majesty, King François.*
> *Since leaving my post as English ambassador, François seems intent on making a friend of me. He must think I hold secrets about Henry and his court that will aid him in his enmity of them. Despite my wish to settle down in a quiet part of Holland, or even Flanders, he wishes me to reside in France.*
> *I have pointed out to His Majesty that I am still in the service of the Holy Roman Emperor Charles, and that my visit must soon be curtailed. He takes this with good grace, but insists on my company at his table each evening. God save me from French cooking, which relies on the most intricate sauces to bolster its taste. I long for an Austin Friars breakfast.*
> *Each evening, François questions me about England, the royal court, and the customs of*

the land, and I tell him as little as I can. In return, he loves to boast, and enjoys a really good gossip. So it is that I can throw some light onto this ghastly business of the severed fingers, and an explanation as to why no thumbs made an appearance.

François boasted to me, this last evening, of how he did give great insult to Henry this last month. His ancestor sent tennis balls to mock another Henry as indolent, and he sent the fingers to aid your Henry in his counting... thus implying that the king is lacking in intellect. A feeble jest, I think. I made so bold as to ask why no thumbs were sent, and François told me that his advisor wished to leave his prisoners with their thumbs.

The king does not know, or care why his man acted thus, and I am at a loss to understand what is afoot. It seems that the prisoners are English soldiers. Deserters, or prisoners of war, taken in battle? I cannot say, but this much I must reveal to you in all its horror. This advisor, Jacques Cordelier, le Comte de Avion by name and title, has hanged all but a dozen of these poor Englishmen, and has sent the survivors to one of His Majesty's strongholds, the fortress in La Rochelle.

Perhaps your spies might find out more, but I am now at the limit of my ability to uncover anything further. Were Gomez still in my employ, I would hope to do more for our cause.

Your devoted friend,

Eustace Chapuys.

Will hands the letter to Miriam, who is just back from overseeing the loading of her provisions barges, destined for the many market stalls she owns all across the south. She reads it, and hands it back.

"Then that is that," she says. "Those poor men were ill used, and then hanged. It is sad, but that is what men do in war."

"The king expects a report," Will tells her. "He will not accept one that shows the French disdain of us. Nor will he accept that we are powerless against our enemies. He will demand we act. Though God knows how."

"Tell him it cannot be done."

"Tell the king 'no'?" Will sees that his wife speaks out of frustration, and that she knows Henry will have his way. "You know how he recently empowered Cranmer to rid England of any who spoke out in support of the Roman church?"

"Yes, and I think the archbishop was a brave man to do as he did. He arrested fifty men, and had them confined in the Tower of London. When Henry demanded their deaths, the archbishop refused him, and demanded in return that they were all spared, after being given a fright. Henry heard the word 'no' then, did he not?"

"Yesterday, the king visited the Tower, and had all fifty men paraded before him. Then he informed them that Cranmer had interceded, and they would not be killed. He asked if any would recant their faith then, and two of them did, and were released at once."

"A just outcome," Miriam says.

"The other forty eight were then blinded with hot irons by Master Wake. He tells me that the king grinned throughout at his cleverness. Not one of the men was executed."

"Dear God," Miriam says. "What then? Are they released?"

"Turned out to beg in the streets, I suppose," Will tells her. "So, do not tell me that the king can be reasoned with.'

"No, but he can be circumvented," his wife replies, hardly able to control her anger. "I shall give orders for the men, and their families to be cared for. We will find work for those who can, and give succour to those who cannot. The children shall receive an education, and found positions with the company."

"Do it quietly," says Will, "or we may come under the same suspicion. The king is ..."

"Mad?" Miriam asks. "Or simply power mad? I hope you did not know what he intended?"

"Dear Christ, woman!" Will feels his cheeks suffuse with blood. "You know me better than that. Now, I must ponder on what to do if Henry demands I take the fortress at La Rochelle."

"I know the fortress at La Rochelle," Miriam says. "One of my captains runs a full laden cog into there every month. He takes in Portuguese wine, English cheeses, and eastern spices, and he brings out salt bricks. There are salt pans all along the seashore."

"What is the place like?" Will asks, and Miriam knows that he means the question in a military way, and answers in a like vein.

"The town has spilled out, over the defensive walls, but the fortifications are strong. A thirty foot stone wall runs around four sides of a rectangle. There are three new built bastions to the north side, with cannon at each embrasure. The inner fortress is a solid stone keep, with a deep moat, fed by sea water. Again it bristles with cannon. It would take five thousand men, with cannon and siege ladders to stand any chance of getting inside."

"We are still at war with the French," Will says. "The king might decide to storm the place, if he thinks Englishmen are being mistreated there."

"Henry does not give a fig," Miriam says. "I doubt he would blind fifty men, then lift a finger over saving a few wayward soldiers."

"I agree, save for his sense of personal honour," Will tells his wife. "If he sees this as an attack on his honour, he will want to act in a way that rebounds on François, and makes him look foolish, or cowardly."

"That is all well and good, but I doubt François has any idea what is going on. We do not know why this Cordelier hangs men without a thought, yet keeps some back. Men without fingers are hardly a valuable commodity, are they?"

"I shall report to the king, and hope he does not want me to sack the town," Will says, glumly. "I do not want to lose half of my Examiners in a futile attack."

"Then be careful how you speak with Henry, my love. Do not let him become angry, or he will act rashly. Hint at a safer way…if there is one… and let him think it is his own idea."

"Madam, you would teach me how to handle the king?" Will says, tongue in cheek, and Miriam smiles and kisses him.

"Why not, for have I not '*handled*' you for these last thirteen years?" She places a hand on his cheek, and wonders at how this man can command her soul so completely. "Now I am older, and wiser."

"Thirty two," Will says, softly, "and you still look just like that eighteen year old girl I met on the ferry boat. One look, and I was lost."

"Really?" Miriam jests. "I thought you had scarce noticed me."

"You tease me now," Will says. "Am I still a callow youth in your eyes?"

"Oh, you were never that, my sweetest darling," Miriam replies. "I saw a man… a man whose very look spoke of a violent life, and whose very voice instilled confidence in me. I knew I must marry one day, and that my circumstances meant I must find a strong protector."

"Oh, then it was not for love then?" Will makes a face at her, and she laughs.

"Handle the king well, my love," she concludes, "and delegate to one of your able captains. I do not want you trying to force your way into the fortress. War is for wild young men, and you are an old married man. Let Jeremiah Cord earn his spurs."

"If I can make it so, I will have the king do nothing," Will says."For I do not wish to risk any lives in some foolish prank to get back at the French king."

*

"We must certainly get back at François." The king is quite adamant about it. "He sends me fingers, damn it, and it is an insult that must be redressed. Can we attack from the sea?"

"I have spoken with one of your best sea captains, sire, and he assures me that our ships would never get out of the harbour. The batteries of cannon would sink our men o' war in a trice."

"Then we can land troops further up the coast," Henry says, as he stabs a finger at the map spread out across his desk. "Here is a likely spot, and it is only ten miles from La Rochelle."

"Yes, but that means we are within easy marching distance of Rochefort, were there is a garrison of two thousand heavy cavalry. We would be caught between to forces and crushed."

"Yes, just as I thought," Henry grumbles. "I think we must think of another way."

"Ah, I see where your thoughts are going, Hal," Will says, and TomWyatt agrees.

"Yes, you see it even before we do, sire," the poet says, just as Will has asked him to. "Some clever trick, no doubt."

"Why yes, you understand my mind. We can use trickery, can we not?" Henry says.

"Like stealing into the harbour in some way?" Will prompts. "Perhaps using some small boat?"

"Does not your lovely wife own several cogs?" Henry asks.

"Good Lord, yes!" Will slaps a hand to his forehead. "You are right. We can use the cog to get a small party ashore without suspicion. It might be that the cog is trading?"

"Then once ashore you can fetch my captive men back to England, and I will use them to humiliate François."

"A masterstroke, Hal," Will says. "I shall see that a a party of my best Examiners is readied."

"Let us not leave anything to chance," Henry tells his Chief Examiner.

"Lead them yourself, Will. You never fail me."

"Of course, sire," Will says. "Just as you wish." There, the deed is done. There will be no fruitless storming of an impregnable citadel, and no loss of hundreds of lives. Just a few men, intent on using guile over force to get their way.

Now all he must do is explain to his wife why it is he, again, who must take the lead. He knows how she will take the news, and he agrees with her concerns. One day, his luck will run out, and he will not come back.

The plan is a simple one, and calls for no more than ten men to carry it out. It is a foregone conclusion that Mush will want to join him, and Tom Wyatt will be eager to risk his life again. Will sees that as well as guile, they must have a few men able to act quickly if the enemy's suspicions are aroused. To this end he will ask Jeremiah Cord to volunteer himself and six of his best Examiners.

"Sergeant Barry and I will provide the brute force," Cord says when he is approached. "Though the others have finer skills. Corporal Jones... Hwyll is Tam's brother... can open any lock ever invented, and Trooper Cope speaks the Froggy lingo like a native. Farmer and Ross are both handy with throwing knives, and Trooper Tate is a marvel at getting through tight places. He was a chimney man before the magistrate spared him hanging and sent him to us. The skinny bugger can get through the crack of dawn."

"Chimney man?" Will asks.

"Yes, he'd come down a chimney like a ferret down a rabbit run, and rob all he could. They only caught him when his woman turned him in for he reward. Women, eh, General Will?"

"Then we are ten," says Will. Jeremiah's musing about women makes him wonder how he can best inform his wife that he is, once again, the chosen man. He must grasp the nettle, and tell her how it is. It is a short walk from the Examiner barracks to Draper House, and Will takes it slowly. He is unhappy at having to upset his beloved Miriam with this unexpected news. He goes into the great hall in search of her, and finds her standing by the long dining table.

Laid out upon it is his best sword, his dagger, and a pair of excellent pistols. Miriam sees the look of relief on his face as he realises that she already knows. He picks up the sword, a German made killer of men that he won after slaying the Irish lord it belonged to, and buckles it about his waist.

"There," Miriam says. "Now you are complete. Try not to be first in every fray, and come back to me. I cannot live without you, my darling."

"There will be no bloodshed," Will reassures her. "We shall slip in, rescue the prisoners, and return home. Then Henry can play his stupid prank on François."

"They are like children," Miriam says, but more malevolent, she thinks. "One day, we might have a better man on the throne."

"Edward is still a small child," Will says, "but the queen tells me he is a fine lad. She speaks highly of Elizabeth too, but finds Mary to be stiff necked and overly zealous. Though I fear Henry will live forever, despite his rotting leg."

"You fear?" Miriam smiles at her husband's choice of words. There is a small, polite cough from the door, and young Al Varney, a street urchin in training to become a footman, is there.

"Pardon me, Milady, but there is a messenger. He is from Sir Richard's household, and he bids you and the master come quickly, for his master says that today is his day for dying."

"God's sacred teeth," Will growls. "Not this nonsense again. Must the fellow die every month? I swear, were he not a dear friend…"

"Hush, husband. Let us humour Richard, and so talk him into a better frame of mind. It is only that he misses Jane Boleyn so much."

"Then we must hurry. I wish to

take the ebb tide, and my men are waiting."

Richard Cromwell's house is on the river, and it is one of those built by Miriam Draper, some ten years before. She and Will take a boat downstream, and arrive just after noon. They arrive just as Mush and Tom Wyatt turn up. They too have been summoned by worried servants.

Cromwell's steward meets them at the door, his face a mask of concern. Apart from the thought of losing his position if Cromwell dies, the man actually likes his master and wishes him well.

"He's proper bad this time, sir," the man tells Will. "He refuses food, and is in his bed again. All he talks about is as how he was pledged to Lady Jane, and how she was murdered by the king."

"Christ," Tom Wyatt groans. "Is any woman worth dying for?"

"Don't be a fool," Miriam snaps. "Have you never wanted to die for a true love? Did you ever really love your precious Anne Boleyn?"

"With all my heart," the poet says, tartly. "But mine is an undying love."

"A cheap jest, Tom," Mush says. "Let us go up and turn our Richard out of his bed."

They climb the steep stairs, and bungle their way into the large front bed chamber. Richard Cromwell is in bed, propped up with down pillows, and he looks to be in rude good health. He smiles at them.

"This is most fitting," he says. "That all my best friends are here for this moment. Will, you have my last testament safe?"

"It is lodged with Rafe Sadler's practice," Will replies. "As safe as can be."

"Excellent," Richard says. "Then let me bid you all farewell. Has any man ever had such loving friends? Has any man ever lived so full a life?"

> *"Listen to the great bear groan,*
> *like all those creaking gates,*
> *the more our bear loves to moan,*
> *and his own death he venerates."*

The poet waits for someone to decry his doggerel, but the chamber is silent. Even as they think to cheer their friend up, and raise the cloud from over his head, the Angel of Death slips in, and takes his soul.

Sir Richard Cromwell, advisor to the king, statesman, warrior, and friend, has suddenly breathed his last. Will cannot speak with the horror of it. He closes his friend's eyes, and finds two copper coins to put on the eyes. Miriam falls to her knees, and tears the neck of her dress open.

"*Why boasteth thou of your death, o mighty man? The Lord God's goodness endureth for ever and your soul will be ever with Him. Amen.*"

Tom Wyatt and Mush stare at each other in mute shock. It has happened in the blink of an eye. Richard Cromwell, a giant amongst men, and their greatest friend, is dead. Mush feels as though a dagger is in his heart, and he almost chokes with grief. Then Miriam begins to chant the sacred words of the *Kaddish*. After a moment, Moses, the son of Mordecai casts aside his 'Mush' persona, and joins in.

As the alien liturgy fills the house, Will Draper goes down to reassure the servants. In his will, Richard has made a bequest to give each of them enough money to support them until they can find another position.

"Those who wish may come to us at Draper House," he says. "Work will be found for you all."

"This is a bad day, Your Lordship," Richard's matronly housekeeper says, between wracking sobs. "I am sorry. Thank God above that poor Master Thomas is long gone, for this would break his heart."

Dear Christ, Will thinks. How can I tell Tom Cromwell? The woman is quite right, and it will break his heart. The dilemma is solved for him when he returns to the chamber where Richard Cromwell is laid out. The binding woman has been, and the body is prepared for burial, whilst Miriam is busy composing a message for the king.

'Henry must be told of Richard's death," she tells her husband. "He has been a faithful servant to the king, and His Majesty will wish to know. I shall take a cog to Antwerp this very afternoon, and break the news to Master Tom. I shall stay with him until he is over the worst of it."

"I do not understand it," Mush says. He is sitting in a darkened corner, with his head in his hands. "There was no ailment. Richard did not have any sign of an illness, save for his stubborn wish to die. Can a man will himself from this world?"

"You saw," Will tells his brother in law. "It was as if he had chosen the moment. I doubt we could have done anything to stop him from dying."

"Why though?" Mush wishes to find an answer where none exists. "He was rich, and in the king's favour. His friends loved him, and his enemies feared him. He could have had another twenty years ahead of him, had he wished it."

"When Lady Jane died, so did he," Miriam says. "Love can kill just as well as a sword, and Richard's death must be laid at the king's door."

Mush knows this, and hates Henry for it. Jane Boleyn's transgressions were not enough to warrant execution, but the king could not allow her to live. She kept herself from his bed, and scorned the king's desire for her by taking other lovers. To sleep with

Richard Cromwell, and then Tom Culpeper, was to place them above Henry, in his eyes, and the insult was enough to condemn her.

"The king could have shown clemency," he says. "Had he but banished her from court, my friend would have found a way to be with her, and so stay alive. Instead, he condemns her to the axe, and loses the loyalty of his best minister. The man is a loathsome bastard, and I do not see how I can remain loyal to him."

"You must remain loyal to your family, and your friends," Miriam tells her brother. "You must see that they prosper, and that means you must show a certain face to the king. Let him feel your disgust of him, and he will destroy you. Can you pretend to love him still, brother?"

"I must," Mush replies. "Though my earnest wish is to curse him for his callowness, and slit his worthless throat."

"I know," Miriam says. She understands Henry well, and knows that his actions are the result of his overweaning desire not to look foolish. It is a hard thing to be a king, for you must seem to be perfect in every way. Let the façade slip for one moment, and all your human frailties might be exposed. "We expect the king to be all powerful, then complain when he acts on his own omnipotence. If we demand humanity from Henry, we will be sorely disappointed. The man is less than he should be, and he hides inside the shell of the king. Now he must be told of Richard's death."

"Let me take the news," Mush says. "Then I might search his face for any sign of remorse."

"Very well," Miriam agrees, "and I shall take ship for Antwerp. Master Thomas must hear this news from me, before some official broadcasts it to all and sundry."

"God's speed, sister," Mush says, "and let us get this black day behind us!"

*

The Duke of Suffolk sits by the well banked fire in Queen Kathryn's private chambers, and listens politely as one of her ladies in waiting reads from some fanciful romance that is being passed around the royal court.

"And so, the Lord Roncival did come to Castle Darkness, and seek entry," the girl reads, as she moves her finger across the printed lines. "The Dark Lord of Castle Darkness looked down from the highest tower, and saw that the knight errant had come, as the old prophesy predicted. Though it meant his doom, the evil master of the castle was loathe to give up his kingdom without a fight."

"Thrilling," the Duke of Suffolk mutters, as he stifles a treacherous yawn.

"'For prophesies can be wrongly read', the wicked tyrant thinks, 'and so allow for an escape from that fate that the Lord God has decreed'. He girds himself in his finest armour, obsidian black, and made by the very demons who stoke the ires of Hell."

"Most exciting," Suffolk says, encouragingly. "One can only wonder how poor Roncival might overcome the wicked Dark Lord. Do continue, my dearest Lady Clarissa." Suffolk's literary interest seems genuine to the lady, but she does not see that the duke's interest lies more in her slender figure, and pretty face. "You read beautifully."

"My father insisted that I lean to read and write," Lady Clarissa replies. "Though I seldom need the skill, save when I must read the queen's letters for her, or when a new romance comes to court. This Roncival is a most devout knight, I think."

"Yes, he spends his days searching out some damsel in distress, then he saves them… and then what?" Suffolk raises an eyebrow. "He saves them, and rides off into the dusk. I do not think this is as realistic as it might be. Surely, so great a hero would expect a lady's generous favours?"

"The book does not say so," Lady Clarissa says. "Sir Roncival remains chaste in all his adventures."

"Then he is a gallant fool," Suffolk mutters. "For it is only natural for a man and a woman to swap affections after some wonderful adventure is concluded."

"Yes, I see that," Clarissa says. She also sees that Charles Brandon, Duke of Suffolk, is hinting at a liaison, and she is flattered. She glances across at the only other person in the chamber, and sees that the elderly Lady Madge is dozing in her chair. "One often wonders how it would be to be *fulfilled* by some handsome rescuer."

"Is it not natural that a man and a woman might become attached… as we are through your reading tome… and thus wish to further their friendship?"

"It is, sir," Lady Clarissa replies, and wonders how long winded the duke intends to be. She is quite ready to forego much of the courting ritual. "I am sure that we are friends enough to realise how much we wish to … succour… one another. Might you have a private chamber, where I can visit you, discreetly?"

"I have a chamber but three doors down, my dear," Suffolk tells her. "Is your gallant husband at court?"

"Alas not," Clarissa replies. "He is in far off Dublin, and I am left to my own devices. Oh, how the evenings do drag on, and the nights seem soulless, and devoid of any real… fulfilment."

"Poor girl." Suffolk sighs, exquisitely. "Poor, dear, girl."

"Dear Charles."

"Might I prevail on you to…"

"Yes. I will come to you in one hour," the girl says. "My heart is overflowing with wanting, sir, and I fear you must labour hard to satisfy my desperate needs. Can any lady want for more, and wish for time to fly?"

"Oh, I shall devote my very being to giving you that satisfaction you desire," says Suffolk. He has not lain with a woman for several weeks now, and he is eager to bed Lady Clarissa, who has several glowing references from his friends. He stands, and stretches. "Goodness, but I am tired. Might I excuse myself, and retire to my private bed chamber, which is but three doors down from here?"

"Of course, My Lord. I too am tired, and think I might also be abed soon." They exchange a glance, and the deal is done. The girl will spend the night with him, and in return, he will be generous towards her. A pearl necklace or a new gown will express his gratitude, and ensure further trysts, if he should wish.

"Goodnight, Lady Clarissa," Suffolk says, loudly enough for the old lady in waiting to hear. He leaves the warm chamber, and collides with Mush Draper.

"Are you hurt?" Mush asks even as the duke staggers back.

"Damn me, Mush, but must you run about everywhere, like some capering court jester?"

"I must," Mush replies. He is quite out of breath, and he is relieved at coming upon a good friend. "We are well met, Charles, for I have need of your friendship with the king."

"How so, old friend?" Suffolk asks. "You wish me to intercede with Hal on your behalf?"

"No, no that," Mush tells him, "but rather to be there, with me, so that I might impart my news to him without fear of losing my temper."

"You intrigue me," Suffolk says. "I can attend you on the morrow. For now, I am about an assignation… of a romantic nature."

"I must beg you to come in to the king with me at once," Mush says, "for my news will not wait. I must impart it, and race to join Will at the docks. We are for France this very evening."

"As I am meant to visit Paradise," Suffolk complains. "Lady Clarissa Camberley looks favourably on me, and wishes to share my bed this very night."

"I know of the lady's lewd reputation," Mush says, without thinking. "You can rejoin the queue at any time. I doubt she will care who is next in line. One day, her husband will discover her behaviour, and he will have to call out half the men in court."

"Damn you, Mush," Suffolk

curses. If the lady is so profligate with her favours, he might just as well visit one of the sweeter whores who ply their trade in Whitehall and save himself the cost of a piece of jewellery. "What is so important that it cannot wait?"

"Richard Cromwell is dead." Mush is not one for subtlety, and he blurts out the harsh truth without any further preamble.

"Dear Christ!" Charles Brandon is stunned at the news. He has been a friend to the younger Cromwell for a dozen years, and they have diced, roistered and fought their way through many adventures. The great bear of a man was easy to love, and easy to fall out with, but always, no matter what, they would reconcile, and work together to help Tom Cromwell, and to further the cause of the Austin Friars cabal. "When… how…?"

"An hour since, and he did not die of any malady a doctor might diagnose," Mush tells the duke. "Miriam says that his heart just broke."

"I cannot believe it," Suffolk says. "The man was my rock. Whenever I weakened, or found myself at a low ebb, I would seek him out. His strength would lift me. Now he is gone… and I did not even get to say goodbye."

"Come with me," Mush urges. "Henry must be told."

"Yes, I understand," says Suffolk.

"Though I doubt the king will bemoan Richard's passing. He has only enough compassion to spend upon himself."

They walk the fifty paces down to the outer court, and enter. A few gentlemen still loiter, in the hope of some favour coming their way, but the usual hubbub has wained. The two guards on the inner door recognise the duke, and pull open the chamber's doors for them. Suffolk puts a hand on the small of Mush's back and urges him into the king's presence.

Henry is seated at a low table, with his leg propped upon several cushions. Queen Kathryn is seated next to him, and Rafe Sadler is in the third chair. The Privy councillor, and principal advisor to the monarch, is dealing out cards.

"Ho, now see here, Sadler," Henry says. "We have two more to take a hand at playing a round of 'Queens'. Come, my fine lads, and play a hand with us."

"My pleasure, Hal," Charles Brandon says, in his 'hearty' voice. "But Sir Mush Draper is with me, and I fear he has some terrible news for you."

"Is it the Scots?"

"No, sire," Mush says. "It si…"

"The French, then?"

"No, sire, I…"

"God's teeth, can it be that Calais is under attack?" Henry is quite prepared to go through everything that has ever worried him, but Queen Kathryn is a woman of a sensible nature, and she intervenes.

"Hush, my dearest one," she says to the king. "Let the poor boy speak, and so save you from guessing all night. Pray speak up, Sir Mush."

"Your Majesty, Sir Richard Cromwell is…"

"A damned swine," Henry curses. "He stays away from my court as he sees fit, and I find myself having to beg his company at dinner table… like some poor supplicant. Well, I find that I do not need his expertise as much these days. Now he is away again, I see. What excuse does he offer for his latest absence?"

"He is dead, sire," Mush says, bluntly. "He felt unwell, and took to his bed. Within the hour, he died."

"The poor man," Kathryn says, and Rafe Sadler finds that tears are pouring down his face.

"What's is this?" Henry grasps that he is in the presence of some great sadness, and he cannot understand natural grief from his minister. "Tears, Rafe? By God, but the Dick Cromwell I knew would scorn such womanly distrait. He was the only man ever to best me at arm wrestling… though I was ailing with an ague at the time. We would test ourselves with hugs, and feats of strength, until we called it quits, and the man could drink a lake of wine dry. He was like a great bear, and never a man was born who did not like the fellow. How can he be dead? I would have forbade it, had I but known. Damn me, I would have refused the Angel of Death entry into my kingdom for *his* sake." The king thinks this show of bluster will put him in a good light, but he cannot understand true sorrow, never having felt it… save for himself.

"Forgive my tears, sire," Rafe says, "but I have lost a blood brother this day. Richard Cromwell was a giant amongst men… and I loved him. The world is a lesser place without him in it."

"We must see to his funeral, gentlemen," Queen Kathryn says. "He was a loyal servant to my husband, and his passing must be well marked."

"Richard leaves a will," Mush tells her. "In it, he does specify where he is to be laid to rest, and how his fortune is to be dispersed."

"Fortune?" Henry says, and his ears prick up. The man was a Cromwell, and that means that there is money to be accounted for, or so he thinks.

"Mush uses the word advisedly," Suffolk puts in. "Dick Cromwell was the most honest of public servants, and his worth was little more than the generous salary granted by you, Hal. Though I do believe he has left you the choice of his most excellent stallions."

"Has he, by God?" Henry smiles at this. Already, he forgets the loss of his finest advisor, and wonders which horse he might find to be the best. "What a good hearted fellow. Though it would be a pity to break up his stable. Perhaps the executors might allow me to take all of the beasts, to save them the trouble of finding new homes for them… at a nominal rate, of course. Now, let us play cards."

"Forgive me, Your Majesty, but I must excuse myself," Mush says. He wishes to shout at the king, and tell him how heartless a swine he is, but he does not. "I am for France this evening, and hope to join Will Draper in the freeing of some cruelly treated Englishmen."

"Oh… that?" Henry moves on from one thing to another with ease, and the horrible affair of the fingers is already becoming a bore to him. "Yes, we must do something… something or other. So, off you go, my little monkey, and do your duty." The king turns away, and gestures for Rafe Sadler to deal out the cards again.

Mush stares at the back of Henry's neck, and sees where he might place the point of a knife. One gentle stab at the nape, and England will need a new king, he thinks. Then he shrugs, turns about, and strides out of the throne room. Henry is spared, simply because he is of so little worth as a man, and Mush would gain no honour by his death… just satisfaction.

"Damn me," Henry moans. "Did you see that, my dear?" The queen frowns, and wonders what she missed. "The fellow left my presence, without bowing. Am I then to be thus insulted?"

"No, my love," Kathryn says. "The poor fellow has lost his dearest friend, and his mind is clouded. There is no insult meant to you. The boy loves you, Henry."

"Of course not," Suffolk agrees. "You have no greater supporter than Mush Draper. Why, this very night, he sails to France, where a dozen of your most loyal men intend storming the fortress of La Rochelle."

"Damn me, Charles, but we should be with them… as I was at the two battles of the spurs… and when we broke the French outside Amiens."

"We could still catch them, sire," Rafe says, and the king blanches.

"If only," he splutters, "but no. It would make folk think I doubted the leadership ability of dear Draper. I must content myself with the time I thrashed the French, twice, and turned back the Moorish hordes with so few men."

Surrey wonders at how powerful the dose of poppy juice is this time. Henry is convinced he was at the second battle of the spurs, and even present when Will Draper and his men broke the Malatesta's brother's army in Flanders. AS for him defeating the Moors… he can only guess as to what is in the king's fevered mind.

"You have warred enough, Hal. Besides, your wound stops you from charging home. Let it heal before you lead any more forays. As for me, I fear I am just too old for it all. I am fit only for the life of a gentleman farmer these days. Though I do devote some of my time in helping those who are in need. This very evening, I am ministering to a poor soul in need of comfort."

"Really?" Henry struggles to think of his dissolute childhood friend as a philanthropist. "And does this poor lost soul have nice juicy titties, Charles?"

"My Lord!" Queen Kathryn expresses her shock loudly. "Such talk is not fit in this place, and in this company."

"Bugger it, Kathryn, but I mean no harm," the king replies. "It is just that my dear old friend always has a girl about the place. Confess to it, Charles, and name the wench."

"You do me an injustice, Hal," Suffolk says. Now I Must dash, lest they start the prayers without me."

"Yes, you are excused, Charles," Queen Kathryn says, and she takes him by the elbow and guides him to the door. She drops her voice to a whisper. "Do give Lady Clarissa my regards."

"Thank you, madam," Suffolk replies. "I shall say a prayer for you... when I am upon my knees!"

Revenge and Small Wars

Captain Stubbs guides his cog right up to the Draper Company's private jetty, and moors her fore and aft. He knows why Lady Miriam is here before her usual time, and he does not relish her task. Even so, he offers to accompany her up to the *Palais de Juis*, and help break the terrible news.

Miriam refuses his kind offer, because she understands about grief. It is an emotion of such intensity that it should be shared with as few others as possible. In her faith, it is the women who tear their clothes and throw ashes on their heads. It is the women who wail and beat their breasts.

"Master Thomas," she says, and the ageing man looks up from the ledger on his desk. "I do not know how to tell you this without causing you pain, so I must simply say it. Richard is dead."

The words hang, like a fog, over the chamber, and the silence that follows them seems to last for an eternity. At last, and with tears in his eyes, the older Cromwell speaks.

"Was he murdered?" It is the first thing that comes into Tom Cromwell's mind. There is always someone wanting to harm them, and there must be blood for blood.

"No, it was not murder," Miriam tells the shocked old man. "He simply closed his eyes and faded away. I fear he was too unhappy to carry on in this world."

"You mean his great heart was broken?" Thomas Cromwell shakes his head in disbelief. "I do not believe it. Yes, losing his dearest Lady Jane laid him low, but a man does not die for love quite so easily. Was he wasted away… or sickening for something?"

"He was not wasted away, certainly," Miriam replies. "For I sent around food from my own kitchens every day, and my serving girl reported that his servants swore he always ate it up well enough. Nor was he ailing in some malignant way."

"Then he just declined?" Cromwell asks. "Was he grey of pallor, or listless?"

"Mush tells me that he would often take to his bed, as if exhausted," Miriam says. "The last time I saw him, he was ashen faced, and listless. I fear that his lost love must have drained him."

"Just so, my dear," Cromwell agrees. "How else can a man of such stature be brought down so low? Is there a will to be read… or instructions to be followed?"

"There is," says Miriam, "but the instructions are so concise that there is no room for misinterpretation. Rafe Sadler tells me that his children are well cared for, and that even the king is to be the recipient of a fine stallion."

"What about his papers?" Cromwell asks. It is obvious that so well placed a man must have important documents and secret files in his possession.

"Richard appoints a certain Master *Tomas Cornelis* as the executor of his remaining estate," Lady Miriam tells him. "That means all of his papers are yours to dispose of as you wish."

"That is for the best," Cromwell says. "I dare say that my nephew lists down his many contacts, and has details of secret things which are best kept within the family. Can you arrange for everything to be sent here to me, as soon as possible?"

"Of course." Miriam finds it hard to say that which is in her heart. "I loved Richard like a brother, Master Tom, and I know that he was like a second son to you. It is a sad thing when we outlive our own children. Shall I stay and keep you company?"

"No, I would rather sit here in silent contemplation, my dear." Cromwell wipes the tears from his eyes with the cuff of his sleeve. "Let me mourn in solitude. You must be tired."

"I am." Miriam is, in truth, exhausted from the events of the day, and the unexpected sea voyage, and now, she longs for her bed. "If you are sure…?"

"Off to your bed, my sweet girl," Cromwell tells her. Then he raises a hand to have her wait a moment. "If Richard was as like to a son to me, then you are my daughter. I can love you no better. There, it is said… now be gone, and rest yourself. Tomorrow will be another busy day."

Miriam withdraws, and Cromwell sighs at the terrible news she brings to him. Then he picks up a tiny bell that sits on the edge of his desk, and tinkles it twice. After a moment, the door opens, and two men come in. Kel Kelton, when not about Cromwell's business, is to be found in an adjacent room, waiting for his master's instructions. This evening, he is with company, for Alonso Gomez, who seems to be in the employ of everyone of any worth, is here to report to Thomas Cromwell.

"Master?" Kel asks. "What is it?"

"Richard is dead."

"*Madre mio*!" Alonson Gomez curses. "How was it done… by some treacherous ambush? Señor Richard is not so easily caught out."

"He died in his bed, of a broken heart," Cromwell tells them, and Kel Kelton snorts with disbelief.

"No, sir… that cannot be."

"He is a great man," Gomez agrees. "Such fellows do not pine away."

"My thoughts exactly," Thomas Cromwell says to the pair. "I want you to go to England, and find out why my nephew is dead. If, indeed, it is from a heart that is broken, I must accept that diagnosis, but if it is not, then I must have the entire truth of the matter. I cannot accept Richard's death at face value. You understand?"

"Yes, sir," Kel replies. "I shall sail at once."

"And I shall be with you," Alonso Gomez says to him. "If Richard is dead, I too must know the reason why."

"Thank you, Gomez," Thomas Cromwell says, sincerely. "Do not let Miriam, or any of the others find out what we are about. I do not wish to cause upset without just cause. They will see that the proper homage is paid to my dear, dead, boy, and that he has the finest funeral ever seen in London, whilst you two will attend to the seamier business, with discretion."

"Señor, I shall be like a shadow," Alonso Gomez replies. "We shall discover the truth for you, and see that all is well."

*

Rob Buffery is in his fortieth year, and too old for such capers, but when the call comes to help Will Draper storm one of the most impregnable fortresses in France, he takes down his broadsword from above the fireplace and hones a fresh edge onto the blade. He kisses his woman goodbye, and bids her look after his thriving Cambridgeshire inn well in his absence. She knows well enough that it is impossible to dissuade him, and just offers up a silent prayer for his safe return.

The brawnily built ex soldier makes straight for the quayside in Tilbury, where he knows that Miriam Draper's sleekest cog awaits his arrival. The huge figure of Captain Jeremiah Cord is standing at the gangplank, and he waves in welcome.

"Good day to you, Master Buffery," he growls. "The sky looks black to the east, and our sailing master thinks we might hit a little foul weather in the Bay of Biscay. I hope you have good sea legs."

"Do not worry on my account, Captain Cord," the soldier cum inn keeper replies, with a broad grin on his face. "I have crossed the English Channel a score or more times, and in the most turbulent weather. Are our troops already assembled?"

"If you call a dozen men a troop, then yes," Cord tells him. "Apart from we two, there is General Will, Captain Mush, Colonel Beckshaw, and that strange poetic fellow, Tom Wyatt. Then there are my volunteers from the Examiners. Six men, all sergeants with experience behind them."

"Twelve of us?" Rob Buffery frowns at this news. He knows about La Rochelle, and doubts the garrison is less than six hundred men strong. "Then the odds are only fifty to one against us. I dare say we might cope, if we pray hard enough."

"Have faith, Master Buffery," Jeremiah Cord replies. "General Draper has a plan. We will triumph, no matter what the odds."

"Ah, a plan," Rob says. "I do love a good plan. Pray, explain it to me."

"Oh, I do not yet know what is in the general's mind, but I am sure it will be something quite brilliant."

"Of course." Rob Buffery recalls previous skirmishes he has fought in the company of Will Draper, and he seems to recollect that tricking the enemy into attacking his own hidden cannon, or concealed cavalry, plays a large part in the man's military planning. The idea of throwing a dozen armed men against a fortress manned by a regiment of the best French troops seems like one of his least cogent ideas.

"I suppose we must do our best to save these poor prisoners," Jeremiah Cord says. "These French are such dogs to do what they do."

"You mean cutting off their fingers?" Rob Buffery gives a shrug. "We cut of a man's hands for coin clipping, or stealing a king's deer, but why take the fingers, yet leave the thumbs? What use is that?"

"Yes, General Will agonises over that too," Jeremiah replies. "He thinks there must be some intricate plot behind it all, and he worries at not knowing what is afoot."

"Or 'a hand'," Rob Buffery says,

and they both laugh at the jest. "I suppose there is only one way to discover the truth of the matter, and that is to storm the walls of La Rochelle, overcome hundreds of heavily armed soldiers, and free the English prisoners. Then we can ask them why they had to forfeit their fingers."

"Just so," says Jeremiah Cord. "It's a rum business, and no mistake."

"Did you hear about Dick Cromwell?"

"No, what about him?" Cord asks. "I once arm wrestled him, you know. I would have won, but my elbow slipped, and the bastard refused to let me try again."

"He's dead."

"What?" Jeremiah Cord considers this for a while, then curses. "Damn me, then I'll never get a re-match, and I must confess… my elbow did not slip as I said. The man beat me fair and square."

"That is a most gracious confession, Captain Cord." Will Draper is behind them, and his approach is as silent as a cat stalking its prey. "Richard Cromwell was quite the bravest, and the strongest, man I have ever known."

"No offence, General Will," Cord says, as he comes to a smart attention. "Men such as him and me… well, we like to rattle each other's cages, and goad one another into feats of strength. If I lost to him at arm wrestling, I might triumph at jousting, or fighting with a stave. Now I shall never have the chance to try him out. He was no great age, sir, and I must ask - what was it that bested him?"

"Love," Will Draper says. "It seems he did die of a broken heart."

"Women, eh?" Rob Buffery growls. "Was ever a one worth it… even since Eden?"

"Saving my own dear wife," Will replies. "I suspect not."

"Your wife is different," Buffery tells Will. "I saw that the first time I met her, back when she was out and about, delivering her own wine. Lady Miriam is, by our stupid English laws, less than a man, but far more than any woman. I wager you thank God daily for her taking you on as her husband, General Will."

"You put it so well, Rob," Will answers, with a wry smile. "She makes my fortune for me, employs one half of London, and feeds the other half. She can calculate a profit, speak Latin and French, and bargain in six other languages, yet any common shepherd has more legal rights than she."

"We live in a strange world, sir," Jeremiah Cord says. "Why, this very day, we set sail to sort out the puzzle of why honest Englishmen lie in French dungeons, with their fingers stolen from them."

"By order of the king," Will says,

"and that is all we need to know."

"Why then does Henry not send Norfolk and his thousands against the fortress?" Jeremiah Cord likes a good fight, but cannot understand why the odds are so uneven. At that moment Tom Wyatt comes running down the quayside, with a dozen men in pursuit of him. The poet reaches the gangplank, and turns to face those who give chase.

"Thomas," Will says, and slips a hand to the sword at his belt. "Who are these friends of yours?"

"Brothers, cousins and the husband of a certain lady... a lady who assured me her spouse was in Ireland for another month," the poet says.

> *"Tho' oft we lay and loved so well,*
> *our tryst was known, and truth to tell,*
> *the husband knew, and his anger grew,*
> *until he swore to run me through."*

Will Draper sighs at his friend's almost suicidal love life, and motions to both Cord and Buffery. They move out to right and left, and so form a formidable shield between the poet and his pursuers.

"Good sirs," Will calls to them, "I well understand the anger you all feel at the way my friend here has debauched a married lady, and I am here to offer a solution to this situation. Is the offended husband here?"

"That I am, sir," says a man who looks like a professional soldier. He is a little under six feet in height, and is of a muscular build. "The name is Fairfax, and this lecherous rogue has been swiving my dear wife for many long weeks."

"Not against her will, I suppose?" Will says to the man. "For she has not complained of his attentions, I believe."

"You seek to insult me, sir?"

"No, I simply seek to inform you that it takes two to make a man into a cuckold." Will sees his jaw clench, and one hand slip to his sword hilt. "I believe you have a just complaint against Thomas Wyatt, but these other gentlemen do not. I cannot allow them to fall on my friend unjustly. Let them withdraw, and you may challenge our adulterous poet, man to man."

"Or are you scared of me?" Tom Wyatt puts in, rather unhelpfully. Sir Rupert Fairfax roars in anger, and draws his sword.

"Back, my friends," he commands. "Let no man interfere in this business. Draw, poet, and let us settle this, man to man."

"First blood?" Tom Wyatt asks the man. The matter is a serious one, but not one of such magnitude that it needs to result in the death of one or the other.

"Very well… first blood," Fairfax agrees, and Tom Wyatt reaches inside his doublet. A moment later, he withdraws his hand and flicks his wrist in one fluid motion. The leather covered sap, filled with lead, smacks Fairfax in the face, and brings fresh blood to his nostrils.

"My victory, I believe," the poet says. "Now, be about your business, sir. Your wife is not one to be left alone, and you should either spend more time at home, or have her put into a nunnery."

"You cheat, sir!" Fairfax snarls, as he dabs at the free flowing blood. "You are no gentleman."

"Sir, a gentleman would not have swived your wife," Will Draper tells him. "Now, the course is run, and you must withdraw. If your followers wish to contest this with us, I must warn them that I have a company of men within whistling distance. They are not gentlemen either, and will not consider the niceties of 'first blood' as they do slaughter."

"Come away, Fairfax," one of the wiser heads calls. "We do not want a bloodbath over that faithless wife of yours."

"Damn you, cousin… do you hold honour so cheap then?"

"Hers, yes," someone says from the rear of the small crowd, and several men laugh. Fairfax makes as if to draw his sword, then turns on his heel and strides away. His humiliation is complete, and it is his wife who will suffer from his anger.

"You have made a bad enemy there, Master poet," Jeremiah Cord says. "He will not rest until he has his revenge.

Yes, he is a bad enemy."

"Are there are any 'good' enemies to make, Captain Cord?" Wyatt replied, and he runs up the short gangplank. "I do not see your company of men, Will. I hope you were not lying to poor Fairfax."

"Oh, shut up, you damned fool," says Will Draper. The poet's flippancy ires him, so close to his friend's death. He wishes to mourn, but instead, he must put his sorrow aside for the king's sake. "We must be under way soon. My agents tell me that the best time to strike at La Rochelle is three days from now."

"Really?" The poet is surprised by this, as the fortress is unlikely to throw open its gates at that time. "Has Mistress Pru made one of her marvellous predictions?"

Something like that," Will tells the poet, with a wide grin on his face. "Now, let us bid our captain get underway. I am getting too old for these adventures, and would prefer to have this one concluded without more ado!"

"Would that Richard was with us," the poet says with deep sincerity. "For never was there a man like him in a scrap. In battle he was worth twenty good men, and his friendship was as like a wall of steel about those he chose to call 'friend'."

"We shall all miss him sorely," Jeremiah Cord agrees. "And that fierce blackamore too. For when Ibrahim the

Moor and Master Cromwell stood beside me, we were nigh unbeatable."

"He is a week into his voyage to the New Found Land by now," Tom Wyatt says. "I hope his horses fare well, and soon populate the new lands with their equine off spring."

In his heart, the poet wishes he were going to the land discovered by Cabot, years before, and claimed for England, rather than to La Rochelle, and he envies Ibrahim his adventure.

*

Captain Isaiah Hawk knows how to handle a ship and her crew, and he has been one of the famous Draper Company captains for almost ten years now. His devotion to Lady Miriam, and the sprawling empire that is the Draper Company is unquestioned, and his skill in navigating dangerous waters is renowned amongst his peers. He is familiar with all of the seas from France, down to the African coast, and even into those dangerous waters governed by the Ottoman Turkish Empire.

So, when he is commanded to sail across the vast Atlantic, in search of the New Found Land, he shows not a hint of the dismay he feels at the quest. It is only now, three days out of port that his worries begin to mount. He and the other four captains in the small flotilla are under the overall command of Ibrahim ben Rachid, a soldier of fortune, and confidant of Lady Miriam.

Everything about the man is strange, Hawk thinks, not just his ebony coloured skin, or exotic way of talking. He sometimes refers to himself as 'Prince Ibrahim' and changes his name like others might change their doublet. He uses both '*ben*' and '*äl*', as he sees fit, when both mean much the same.

"I prefer the Hebrew '*ben*' when not amongst infidels, and I adopt the '*äl*' if I fall in with those followers of a more rabid form of Islam," he explains glibly, if pressed. Hawk does not like the fellow, at first, but if Lady Miriam trusts the handsome black man, then her ship's captains must too.

It seems, according to the Moor, that there is to be a change of plan. Lady Miriam has never had any intention of settling in the New Found Land again. Instead, according to Ibrahim, she has a better plan… a scheme that will actually result in a vast profit for all concerned.

"Damn me, Lord Ibrahim," Joseph Cottershaw curses. He is in command of *The Primrose*, a sleek twenty gunner meant to offer protection to Hawk's much bigger, yet slower, craft, *The Prince Edward*. "Why does not Lady Miriam trust us? To have us think we are off to the Americas, and then have us change course for Tangiers is a strange business indeed."

"Not so, Captain Cottershaw," Ibrahim lies smoothly. "She fears that spies might guess our plans, and so she gives out that we are bound for the New World. Thus we are free to set sail for our true destination unhindered... the Barbary Coast."

"But why?" Noah Bright asks. He commands *The Seagull,* another man o'war. "*The Prince Edward* is a merchantman, filled with trade goods, farming tools, soldiers, and supplies. She carries fifty excellent horses... both mares and stallions. I can see why *The Seagull*, *The Primrose*, *The Seafarer*, and *The Royal Jane* might prove their worth on the Barbary Coast, but Captain Hawk, though the best seaman amongst us, is not rigged to fight off marauding Corsairs."

"Nor will he have to," Ibrahim explains, as if the plan was Miriam's own. He has failed once when trying to establish a settlement in the New Found Land, and he has no wish to lose many more lives trying to prove there is an easy, navigable, western passage to far off Cathay. "We are going to the free port of Tangiers, where we will trade our horses for gold, and barter away all of the supplies we now carry. The port struggles to import decent cannon and muskets, because of the disruption caused by the wicked and vicious Barbary Coast

Corsairs."

"Will not those very same pirates seek to stop us?" Captain Hawk gives voice to an obvious flaw in Ibrahim's thinking. "Might they not fall on us, and plunder our wares?"

"If they knew of our coming," the Moor tells the gathered captains. "We have the element of surprise on our side, and we will sail into Tangiers harbour, unopposed."

"Where we sell our wares, and make a fine profit, no doubt," Captain Noah Bright says, somewhat caustically. "Then what?"

"We offer our services to the city," Ibrahim the Moor explains. "Lady Miriam commands me to hire our fleet out as mercenaries, with the intent of ridding the infamous Barbary Coast of its piratical curse. We shall become the Tangiers own navy… for a price. Lady Miriam thinks we might make a fine bargain… charging either by the month, or by each Corsair raider we sink."

"These pirate ships number in their hundreds," Captain Hawk complains. "We are but one merchantman, and four middling sized men 'o war. In any sea battle we would be surrounded and taken with ease."

Ibrahim has his answers ready. Behind the great lie, that he acts for Miriam draper, he can expand on a scheme that he has thought about ever since the expedition to the New Found Land was mooted to him, some months before.

The sale of the English fleet's cargoes in Tangiers will raise about three thousand pounds, and the horses another thousand. The money is to be used to purchase such exotic goods as can only be found along the North African coast. Unusual timber, spices, the mysterious *Khat* leaf which induces euphoria, when chewed, precious jewels mined in Abyssinia, and rare trinkets made by Nubian women on the banks of the mighty Nile. The three or four thousand will be worth thirty times the amount, once back in England or, perhaps, the port of Antwerp.

It all sounds quite wonderful to the five experienced captains, who envisage generous shares all around… except for one problem.

"We can probably get into Tangiers easily enough," Hawk comments, voicing the fear of every man there, "but will not these roving Corsairs hear of our venture, and be watching for us when we leave the port?"

"I hope so," Ibrahim ben Rachid replies. "For our plan depends on their wish to plunder our ships, and on their greed," the Moor says. "They have no single leader… these wild Corsairs… but stalk the Barbary Coast either alone, or in pairs. Each pirate ship has its own small harbour, which they jealously guard, even against their fellow pirates. We must draw them out, piecemeal, and destroy them."

"For pay?" Captain Noah Bright asks. "We risk our ships, and our lives, for a few silver coins each week?"

"And for the Corsair bounty," Ibrahim tells him, with a smile, and a sly wink of the eye. "These rogues do not trust one another, and keep their plunder to themselves. I wager that most of these ships keep their treasure in their own holds. Once we capture one of them, their treasure becomes our very own property. Imagine how rich we will become if each pirate has the plunder of several months in them."

"And if we are beaten?" Hawk is careful over giving his full support, for he is a merchantman, and his ship is not rigged for a sea battle.

"Most of these pirate crafts are nothing more than captured merchant ships, crudely converted by having a few cannon mounted on their decks. They lack speed, and most can only boast a half dozen cannon and a fighting complement of fifty, or sixty men. Most of the crews are renegade Spaniards, outlawed Venetians, and Egyptians. They seek to inspire terror in their poor victims, but have little stomach for a real fight."

"You seem knowledgeable about

these rogues," Hawk says.

"I was a captive amongst them for a full year,"the Moor lies, smoothly. He was first mate on a Corsair raider for the year, and only left to accept a better offer from an evil minded Spanish cardinal. "I escaped, and made my way to England. May God bless Lady Miriam for setting me on a righteous path."

"Amen," the captains murmur, and the new plan is accepted. If Ibrahim speaks for the Draper Company, then they must follow his lead.

*

Kel Kelton attends the funeral of Richard Cromwell, with Alonso Gomez by his side. They make a pretty pair, and they are avoided by most of the mourners, who do not know of Cromwell's life when not playing the loyal courtier. They see two cold hearted killers, and they are not far wrong.

The mourners are few, because most of them are spread about the world on Draper Company business. However, Lady Miriam, and Richard's cousin, Sir Gregory Cromwell, the Baron Cromwell of Oakham since 1540, have arranged a fine send off for the giant fellow.

The service is strictly Church of England, and it is soon over with. Then Richard's remains are placed in the church of Saint Peter and Paul. Bags of copper coin are scattered from the tower of the church, so that they cascade down onto the hundreds of poor Londoners below, as if from Heaven.

At each street corner, Lady Miriam arranges for huge tureens of hot soup, and fresh baked bread, to be waiting for any who wish to eat. The food is all free, and in return the hungry folk of London need only offer up a short prayer for Richard Cromwell's soul.

The small procession of mourners, no more than fifty in number, proceed down Peter Street to the waterfront, where barges are waiting to convey them to Draper House. The five craft cover the distance in a stately, almost silent procession. Once at the private Draper jetty, the guests arrange themselves, without thinking, into the order of their importance to the proceedings, and their stature within the court, and they troop up the long lawn to the great hall.

Most imminent amongst them is Queen Katheryn, who represents her uncaring husband, and beside her, the Duke of Suffolk, who wishes to honour his friend.He is the foremost nobleman, because the Duke of Norfolk knows better than to show his face at the funeral of a man who has been such an enemy over the years.

After them comes Sir John Russell, Sir Rafe Sadler and Eustace Chapuys, who is visiting England, much against his own master's wishes.

"I could not stay away, my dear," he tells Miriam who is beside him in the procession. They link one another affectionately, and in mutual grief. "I see that Gregory is here with his wife. The boy is doing well for himself. Not yet twenty three years old, and he owns half of Leicestershire, and ten thousand sheep."

"I think his love match helps," Miriam says, shrewdly. "His marriage to Jane Seymour's sister makes him close kin to the king, and it saved him when his father fell from grace."

"You English are a cruel race," Chapuys mutters, and she smiles.

"I am not English, Eustace," she reminds him. "Though my children are, through their father."

The group come into the great hall, where a funeral feast is laid out for the mourners. It is a 'help yourself' banquet, but the queen cannot be seen to serve herself. Miriam and Pru hurry forward to seat her, and see she is served, so that the others may also eat.

The guests break up into smaller groups, and exchange stories of the man they knew, either of his bravery, his strength, or the kindness he always showed to those he loved well.

"Farewell, old friend." Suffolk raises a glass into the air, and proposes a toast. "May you be in Heaven long before the devil knows you are dead!"

*

In one corner Kel Kelton and Alonso Gomez consider how best to proceed with their own investigation. They are charged with finding a murderer, and are eager to get on with the task.

"The body bore no marks of violence," the Spaniard says. "Nor was he convulsed. Richard spoke of his own death many months before, and seemed to welcome it. His strength began to wane from that moment on. Could he have been poisoned?"

"How?" Kel asks. "There were none of the signs… discoloured skin, fetid odours and contortion of the features."

"If given in a large, single dose, poison can do such things, but administered in small amounts?"

"Dear Christ, but that may be it. Though who might have access for such a wicked scheme?"

The Spaniard shrugs his shoulders, but he will find out, and then there will be Hell to pay for someone.

*

Lady Miriam cannot believe Richard is dead, and she wishes her husband, her brother, or even Ibrahim was there with her. Each man is away for different reasons, and she must cope alone.

It is then that she notices the two men
lurking in the quiet corner, and beckons
over Chapuys.

"I see them, Miriam," he says.
"They claim to be mourners, but I fear they
are looking for revenge. Gomez swears not,
and I must seem to believe him, for he was
ever loyal to me."

"I am almost past caring," Miriam
says. "As the Draper Company grew, I
thought we would turn away from violence,
and grow into respectability, but it will not
happen in our lifetime. Perhaps our children
will reap the benefits?"

"Violence and intrigue are with us
still," the old diplomat agrees, yet he
dissembles, for that very day, he has used
his influence to aid Will Draper in his own
appointed task. Rafe Sadler saunters over,
as if to pass the time of day with Miriam,
but his voice drops to a whisper.

"Lady Miriam… Robin Askey, the
king's squire, tells me that Surrey has been
boasting, whilst drunk, about a great plot he
has undertaken. Robin cannot find out what,
but worries that it was spoken of only the
day after Richard died."

"God's teeth!" Chapuys curses. "If
Norfook's son is involved…"

"It might be some plot to defraud
the navy for all we know," Miriam says. "I
shall advise Will, on his return, but for now,
we should let Kelton and Gomez seek out

the truth, and see what they uncover."

"My lips are sealed," Chapuys says.

"As are mine," Rafe adds. "Let us hope they find proof positive, and do not pass sentence without a trial!"

11 Conclusions and Verdicts

The lone merchantman seems to be in trouble, and the Corsair, a converted cargo ship with two cannon strapped onto her deck closes in for the capture. The ship has lost the wind, and lies at the mercy of the oncoming sea wolf.

"Hold steady, Master Mate," Captain Hawk says to the man crouching at the rail. "Let them come alongside before we reveal ourselves."

The Corsair sees that their quarry is done for, and sweeps alongside, ready to board. It is only in the last moment that the pirate captain sees the trap. Another ship, sleeker and faster, appears from behind the headland, and cuts off their retreat, whilst armed men spring up on the becalmed merchantman, armed to the teeth.

The fight is brutal, bloody, and one sided. Caught between two enemy ships, the Corsair is soon overwhelmed, and Ibrahim ben Rachid boards her to the cheers of his own crews. A victorious admiral is a loved admiral, and the plunder from this, and another four pirate ships is enough to make them all wealthy men.

The Corsair captain, a renegade Spaniard from a rich family, is spared for later ransom, but the rest of the pirates are hanged from their own masts, as required by the Tangiers Council who pay the English fleet's wages.

Ibrahim, once Prince of Kush, and now Lord Admiral of the Fleet, is pleased with this last victory, for he has lost no men, and only two in the whole campaign, and gained considerable wealth. The hold of the Corsair ship is filled with gold and silver coins, captured from an Ottoman Turkish slaver, but the day before.

The treasure, meant to be used to purchase slaves from the Tangiers market will now go towards saving the Moors neck when he sails home. He disobeys Miriam's orders, and for that, she may well demand he be tried for piracy and theft of her fleet.

Instead, he returns home with over one hundred thousand pounds in gold, silver and precious spices. Her share, as owner, will come to fifty thousand, whilst he can expect to clear twenty five for himself. Each captain shall have a thousand, and each crew member a hundred… or ten years wages for three months work.

Even the burgesses of Tangiers will rejoice, as the power of the Barbary pirates is broken for the next year or two, and they can expect good trading times ahead. Furthermore, the free port will employ four English volunteers who will help train the new Tangiers navy in the art of loading and firing cannon, and seamanship.

The English fleet shall return home with letters of commendation from the Tangiers authorities to both the Draper Company, and to to their beloved ally, Henry, King of England, France and Ireland. The king will rejoice, as the title confirms his claim to the French throne by another power.

"Well lads, are we ready for home waters?" the Moor asks, and the crew acclaim him again.

"We are, Admiral Ibrahim," Captain Hawk says, softly, "where I shall enjoy watching you try to explain matters to Lady Miriam. You lie well, sir, but not well enough to fool an old hand such as I."

"Perhaps not, Captain Hawk, but if I end up dangling on a rope's end, then so shall you. The others believed my lies, and still do, whilst you knew all along. Why did you not stop me at once?"

"I was but one ship."

"Had you voiced your fears, or even demanded to see my letters of commission, the others would have put me in irons at once. How will you have it, Hawk… watch me hang beside you, or support me, and live to spend your gold?"

"Oh, I will speak up for you, sir," Hawk says. "I will say you led us to Tangiers only because of adverse weather, and the unwillingness of the crew to sail across the ocean… for a price."

"Your share will be enough to buy your own merchant ship, ten times over, Hawk," Ibrahim replies. "How much gold does a man need?"

"Enough to fund a share in the next voyage to the New Found Land," Hawk says.

"Then you are a fool, for there is no passage to Cathay that way." the Moor says, smiling at the captain's foolishness.

"No, but there is timber to be had, and furs," Hawk says, "and land. So much land that every farmer in England could have a thousand acres, and still it will not run out. Then there will be silver and gold to mine. The natives will know where to look."

"You mean it?"

"I met this Spaniard," Hawk replies. "His tales convinced me. I am for the New World, if Lady Miriam will only let me buy a share."

"Then I shall invest my money too," Ibrahim says. "I shall buy a double share, and sell one out in hundredth parts to any of our crews who will sail with us."

"Then you really would go again?" Captain Hawk is bemused, for the man was not for travelling so far abroad before.

"You are the steadiest man I know, Hawk," Ibrahim says. "I doubt we can find a western passage to the East, but who cares? The land will provide everything you say it will. If you and I think it can be done, then it can be done, and we will all become as rich as kings!"

*

Miriam Draper's single masted cog bobs up and down on the waves outside the harbour. The crew use a drag anchor to keep the craft in place, whilst Will Draper and his small band of men make their final arrangements to invade the great fortress of La Rochelle.

"Remember that we are not here to fight," Will tells his men. "If we must, we must, but the plan does not call for it. We can do this without violence."

"Most commendable," Tom Wyatt says, "but I doubt that the French garrison will open their gates and invite us in."

On the contrary, my friend," Will Draper replies with a wry smile on his face. "That is exactly what I expect them to do. In the chest you sit on, there are a dozen uniforms of the French Royal Arquebusiers Regiment. We will dress ourselves up in them, and march right up to the front gate. Those of us who speak French will deal with the guards. I have a forged document which instructs us to reinforce the garrison in their hour of need."

"Their hour of need, you say?" Mush is as puzzled as the rest of the small company.

"Yes for, with luck, most of the French garrison will be marching down the coast to defend the town of Rochefort from attack." Will sees the blank looks on their faces and grins at their confusion. "Some days ago, Eustace Chapuys contrived to have a letter he meant for the Holy Roman ambassador in Paris to go astray. The French have it, and within, he mentions seeing many ships being made ready to land troops in France again… at Rochefort to be exact. A dozen of Miriam's cogs, and several merchantmen are anchored off the coast, but in plain view, to support the tale."

"Will they believe it?" Tom Wyatt asks.

"Think about it. Information from the Holy Roman Emperor's man in England, then a fleet showing up. Besides, my agents have been spreading rumours of such an attack for the last week. The French are feeling very clever just now, after Norfolk's poor showing. They will think to lay a trap for our army as it lands, and destroy it."

"Then we are at an advantage, providing they fall for it," Mush says.

"The colonel in charge of the troops in Rochefort will see the fleet, and believe it," says Will, "and he will send for help. the nearest available men are inside La Rochelle. The fortress's commander dare not ignore such a plea, and I think we will find the place stripped of every fighting man he has, save for a few men to guard the gate, and their prisoners."

"Yes, I think it will work," Jeremiah Cord puts in, "which means we miss out on a good fight, sir. The lads will be disappointed."

"I hope so," Will replies. "Once inside, we must seek out the English captives, and take them down to the harbour, where our cog will be waiting to take them all aboard. Any questions?"

"What if the commander of the fortress refuses to help Rochefort?" Tom Wyatt asks.

"And risk the anger of King François" Will says. "I think not."

"True enough," Tom Wyatt concedes. "He was furious at the recent reverses, when his army ran away like rabbits. If any of his men ever do the same again, he will have them torn apart between wild horses. It is an unpleasant death, and one that must distress the horses!"

"The Chevalier de Angoulins is renowned as a brave, though pedantic, commander of troops, and he will obey a request for urgent military aid. He will also leap at the chance of crossing swords with the Duke of Norfolk's soldiers," Will continues. "By the time he realises he has been duped, we will be back at sea again, and making for Tilbury under full sail."

"There are too many 'ifs' and 'buts' for my liking," Rob Buffery grumbles, "but if you think it a good plan, General Will, I shall be at your side all of the way."

"Trust me," the Examiner General says, "for what could possibly go wrong?"

*

The Chevalier de Angoulins is at the head of his six hundred and fifty troops, and within easy marching distance of Rochefort, when a deputation of prominent citizens from the town come galloping towards him. They are the bearers of some very interesting news.

"The English fleet is gone, sir," the leader of the deputation informs the Chevalier. "A sudden squall blew up, and they sailed away as it struck."

"And the *Duc de Norfook's* army?" the Chevalier de Angoulins demands. "Are they ashore, and fortifying a camp?"

"They never landed, sir," the same man replies, joyfully. "Our town is spared!"

"Or this promised invasion is a wild fancy," Angoulins says. "Then I must return to La Rochelle and resume my usual duties. Though I regret not having the chance to fight against the renowned *Norfook* and his troops."

The order is given, and the entire force turns about in the muddy road, and begins the short march back to their heavily under-manned fortress.

*

"What have you discovered?" Alonso Gomez asks Kel Kelton. The Englishman is less noticeable than the Spaniard, who actually looks like the evil cut throat that he is, so can ask questions without arousing too much suspicion.

"Only as much as we already know," Kelton complains. "Richard Cromwell was beloved by all, save those who count as his enemies, and most of them are already dead, or in hiding. Only the Howard family still bear him any serious ill will. Both Norfolk and Surrey hated him with a vengeance, but their recent attempts at bringing him down have all failed, miserably. In fact, the king will not listen to anything these two lords have to say, these days."

"Then you think it is one of them who has murdered him?" Gomez asks. Kel Kelton can only shrug his shoulders at this, for he has no idea if either man is implicated or not, or even of how the wicked deed was done.

"All we know, for sure, is that Cromwell took to his bed, and announced his own death… as if he had some foreknowledge of the deed."

"Yes, that is so," the Spaniard replies. Then he curses under his breath. "Here comes my old master, Chapuys. I love the man like a father, but I cannot have him meddle in our business. He is a man of high morals, and he will seek to dissuade me from my mission of revenge."

"Good day to you, gentlemen," Chapuys calls. "I trust you are both well?"

"Well enough, My Lord

Ambassador," Kel replies, and the little Savoyard shakes an admonishing finger at him.

"I am no longer an ambassador, my dear Kel," he says. "You must call me either Chapuys, or Eustace... as is your desire. Now, what is afoot, my fine fellows? You both look like conspirators against something or other, and I cannot help but wonder at your strange pairing. Can it be that a certain gentleman in Antwerp has put you together for a most important purpose?"

"No sir, we are but friends who have been thrown together for no good reason. Our only intent is to find some comfortable inn, and drink to the memory of poor Master Richard Cromwell." Alonso Gomez is uncomfortable with the lie, and Chapuys nods his head at the obvious falsehood.

"Then you are not for discovering the truth behind poor Richard's strange death then?" the Savoyard says, and he notes the look on Kelton's face. "I am not atall convinced it was natural causes."

"You perceive our mission then?" Kel says, and Chapuys nods his assent.

"Of course. Tom Cromwell cannot accept this ridiculous tale of his nephew dying of a broken heart. Poor Richard was often sick these last months... weak, and often tired. I think it was one of two things... both using poison. He either killed himself, or someone killed him. I do not believe that dearest Richard would destroy his immortal soul by an act of self murder. You have a suspect?"

"We think it either Norfolk, or his son." Kel admits this, but doubts he can give any proof.

"I do not doubt that either would kill Richard if they could," Chapuys says, "but they do not have access to the kitchens, do they? I mean to say, who would have access to Richard's food, and not be suspected?"

"We know not," Gomez admits. "If it is poison, he either drank it, or ate it."

"Then you must look to his household servants for an answer," Chapuys says. He cannot have his old servant arrested for trying to kill dukes and earls, and he hopes his advice will keep the two men occupied until Will Draper returns from his own mission in France. "See who is a recent addition to the staff, or find out if anyone has been dismissed in the last month or two. Speak to the most trusted of them, and ask who they might suspect. Build a case, my friends, and then bring it to the King's Examiner for justice."

"Richard's people have been with him for years," Kel says. "Most are from the old Austin Friars days, and they love him like a son. They are all loyal to him."

"Perhaps one was not," says

Chapuys. "Perhaps they are indebted to *Norfook* and thus compelled to do his bidding. Or they might simply have taken a bribe. Yes, I know… his people are better than that, but what if one of the serving wenches has a new swain, and that new swain is a *Norfook* agent? You see what I mean? There are many avenues to search down, my friends. So, search away, and may God be with you."

"What if it was not poison?" Kel asks.

"Oh, he was poisoned," Eustace Chapuys tells them. "Whilst the body was laid out, and ready to be embalmed, I brought in a physician… a clever fellow known to a certain gentleman in Antwerp, and he did an examination of all the vital organs."

"Dear Christ!" Gomez crosses himself at such an act. "It is an unholy thing to do to any man, dead or alive, master."

"Perhaps, but it threw up some strange things," Chapuys continues. "For instance, the lining of the stomach was scoured, as if subjected to some caustic potion. The liver was almost black, and the heart was much enlarged, as if treated with something quite acrid."

"What does this mean?" Gomez asks.

"It means he was poisoned, but over a long time," Chapuys says. "The stuff worked away at him like an evil spirit, killing him inch by inch." The Savoyard opens his purse, and counts out thirty small, silver coins. He hands them to Gomez, who can only nod his head in understanding.

No words need to be spoken, for it is an old custom where he comes from. The thirty pieces of silver are to be stuffed in the mouth of this Judas, as the sentence is carried out.

"Ben Greyson is the cook. He worked for Cardinal Wolsey, years ago."

"You suspect him?" Chapuys asks, and Kel shakes his head.

"No, I do not. Why would he want to harm his master?" he tells the thoughtful Savoyard. "Richard paid him handsomely, and they would often spend the long evenings drinking wine, and swapping tales of their past. Ben could easily poison Richard's food whenever he wished, but I doubt he ever would."

"Then who else can we look at?" Chapuys demands of them. "His death cannot go unavenged, for obvious reasons."

"Obvious, master?" Gomez is a dangerous, and shrewd man, but the vagaries of these English intrigues can often leave him quite confounded. "In what way do you mean?"

"If Richard's death goes unpunished, then whomsoever is responsible will think themselves and their wicked deed to be undetected. This will encourage the fellow to widen his net, and destroy all of his enemies by the same process. He has someone within our circle of trusted people, and that person can strike again and again, if we do not stop him at once. I care not who the killer is, my friend, but they must be uncovered, and utterly destroyed…as publicly as possible. A public hanging, or a burning at the stake would terrify others away from going against us."

"Then let us test Master Richard's servants and friends without fear or favour," Kel tells the ageing diplomat. "We must look even into his blood relations: for did not Cain slay Abel, and Romulus put an end to his own brother, Remus?"

"Quite so, Kel, but I doubt his family are to blame. His wife lives in quiet solitude, given all she needs by her absent husband, and his children are all pampered, and supported, like princes of the realm. I suggest you start with the servants."

"Might I question them in the Spanish way?" Gomez asks, "or must I go gently?"

"No finger breaking, or hot irons," Chapuys replies. "Though once their guilt is established beyond doubt … I leave their mode of punishment to our friend in Antwerp, for he is closest in blood to poor Richard."

"Then let us get to it," Kel says. He

has no great love for Richard Cromwell, but he is devoted to Tom Cromwell, and wishes to impress him with his zeal. "We dare not let these people think we are bested by them. They are laughing, and think they have escaped our wrath."

Oh, we shall find our murderer," Alonso Gomez vows. "Richard and I were friends, and I will have my moment. By God, I swear it!"

*

"*Ouvrez la porte. Nous sommes sur les affaires royales.*" The accent is northern sounding to the guard on the gate, and this lends veracity to the man's claim to be fro the royal court. After all, he reasons, how few of those Paris bastards ever bother venturing as far south as La Rochelle, unless forced to it on the king's business? Still, why make it easy for the stuck up Parisian officer?

"*Permittez-moi de voir vos documents, mon siegneur,*" the guard replies. It costs nothing to flatter, and the leader of this small troop might be some kind of a lord. His polite reply may earn him a couple of silver coins for his trouble.

Troop Sergeant Alan Cope speaks good French, learned when serving in the north of the country, but he does not think he can fool this Frenchman for long. He hands over the forged documents, given to him by Will Draper, and insists on being admitted to the fortress. The commander of the small guard left to watch over the fortress can see nothing wrong with the papers, though he cannot actually read, and he admits the King's Arquebusiers without more ado.

Once inside, and it is an easy matter for Will, Tom Wyatt, and Mush to slip away, whilst Cope, Cord, and the rest occupy the few guards. Will leads his friends down into the fortress cellars, in the belief that the dungeons will be there. Sure enough, the English rescuers find a row of unguarded cells, each occupied by a half dozen captives.

"English?" Will hisses, and voices answer him from the gloom.

"Dear God, sir, but are you here to save us from our terrible fate?" says a rough north eastern voice. "These bastards are beyond all forgiveness."

"We are here to take you safely home, lads," Mush replies.

"And our fellow captives too?" the man asks as he is released. I cannot see these poor wretches left to Jacques Cordelier's tender mercy. See how he treats us, master?" The man holds up his mutilated hands to show stubs where fingers should be. "The bastard knows French folk will pay good money to see we English, maimed and held captive. They laugh at us as we try to pick up our food or hold a cup."

"Bring the torches nearer," Tom Wyatt says, and he looks into each cell. "Dear Christ, what is this?" He steps back in horror. In one cell a young woman sits, and her eyes are stitched shut, whilst beside her is a boy with contorted limbs, and another with a hunched back.

"Cordelier's freak show," the man says. "The filthy swine collects oddities... or creates them... and puts us out to tour the land. We are to be gawked at for a penny or two, all over France. The man has many such shows, and makes a pretty penny from them."

"Hush man, and let us get these cells emptied of their infernal contents," Will Draper says. "You must come with us now, for we have a boat waiting. Let any of these poor wretches wish it, and they can join us too. I can take them to England, and promise them a better life than any Cordelier can inflict upon them. God curse him!"

The cells empty, and twenty-five captives are ready to escape their awful fate. Even the cripples are carried by those better abled, and they mount the steps back up into the main body of the fortress.

Will is first to break out into the light. He blinks and tries to see what is about him, There is the unmistakeable click of a pistol being cocked, and then a flurry of others. He squints, and makes out his men, surrounded by a company of armed French soldiers.

"M'sieu, I must demand your surrender," a heavily accented voice cries out.. "Try to fight us, and you must all die. I am the Chevalier de Angoulins, and custodian of this fortress. What is your business here?" Will raises his hands to show they are empty, and he moves further out into the great hall.

"I am the Baron Will Draper, Lord Templar of England, and General in Chief of King Henry's Royal Examiners, sir, here to rescue fellow Englishmen from their captivity. Instead, I find myself in a place of horror, and dishonour."

"Dishonour, *mon General*?" the Chevalier de Angoulins asks. "You come into my domain, by trickery, and you dare to speak to me of dishonour?"

"Not yours, sir, but a certain man by the name of Jacques Cordelier." It is a stab in the dark, but Will can see no other course open, other than to drive a wedge between the chevalier and this rogue, Cordelier. "I am sworn to bring the man to justice."

"Cordelier is here, with me," the Chevalier de Angoulins replies, and a thin, evil looking fellow appears at the officer's side.

"What is this, Angoulins?" the man says. 'you have taken some important men,

I think. A king's officer and his captains. Hang them all, and be damned to King Henry. François will be pleased with…"

"Silence!" The Chevalier de Angoulins senses that something strange is afoot, and he wishes to know what is going on under his very nose. "Englishman, why do you steal prisoners from my dungeons?"

"I seek only to free my own poor, maimed men, sir, but I find your cells filled with such misery that I must try to save them all too."

"Cordelier, what is the meaning of this?" the commander of the fortress demands. "You come to see me, and demand the run of my dungeons, for some dangerous English prisoners to be locked up in, and now… *Mon Dieu* … who are these other people?" He sees the horrible afflictions, and the maimed limbs, and he is sickened by the sight.

"They are my property, sir," Cordelier replies, stiffly. Do not baulk me, or the king will hear of it. Arrest these men at once."

"Chevalier… gentleman, we say in English," Will says. "This man makes a fortune by sending circuses of these poor people all about France, where they are mocked for the price of a copper coin. He is no gentleman. I beg your indulgence. Let me and my men leave. It is the honourable thing to do. If you wish, I can take these other wretches with me to England, where we do not allow such casual brutality to the afflicted."

"This is none of my doing, My Lord Templar," the Chevalier de Angoulins protests. He is a young man, full of the the virtues of honour and fidelity. "It seems that the king's advisor is the one lacking in honour. You may leave, completely unmolested, sir, and take with you any of these poor creatures who wish to accept your offer to go to England. As for this Cordelier monster, I shall write to my dear cousin, who is François' war minister, and condemn his wicked actions."

"Sir, I will gladly take him with us," Will says, "for he has hanged over eighty of my men without trial. In England, he will be given a fair trial, and then executed... if his guilt is found to be so manifest."

"That I cannot allow," the Chevalier replies, reluctantly. "Leave now, with my full consent. It is the very best I can do for you."

"I commend your honourable actions, sir, and I will accept your kindness," says Will. He signals for his men to close ranks about the released captives, so that they might leave the fortress, and return to the waiting cog. Cordelier cannot contain his anger, as his prized possessions are taken from him.

First he is sent on a wild goose chase with that idiot Angoulins, and now, he is robbed of his rights, as his future exhibits are being stolen away. That he has another dozen such groups is unimportant, for this troupe, bolstered by captive Englishmen, is the one that would surely make his fortune.

"Damn you, Angoulins," he cries, as the English party begin to leave. "You cannot do this. The king will hang you for cowardice. Stop them!"

Jacques Cordelier isa man who cannot see beyond his own greed, and seldom understands that there are consequences to every action. He snatches an arquebus from one of the guards, and aims it at Will Draper's back. It is a broad enough target, and hardly ten feet distant.

Tom Wyatt sees the sudden movement of the gun, swinging towards his friend, and he lunges across him, and cries a warning. The muzzle flashes, and the Chevalier de Angoulins curses at such treachery. He draws his sword and, without hesitation, he thrusts it straight into Cordelier's heart. King François' advisor crumples to the flagstoned floor, and the Chevalier steps over his lifeless body, and kneels by Tom Wyatt's side.

"Forgive my countryman's wicked treachery, My Lord. He has paid the price for it now," the distraught Frenchman says.

"You bloody idiot," Will says to

the wounded poet. "What ever possessed you to do that?"

"Would you see me killed in so base a way?" Tom Wyatt replies, and coughs. The lead ball has hit home under the left shoulder, and his lungs feel as though they are on fire. "I thought to save you, because you are a better man than I, and so well worth saving. What would Miriam say if I let you die, old friend?"

"Oh, Tom… you damned fool." Will pulls aside Wyatt's doublet, and looks at the wound. The shot has not passed through, and remains lodged within the poet's body. "It is bad. You need to see Doctor Theophrasus, who is a wonder with such wounds."

"My friend, I am a dead man," the poet says. "Let me finally die, as often as I have attempted before. Let me die for love, at last."

"Not a chance," Mush Draper vows. "Come lads, let us bind our Master Poet up, and get him back to the boat. Doctor Theophrasus will save him."

It is Jeremiah Cord who lifts Tom Wyatt up, and cradles him in his massive arms. The French soldiers are stood down, and the Chevalier de Angoulins escorts them all down to the quayside, where their craft awaits them.

"Forgive me, Lord Templar," the Frenchman says, as Will boards, "but, at least, Jacques Cordelier is dead. I should have acted faster. The man was without a shred of honour."

"You killed the man for us, and that is ample enough, sir," Will replies. "I hope you do not suffer by your action."

"Not I, sir," the French officer replies. "Jacques Cordelier's body will be found floating in the harbour tomorrow. He was often warned about visiting brothels alone, and he must have upset some girl's pimp. That will be in the report to my king Now, God's speed to you all!"

*

The Draper Company cog slips out of the French port, unhindered, and begins the crossing, back to England. Will Draper stands at the prow, and stares out to sea. He hears footsteps behind him.

"Adolphus will save our poet," he says.

"I doubt it not, sir," Jeremiah Cord says. "Mush is with him just now, giving him poppy juice for the pain. I wonder if we might try to cut the ball free?"

"One slip of the knife, and it will kill him," Will replies. "No, the doctor is our only real hope. We must make haste."

"We are full rigged," Jeremiah Cord tells his commander. "Now our poet's fate is in the hands of God.

"Amen to that," Will Draper mutters. 'If you die', he thinks, 'to save my own life, I will never forget it… you damned fool!'

*

In the end, it proves ridiculously easy to uncover who it was who poisoned Richard Cromwell. Kel Kelton and AlonsoGomez do as they are advised, and start with the most obvious suspect they can think of. Ben Greyson was Richard's cook for years, and they question him about how easily his master's food could be doctored. The man scoffs at their thoughts.

"Impossible," he says. "I prepare everything myself. It is a small household, and the task is not beyond me. I see the raw vegetables come in from market each morning, and every cut of venison, beef, rabbit, hare, or fowl is cooked by myself alone. I also make all the sauces, and plated up every meal the master ever ate in this house. When not dining out, he seldom ate in company. Mostly, he just picked at his victuals, and bemoaned the loss of his great love. In the end his heart broke, and he died for love."

"Then the food never left your sight, from being cooked, right up to Richard eating it?"

"Never… well, the food never left my sight until it was being served. Even then, none of the other servants ever served the master with his meals. If I was not able to serve him, for some reason, Mistress Peg would step in, and help me out."

"Mistress Peg?" Gomez asks.

"Peg Buckley," the cook explains. "She was nursemaid to Master Richard when he was a small child, then stayed on to become his housekeeper, after his mother passed on. She is almost sixty, and she loved her master like he was her own son."

"But she would serve him his food, now and then?" Gomez persists.

"Rarely," the cook replies, uneasily. "Mistress Peg would only serve him if he chose to eat alone, in his private chamber. The stairs play havoc with my swollen feet, you see, and she would take up a tray for him."

"Whilst you stayed down in the kitchen?" asks Kel Kelton.

"Well… yes, but it was seldom more than a bowl of soup, with fresh bread, a little of my venison and juniper berry stew, and a half dozen lean lamb cutlets. Of late, his appetite was less than usual."

"How often did she take up a tray?" Gomez asks of the man, and the cook scratches his balding head.

"Not more than once or twice in each month," the cook admits, grudgingly. "Perhaps thrice, of late, but why, by all the gods. would she hurt the one person she loved like a son?"

"I shall ask her," Gomez replies, with a wicked glint in his eye. "Send her in to us, as you leave, Master Greyson."

The old woman knocks, and enters the chamber. She sees the two men waiting, and looks down to the floor, as if in shame.

"You know then?" she asks.

"Yes, we know," Kelton says, glad at so easily offered a confession of the woman's guilt. "Though we wish to hear it from your own lips, Mistress Buckley."

"What is there to tell, sir?" Peg Buckley asks. "I put a few grains of powder onto his food each time. It was a terrible slow thing to watch. He would sicken, then recover… until I almost gave up, but then he took to his bed again, and I was encouraged."

"To continue poisoning your poor, beloved master?" Gomez asks, shocked at the sweet looking old lady's stark tale of murder. "You are condemned out of your own mouth, and it is clear that you must die for it."

"One moment, Alonso," Kel says. "Why, woman? Why did you do it?"

"I had a son," she says. "A fine, hard working lad, he was. He died of the sweating sickness a few years ago, but he left behind a wife and a son. I did all I could to help them, and the mother was a competent seamstress. They got by. My grandson, Walt, is almost fifteen now, and apprenticed to a blacksmith in the village of Stepney.

"One day, a man came to me and told me to put a powder into my master's food. I scoffed at him, and spoke of telling Master Richard. He bade me wait until the morrow, and I might change my mind. That night, my daughter in law was found at the foot of some stairs. Her neck was broken, as if from a great fall. Then the man returned, and told me that Walt would be next, if I did not obey him."

"I see." Gomez frowns at the wicked simplicity of the deed.

"I could not let them kill my own blood... my only blood left."

"Then you poisoned Richard Cromwell?" Kel asks.

"I did, and may God forgive me."

"Do you have any of this arsenic left?" the Spaniard asks.

"No," the woman lies.

"Does this 'man' have a name?" Kel asks, and she shakes her head.

"One man threatened me, and another brought the arsenic. I do not know who commanded them, but it must have taken great wealth to see the deed through to the end."

"Very well, we must leave now, and consider our actions," Alonso Gomez tells her. "Think hard, madam, and come up with some detail that might save your soul."

*

That afternoon, a blacksmith in

Stepney is summoned away to fix a broken axle for the local lord of the manner. As soon as he leaves, a swarthy looking man comes to the forge, and calls for assistance. A big, well muscled young man comes out from the back room, bows most courteously, and asks how he might help.

"Good day to you," the swarthy man says, and he looks about to see that they are quite alone. "Are you Master Walt Buckley?"

"I am, sir," the young fellow says. "How can I be of service to you, master?"

"Like this," Alonso Gomez replies, and he thrusts his dagger up and into the startled boy's ribs. He falls to his knees, and in those last moments, he tries to understand why he is killed like this. He is nothing more than a blacksmith's apprentice, and his own murder baffles him. He groans once, then falls onto his side, and dies quietly.

That evening, news reaches Peg Buckley; the evil news that her beloved grandson is dead... foully murdered at his own forge. One witness swears he saw some sort of a foreigner, and Peg nods her head in understanding at how her own evil act is repaid with even more evil.

It is not enough to kill her in revenge for Richard Cromwell's death, she sees. Instead, she must suffer for her betrayal. Her wickedness is done to save her grandson, but to no avail. They have killed him because of her act, and she must suffer the pangs of guilt and remorse. She goes to her room, and retrieves the brown vial of arsenic powder.

Later, when she does not appear for supper, the old cook goes upstairs to find her. She is sitting in a chair, with the empty poison vial in her hand, and she is quite dead. He closes her eyes, and sends a boy to fetch Kel Kelton and the Spaniard. They come at once, and view the woman's corpse.

"Clear signs of poison," Kel mutters.

"Good, for I did not wish to kill her myself, and I knew you were too weak to do it."

"Damn it, Alonso, but you are a cruel man," Kel snaps. "To kill the boy like that."

"I had to do it. She expected death, but did not mind, because she had saved her precious grandson… by murdering her own master. How is her death at our hands, or on the scaffold, a proper punishment? No, she had to be tormented to death, and that is why the boy died. She dies, knowing that she has caused his death. Now she can rot in Hell."

"What we have done this day… all of it… it will not bring Richard Cromwell back, will it?" Kel says. "When will it ever end?"

"Only with one side winning out over the other," the Spaniard tells his comrade. "I shall kill Master Tom's enemies for as long as it takes me, then I will kill all of Señor Chapuys' enemies for him, and finally… my own!"

*

Thomas Cromwell is officially dead, and has been for more than two years, but it is only now that he actually feels dead. The loss of his nephew, Richard, has stunned him, and made him ponder the meaning of, and the worth of human existence. He finds he cannot be alone since his nephew's death, and he surrounds himself with people at every opportunity. This evening, he has Eustace Chapuys to dine, along with Miriam, and her friend, Pru Beckshaw."

"We should not outlive our children," he complains to his dinner companions. Miriam wants to remind him that his son, Gregory, still lives, and flourishes as a country squire, but she understands that he thinks now about Richard, and the daughters he lost so many years ago.

Besides, she thinks, Richard was his own blood, and his sworn man, whereas Gregory is little more than a shadow of a son. He jousts, just hard enough, when Henry demands it of him, and attends the royal court as little as he can, since his father's 'execution'. He shows no interest in politics or in any of the various plots that circulate about the court on an almost weekly basis. Instead, he would rather sit at home, reading his books, and keeping company with his beloved wife, Lady Elizabeth Seymour, sister of the late, much lamented Queen Jane.

Even though this marriage makes Gregory the brother in law of the king, he does not seek to take advantage of it, and enjoys instead the gentleman farmer role he is suited to. He treats his many yeoman farmers, and artisans with respect and generosity, and in return, they keep his estate in fine working order.

Miriam smiles as she recalls the latest news, that Gregory is intent on building a new church on his land. It will have the finest masons and labourers to complete it within the year. Better still, young Gregory orders it to have the highest steeple in the entire county. The Cromwell name will be linked with the Church of England for ever more, and it will stand for a thousand years.

"Now what is left to me?" Cromwell laments. "Gregory is a dull child, who spends all his money on pews and weather vanes."

"You sound like an old fish wife," Eustace Chapuys complains. "I so regret dear Richard's passing, as do you, but we must not dwell in the past."

"What is left?" Tom Cromwell asks again.

"Your son, and your grandchildren," Miriam says, curtly. "Lady Elizabeth is fertile, and Gregory is a most dutiful husband. A husband who does not roam the world must be a fine thing."

"Gregory thinks me dead, and must not believe otherwise, for his own sake. There are those who would do him harm if they thought I still live."

"Perhaps, but your enemies are few, these days," Miriam says, bluntly. "Look how many have died in these last ten years. Even Henry knows your secret, but keeps it safe to save his own face. Only Norfolk and Surrey remain."

"And Richard Rich... and that new fellow that is suddenly near to the king's inner circle... Sir Anthony Denny." Cromwell thinks he must revise his *Vindicatio*, and see it is updated to include these new men. "Why, we might even have to oppose the Seymour brothers one day."

"You see foes where there are only shadows," Chapuys tells him. The Savoyard knows that enemies still exist, but they are so weakened as to be mere shadows.

"Do I?" Cromwell smiles. "Rich does not care for me, alive or dead, but he fears the Austin Friars name, and all it stands for. They still think my agents are in every place, and know everything, so they tread warily. Rich wants to be Lord Chancellor of England, and he might well succeed. Still, if he and the Seymours do not cross my path, all will be well. There is only one really dangerous enemy left now, I suppose."

"*Norfook*?" Chapuys asks, and Cromwell smiles, gently. It will be sad to see Norfolk go, but it is fated. As for the stupid son… well, it is only a matter of time before he upsets the king again, and that will be that. Henry is a vain fellow, and he will not want those great lords to outlive him.

"No, not poor old Norfolk," Tom Cromwell replies. Henry has both he and the son marked for death. The enemy I speak of is time."

"You fear not being able to complete your great scheme?" Chapuys asks, and Cromwell nods, sadly.

"One day, fairly soon, the king will die, and there will be a struggle for power. Great men, and some not so great, will want to use Prince Edward, and it is up to me to see that the right people triumph. Edward is more precious to me than you can ever imagine, and he must have good, decent men watch over him, until he is of age. I doubt I have another ten years left to me, so must rely on surrogates to keep him on his throne."

"The Seymours will rule young Edward through a Regency," Miriam says. "That is already quite clear. Even the king thinks it is for the best.

"Yes, but who will rule over the Seymours?" Tom Cromwell asks. "Ned and Tom Seymour cannot agree on anything, and often come to brotherly blows. Is that how to run a civilised country? I see pitfalls ahead, and it is for us to avoid them, my dear Miriam. If Edward seems weak, some nobles might seek to remove him, and put a stronger Tudor on the throne of England."

"Whom would they choose?" Miriam asks. "Edward is his father's son when it comes to faith, but Mary is a devout Roman Catholic, and two thirds of the country will not want her."

"Not Mary, but Elizabeth," Cromwell explains to his guests. "She is strong willed, and a confirmed protestant. Still, I speak of 'what if' and that is a game for fools."

"Whatever the outcome, we are but players in the game," Pru Beckshaw says. "Fate moves us as she sees fit, and disposes of us when required."

"A morbid thought," Thomas Cromwell says to Miriam's friend. "Can you then foresee all our ends, dear lady? Speak out, for you are amongst friends, and we do not burn witches in Antwerp."

"I foresee nothing clearly, Master Tom," Pru replies, carefully. "It is just that, sometimes, these things come into my head. I see strange things happen, as if through a silken veil."

"And now?" Cromwell presses her. He is not quite a believer, but any divine help would be welcomed. "Might we hope for happiness and long lives?"

"I see darkness lies ahead. There is an angel above Erato, and the candle flickers. I see you, and you are disappointed with something. You speak, and all men listen. No... I see..." Pru shudders, and opens her eyes. She is dismayed, and looks at the magnificent clock set upon the great mantlepiece. "A half hour to midnight. Too late, for the die is cast, and now Neptune must have his say."

"Riddles within riddles," Cromwell says, but in his heart, he is cold with apprehension. Will Draper is probably at sea, as they eat, and Neptune rules the waves, does he not? Then again, because he knows his mythology, Cromwell also knows of Erato, the goddess of poetry.

It sends a cold shiver down his spine, to think of the two deities, conjoined in malevolence. Then he realises that Miriam is speaking to him in a most forceful manner.

"Master Tom, I am not a political animal," Miriam says, "and I am wealthy

344

beyond avarice. I wish nothing more now than a quiet life, at home, with my husband and children. When he returns, I shall ask him to retire, and live the life of a country gentleman. Let Ned Seymour rule, until Edward is of age."

"Will retire... and give over his power to whom?" Tom Cromwell asks. "You see, my dear, your husband is an important piece on the board. He runs the Examiners, and he must keep a check on the Seymours, until the new king is of an age where he might stand up for himself."

"No, Will shall retire."

"As you say, my dear girl," Cromwell says, and drops the matter. What will be, will be. He knows how Draper's mind turns, and he is content to let Miriam have her dream for now.

"Are you well, Pru?" Miriam asks, and her friend smiles wanly.

"Yes, it was just that I saw water, so much water... then blackness. Tell me, Miriam, Who is this Erato?"

"Some old spirit, or a goddess, I think," Miriam says, and she shivers, despite the roaring fire. Outside, a strong wind begins to blow, and the patter of rain at the windows grows into a veritable torrent. Tom Cromwell listens to the uncaring fury of nature and thinks it not unlike England's own future. The wind becomes a gale, and it batters at the shutters. His England is in for a buffeting, and he hopes it can withstand the raging winds.

"Stormy times ahead," he mutters.

"Indeed," Chapuys replies. "We have heard the passing bell ring for poor Richard... and we must hope that it does not ring again for England. For a ruined England means a ruined Europe."

"Then what?" Cromwell muses. "Whom will say *carpe deum*, and re-build so many broken dreams?"

*

The Silverfish is one of Lady Miriam's sturdiest cogs, and for this reason alone, she is still afloat. The storm, which comes out of a clear sky, strikes, and sends them tossing about the choppy sea like a cork in a barrel of water. The boat is fully crewed, and each man strives to keep at his station.

The cog is not meant to carry so great a load, and there are far too many passengers cowering below the single deck, praying for deliverance. Twice, the Silverfish's wide deck slants over at an impossible angle, and sends passengers and sailors alike tumbling. One man, unable to grip onto a wet rope, slips overboard, with a stifled scream, and another is simply swept from the deck by a raging wave.

Will Draper and his force of rescuers have been too successful in their mission, and they come home with more people than they bargained for. Having set out in clement weather, they now find themselves trying to run before the gale, and reach safe harbour.

Each time they come within sight of land, glimpsed through the squall, they are thrown back by nature's fury. Will Draper has good sea legs, and he fights his way above deck, and through the driving rain to where the cog's captain holds court.

"Where do we head for, captain?" Will asks, above the roar of the storm. The man can only shake his head, and shout back a disheartening answer.

"Just wherever this wind takes us, sir," he yells. "We are far west of our intended port, and might fetch up on the Dorset coast… God willing."

"And then?"

"We pray, and hope to avoid the rocks, until the wind eases. If the storm drives us ashore, I will try to find a safe place to go aground." Will turns back to return to his men, when the hugest of waves breaks over them. He is struck down, as if with a hammer, and he clings to a rope for dear life.

The Silverfish plunges into the next trough, and there is a few seconds respite. Will staggers to his feet, and turns to the helm. It is unmanned, and both the bosun and the captain are gone. He cries out for help, and Jeremiah Cord is first to reach him.

The giant of a man sees at once what is amiss, and he grapples with the tiller, until it is mastered, and the cog is back under their command. Mush arrives, and points aloft. the single sail is beginning to shred, and loose rigging swings about like manic whips. A lone sailor is half way up the mast, with a knife in his hand.

"Brave fellow. He must cut away the sail," Mush yells. "If not, we will be robbed of our mast, and that will be the end of it."

"Then may God have mercy on us all," Will says. Through the unceasing rain, he can see a coast in the near distance, and hopes it is not a jagged hell that they are being thrown against. "Hold fast, Jeremiah, and steer straight for the land. If there is a sandy beach, we must pray it finds us."

The boat crests another wave, and comes down onto a razor sharp rock ledge that rips open the cog's underbelly. In a moment, the hull is filled with water, and everyone comes spilling up onto deck, in a panicking, screaming mob. The Silverfish gives a final shudder, and begins to break apart at the seams.

Some of the crewmen go into the foaming sea, with ropes, and try to struggle ashore. If they can get lines secured, they might yet save their souls, and those of the passengers who can brave the storm.

Some men jump into the water, and try to swim, whilst others, like Will, take a weaker person on their backs, and try to make it along the sodden ropes to safety. Some make it, and others are plucked off the ropes by the howling wind and crashing waves.

Jeremiah Cord puts the wounded Tom Wyatt over one shoulder, and lowers himself into the sea. he grasps the rope with his free hand, and pulls himself towards the shore. He can feel solid ground beneath his boots, and takes another stride shorewards.

Then two sailors appear, each roped to a point ashore, and lift the wounded man from Cord's shoulder. It is just in time, for the giant is frozen, wet, and exhausted. He can feel his hand losing its grip on the sodden rope.

"Hang on!" a voice shouts, but he cannot. His fingers betray him, and the giant of a man is plucked from the rope, and dashed from his feet. He feels the undertow, snatching at him, and he fights to keep his head above the foaming sea. Then he curses out loud, for one of the two seamen passes him, floundering.

Cord kicks towards the man, but he is gone in an instant. Then another body floats into view, face down in the water. The big man, though close to death, grabs at the limp figure, and clutches it to himself.

Together, they float off, at the mercy of an angry Neptune.

*

Comes the dawn, and the Silverfish is now nothing more than a few spars, and planks of seasoned oak, bobbing about on the calmer waters. The Dorset coast is littered with wrecked dozens of fishing boats, a Portuguese trading ship, one cog, and many bloated bodies.

Despite a most valiant effort by the survivors of the terrible wreck, a full third of her compliment, and passengers have drowned; their battered corpses bobbing up and down in the shallows, as sea birds flock to feast on the sudden bounty.

An old sailor staggers down the beach, swinging his arms in a windmill motion, so as to drive the birds away until the dead can be gathered up, and give a Christian burial. In other parts of the coast, villagers go down to the sea and rob the bodies of their clothes, rings and purses.

It is just another way of living off the land for the poor, but many more come to help. It is a party of such men who find the giant, clinging to a rock, half dead with cold, yet holding on to another man who seems already dead. They light a fire, and put the two men beside it, hoping to warm them both back to life.

When Jeremiah Cord comes around, they give him brandy, salvaged from the beached Portuguese ship, to drink, and it enlivens him. His senses return, and he stands up, unsteadily. His saviours beg him to rest, but the Examiner captain cannot. He sets off down the beach to find any of his comrades who might be alive, and in need of help. The giant comes across body after body, some of whom he recognises only by their lack of fingers, or other disfigurement, and others he knows by name. He pulls each body clear of the water, closes the eyes of those he can, and tries to lay them out in a dignified manner.

Then he looks down the beach, and smiles. Two dozen men have started a huge bonfire up, using the shattered mast of the Silverfish, and they are busy huddling around it, trying to bring warmth back into their tired limbs.

Jeremiah Cord waves at them, and begins to run towards these pitifully few survivors. He stops, yards away, and sees who is present... and who is not.

"Captain Cord, is that you, sir?" Troop Sergeant Alan Cope stands up, and beckons his captain towards the bonfire. Jeremiah smiles, and waves a hand behind him. The Examiner sergeant looks at him without understanding.

"Back there," Jeremiah manages to gasp out. "The poet still lives!"

*

Pru Beckshaw wakes up in a cold

sweat. In her dreams she has seen the dark waters again, and now she knows that a terrible fate has befallen her friends. She puts her head in her hands, and begins to weep for the dead.

-The End-

Afterword

In his later years, Henry grew more and more reluctant to abandon his claim to the French throne, and his last war against them was meant to give him his heart's desire. Instead, it proved to be a costly failure, with the French army adopting a policy of steady retreat.

Few engagements took place, and the one described in this book is an amalgam of several indecisive encounters. The one real success was the capture of Boulogne, after a two month siege.

Henry's attack is fictional, and the French put up a spirited resistance, until bombarded, and assailed with tunnels beneath the walls. The king was able to substantiate his claim to the French throne again, and his 'kingdom' was enlarged beyond the area around Calais.

The death of Richard Cromwell was sudden, and came after he took to his bed, and complained of feeling sick. My author's mind conjectures that it might well have been poison, rather than some dull ailment like a bad heart, or the sweating sickness. The details of his will are based in fact, and he did leave the king the pick of his best horses, to curry favour.

Gregory's life is described accurately, from his very happy marriage to Elizabeth Seymour, which produced five children, to his acquisition of land and favour because of his relationship to King Henry. As his brother in law, Cromwell's son was accepted as a loyal and reliable courtier... despite his own father's fall from grace.

There was a great storm off the Isle of Wight in this year, and many ships were driven onto the coast of Dorset. I have moved its timing by a few weeks, but otherwise let the elements be. Sea faring was a dangerous occupation in the mid sixteenth century, and it was made more so by the proliferation of piracy. Famines in China and Africa drove many men to piracy, and they were particularly active along the Barbary Coast, around the Iberian Peninsula, and around the Greek and Italian islands.

In 1544 King Henry gave permission for English 'privateers' to attack French ships. The men of Plymouth attacked the enemy with a will, but soon widened their raids to include ships from Flanders, Spain and Portugal. The fine line between sanctioned raiding, and piracy was blurred, and England's seafaring men earned a deserved reputation for their piratical behaviour.

English dealings with the New World began with Henry VII, who sent Cabot to stake a claim on his behalf, and continued, sporadically, for the next century. Ibrahim is, of course, one of my fictional characters, and he never does get to sail off the edge of the world. The concept of a 'flat earth' was debunked by Portuguese navigators in the 1500s, but the idea lingered on.

One practical advantage gained from finding the New Found Land, was the abundance of fish. From 1540 onwards, Plymouth ships would start to farm the rich shoals to be found off its coast, and thus provide the English fish markets with an abundance of new species.

Again, I must apologise for demonising historical figures to create my 'villains'. Richard Rich was, undoubtably, a perjurer, and a shrew lawyer, but hardly the character I make him out to be, whilst Sir Anthony Denny, mentioned briefly, was a loyal servant to Henry, and a clever Privy Councillor.

Likewise, I must be clear about the Seymour brothers, whom I hint at as being hateful to one another, and grasping. Ned was the clever one, and Tom the more adventurous. Both behaved badly at one time or another, but again, I use artistic licence. For a more factual view of my real historical characters, I must refer you to the many excellent texts written about them.

Anne Stevens

'This Death of Kings' is the twentieth book in the Tudor series, and it is due for publication in the Summer of 2018.

This Death of Kings......

Adolphus Theophrasus is in his seventy sixth year, and his bones ache. He often claims to be half Greek, half English, and half Hebrew. To those who point out that this makes three halves, the old doctor replies that he is a man of considerable girth, and that there is enough room for all three.

Whatever the nationalistic proportions, it is acknowledged by all who know him that he is, in his entirety, a physician of boundless understanding, and consummate skill. In short, he is trusted by every Austin Friars man.

Now, he must perform the most hated task of any physician, and tell those gathered below that the weeks of struggle since his wounding in France, and the terrible shipwreck are done with.

"My friends," he says, as he enters the grand hall, and they turn to him, and see it etched in his features. "Tom Wyatt is dead."

So begins an epic period in the history of Europe... a time that encompasses the deaths of great men, and of kings.

11296597R00208

Printed in Great Britain
by Amazon